GEMMA AND THE ACE DETECTIVE

An apartment building murder
mystery

MARGOT DREW DELANEY

SWARM Publishing

SWARM Publishing

ISBN (POD paperback B & N): 978-1-0670574-0-4
ISBN (POD paperback D2D): 978-1-0670574-5-9
ISBN (kindle): 978-1-7386256-7-3
ISBN (epub): 978-1-7386256-3-5

This version (4) published by SWARM Publishing January 2025.

Auckland, New Zealand

Previously published as *Gemma Cross Day One* as well as *The Body In My Building*.

Contents

1

You might have been right about me, Doctor Foster. Because how else can I explain this? Balancing on a window ledge, fifty feet up, with a cop standing on the street directly below.

As a bead of sweat tickles my nose, the wail of a car alarm pierces the night. I glance down. The officer ignores it, blowing out a plume of smoke, trying to look cool for the two ladies who appeared on his radar a moment ago. He leans against his cruiser, giving it his best, but the women are humoring him. I can tell even from up here.

So, Doctor Foster, I guess now's the time to apologize for my reaction to your expert opinion. At fifteen, I wasn't interested in what anyone had to say, but I can now admit you were onto something. Dopamine most definitely rules my life. Applause, food, sex and wine. I chase the hits, no question. But maybe you missed a piece of the puzzle, Doc, because what about adrenaline? The kick you get from riding roller coasters or picking a fight with someone bigger. Risk, thrill, danger. Faster, hotter, better. Because while I'm usually paddling out for dopamine, sometimes I'm surfing back on adrenaline, for sure.

My leg twitches. Heat swarms my biceps. I may have discovered a new muscle near my scapula. Or maybe it's an old one that isn't happy right now, because I've been out here a while. I take a breath and try to command my body to relax. I've done this a million times, but I'm out of practice and this is stupid. Because if that cop sees me, he might recognize me for what I am.

Correction: what I used to be.

The whomp of a helicopter beats down. Sudden and intrusive, even over the city din. And this time, the uniform looks up. I close my eyes and turn to marble. I become one with the concrete; meld my body to the building. I inhale a slow breath to calm my heart and quiet my mind. But a chopper is old news for this guy, and his attention is already back on his female friends. That cleavage won't ogle itself and thank god for boobs.

I should get out of here. But the spring evening is warm, and the city is humming. Whispering promises of excitement. Anything can happen, all you have to do is show up. No. Like a hero, I call it a night. Maybe I've finally learned when I'm pushing my luck. What do you think about that, Doctor Foster? Progress.

I make my way back using balconies and window ledges but avoiding actual windows. I can't become the peeping Tom (Tammy) of the neighborhood. That'd be a rough introduction to my brand-new life in this brand-new building.

Yes, Doctor Foster, one of these condos is mine.

The doors to the *Aurora* opened this morning. A low-rise with only sixteen apartments and a plain, ugly-trendy exterior—industrial chic?—but the inside is beautiful and modern, with high ceilings and shiny new appliances. This is what people do in their thirties, right? Sort out their shit and settle down. Some get married and have kids, sure, but let's not get carried away.

I drop lightly onto my balcony and slide open the door. I amble past my new Chesterfield armchair, an impulse buy after the unexpected thrill of ordering a three-seater sofa, to the bathroom. After unclipping my safety belt, I peel off my climbing gloves and shoes. Finally, I remove my slate-gray spandex top and leggings set—I have these in eight colors to match different 'occasions'—then kick them toward the spot my hamper will go. I've mostly stayed in hotels until now, and I had no clue how much random stuff I'd need to set up my home.

In the shower, heavy droplets massage my head. I sigh. Epic water pressure. As tension melts from my shoulders, I close my eyes. For the past month, all I've wanted to do is eat, drink and sleep. But parts of me are reawakening, and maybe it's time to get back on the horse. I glance down. Hmm. Not quite ready to ride, though. A bit of grooming to take care of first. A trip to Shoppers Drug Mart tomorrow, for sure.

Pink and fragrant, I pad into my bedroom and pull on boxer shorts and a tank, then kneel beside the suitcase next to the closet. I've unpacked my clothes, shoes, and toiletries—the first thing I do when I arrive somewhere new—but this case differs from the others. For one, it's locked. For another, it doesn't contain clothes. I caress the silver polypropylene exterior. Oof. It makes my fingers twitch and my insides itch. Because I already miss it. Heart pounding, nipples hardening, body tingling. The risk of getting caught. Dopamine and adrenaline, baby. I push away the urge to revisit my tools: grappling hooks, glass cutters, climbing ropes, and a variety of gloves, flashlights and lock-picking kits. I want to admire my babies and revel in nostalgia, but I won't.

Because I'm not doing that anymore.

Thirty-six days ago, I quit my life as a cat burglar. And no, crawling around the outside of a building isn't the behavior of someone who's given up the game. I don't know what to tell you, Doctor Foster. Except, well, dopamine. And adrenaline. And it's my first climb since that blood-spattered shitshow of a retirement gig in which my universe imploded: I almost got busted and my best friend disappeared. All up, I'm doing pretty well, thanks very much.

I stand and lift the case. It's heavy but I'm strong. Maybe the only thing my parents did right was enroll me in gymnastics. My robust but bendy body was perfect for it and I was immediately obsessed. Too bad for me, the parents lost interest as soon as things got real: when I needed someone to drive me to out-of-town competitions, or even to early morning training sessions. I'd cried and begged, but nope. Parents are supposed to love their kids unconditionally, but I can tell you for free that isn't always true. So I kept practicing in secret. Any way I could. I showed up at gyms and snuck onto the mat, hoping they'd let me stay. I joined my school cheer team, sucking back sarcastic responses and nuclear eye rolls so I could continue tumbling. Eventually, my smart mouth and rebellious nature won out, and I was asked to leave. But contorting yourself into weird-ass shapes is like riding a bike, apparently, because when I discovered the exciting world of criminal climbing, my body already knew what to do.

I push the suitcase to the back of the closet and step away.

Out of sight, out of mind, right?

New building, new life. A fresh start. A clean slate.

There's a knock at the door.

Who the hell is that?

2

My past hasn't poked its ugly face into my new life, has it? Or did someone see me out there?

I step up to the peephole. A woman, a complete stranger, with an expectant expression pointed straight at me. I keep watching as she knocks again. I want to ignore her, but now I'm curious.

"Hello, neighbor," she says as I open the door, her bright eyes feasting first on my face, then shifting past to look into my apartment. Boundaries, lady.

Shit. I've just remembered who's back there. He's squirreled away in the bedroom, but what if he strolls out? I step to the right so my body blocks her view. Her brows pull together. She seems both surprised and annoyed that I'm not letting her inside.

"You haven't finished moving in yet?" she says, sounding disappointed. "I love seeing what other people do with their space."

A ping of relief. I guess she didn't see me playing Spider-man. Or my illicit roommate.

"Most of my stuff is still coming," I say. True, I just haven't bought it yet.

"Huh." She tilts her head, studying my face.

I wait, uncertain. Is this normal building behavior? Randos showing up to chit-chat without saying who they are?

"Did I catch you at a bad time?" she adds.

"It's kind of late," I reply, even though I'll be up for hours yet.

A bloom of color crosses her cheeks. "Oh. It's just... we're neighbors, and I wanted to say hello." She blinks her wide eyes at me and I'm clearly supposed to be all like, *no it's fine, please come in* or whatever, but I've never been super interested in other people's expectations.

After a pulse of awkward silence, she pushes on. "I'm downstairs in two-oh-three. Penny Pritchard." She smiles and raises her eyebrows, waiting.

Finally, I nod. "I'm Gemma."

"Welcome to the Aurora," she says with a bright smile. "And nice to meet you."

Penny has choppy highlighted blonde hair, an elfin face, and a petite stature. I'd guess she's around forty. She's wearing a floaty top under a cardigan and neat blue jeans, and she might be the most harmless-looking person I've ever met. But what do I know? I'm a terrible judge of character. It's as if my little alarm bell—the one warning you when someone is shady—doesn't work. I've made some defective decisions in my life. Penny could turn out to be another.

"When I was looking around the garden earlier this evening," she continues, "I noticed the light go on up here. I'm pretty sure only three apartments are occupied as of tonight," she adds. "And I've met the guys in three-oh-one." Her mouth twists. "I suppose others will move in tomorrow and Sunday, but some of these condos are investment prop- erties. The Aurora is supposed to be mostly owner-occupier. It's the reason I bought here."

On this, I guess I agree with Penny. The old Gemma would have hidden away in a large complex, where you have no clue about the lives of the people twenty feet away. The new Gemma opted for a place with the word *community* in its advertising. With a communal area on the roof and a garden out back, the Aurora clearly wants its residents to interact. I probably shouldn't be surprised Penny is at my door.

"Gemma?" Penny tilts her head. "Don't you think?"

Whoops, she's been talking this whole time.

"Um, yes, totally," I bluff.

"Wonderful." She clasps her hands together, beaming.

Is that moisture in her eye? Is she tearing up right now? What the hell did I just agree to?

"How does late afternoon sound? We can plan it all over a glass of wine," she adds. "Or a cocktail." Her eyes twinkle.

I brighten. Random day-drinking. Nice.

"Sure."

"Perfect. Five o'clock?"

"Five o'clock."

Penny smiles, claps twice, then disappears down the hall.

I guess I'll find out tomorrow what we're planning.

3

I pat the pillow. When my fingers find the sleek oblong of my phone, I force one eye open to check the time. Almost midday and I have errands to run before drinks with Penny. Mr. Solomon lifts his gray head and fixes his green eyes on mine. *Are we getting up? I'm only getting up if there's food,* they seem to say. Fair enough, Sol. Like me, Mr. Solomon prefers the simple life. Indulgent, some may argue. If I'm not getting a hit of dopamine or adrenaline, I prefer to be asleep. At the very least, dozing. Sol's three speeds are eating, sleeping, and stretching out in patches of sun. And no, pets aren't allowed in the building, so yes, I've already broken a condo rule. Scaling the exterior is also probably a no-no, so I guess that makes two.

But no way am I abandoning Sol. He's all I have, even though I've only had him for a little while. After what I stumbled into a month ago—Tarantino could have directed that bloody mess—I knew he had to be an orphan. So when I saw him cowering on the balcony, looking up at me with trusting eyes—Sol doesn't appear to be a good judge of character either, so we're perfect for each other—I took him with me. We rappelled away together into the night and now I have a cat. And it's as if we've never been apart, Sol and me.

After we arrived at the Aurora yesterday, he slunk around, sniffing everything and emitting a few growls of displeasure—no one enjoys moving, Sol, no one—but as soon as he found the sunny spot in the spare room he parked himself there and has seemed happy ever since. He'll hang out on the balcony in summer and monitor the birds through the windows when it gets colder. As long as he's good, we'll stay. I just have to make sure Penny doesn't catch sight of him like she could have last night. I bet she's the type to rat out rule-breakers.

"Okay, Sol, let's do this." I scratch the top of his head and watch him extend each limb individually, taking his sweet time. He likes to let me know who's in charge. To remind me I'm not his boss just because I can make food appear.

In the kitchen, I check the refrigerator. Nope, it didn't magically fill with treats overnight. There's something for Sol, though—I could never leave him hanging. I spoon it into a bowl and set it down, eyeing him with jealousy. I wish I had someone dishing out my meals. All up, the life of a cat seems pretty perfect. But I'm not too far off, really. Surely I can manage feeding myself? And if I'm going to be a proper grownup, I should leave takeout city and fill my pantry with actual food.

But that sounds like something you start on Monday.

Still, I need to stock up on wine—I can't show up at Penny's empty-handed, even I know that—as well as something for tomorrow morning when I'll be ravenous from all my sex-ing tonight. After I leave Penny's, I mean. Pretty sure that's not what I agreed to, and she's not that kind of girl.

I should make a grocery list. Bacon, eggs, bread, chocolate, wine, and more Sol food. There. A list. I'm nailing this.

As I walk through the lobby to the exit, my eyes catch on something lying on the ground, almost out of sight. I do this automatically—scope my surroundings for nooks and crannies, threats and opportunities, escape routes. Because in my line of work, getting a sense of your environment is crucial. Whoops, my *old* line of work.

I take a step closer. A padded A4 yellow envelope. I pick it up and turn it over, my fingers pressing against the hard lump in the middle. Addressed to Tom Bollard at the Aurora, but no apartment number. This building isn't large enough to have a concierge, so we have to receive our own deliveries. I hope couriers won't dump packages in the lobby like this; I do most of my shopping online. Retracing my steps back to the mailboxes, I leave it on top for him. Look at me being all neighborly. Gold star for Gemma.

As I turn, there's a rush of motion behind me. Someone hurrying to the door leading out to the garden. A rangy woman, maybe late twenties, with tattooed arms and short shorts and a mop of jet black hair. Is this one of my new neighbors?

"Hey," I call.

She doesn't stop. Should I pull a Penny and introduce myself? Why not? Because a moving truck has pulled up to the main entrance and things are about to get crowded. And who am I kidding? She's hot and I want to meet her.

I find her outside the door, kneeling beside a push-bike, fiddling with the lock. I take in her long brown legs and her capable-looking hands working to untwist the cable.

"Can I help?" I ask, and she jumps, literally, whirling around to fix wide eyes on me. "Sorry. Didn't mean to scare—" I begin, but my words dissolve into laughter. Clips of cats being little weirdos (or assholes) are my favorite time wasters, and she just looked a lot like one. Still does, actually.

"Sorry," I say again, relieved when she also lets out a chuckle.

"My startle reflex has always been off the charts," she says, then holds up the lock. "But all good." She shoves it in her backpack. "Thanks."

"No worries." I study her brown-with-gold-flecked eyes, trying to get a read, but she looks past me, a frown knitting her brow.

"I'm Gemma," I say. "Apartment four-oh-one."

She blinks and nods. "Tobi, hey. Uh...." She looks over my shoulder. "Sorry, Gemma. I can't chat."

But as she turns, her eyes drop to give my body a quick once-over, then rise to hold my gaze a beat longer than necessary. Then she's gone, wheeling the bike through the garden and up to the street. I remain where I am, heart thrumming faster. The hot, cagey, enigmatic Tobi just checked me out. My new life at the Aurora is already getting interesting.

4

The Aurora sits at the end of Cannon Street where it intersects with Bright Street, a block that has a couple of bars and restaurants, a Loblaws with an LCBO inside, and a Shoppers next door—thank you grocery store gods. I cut through the garden and backtrack through a side alley, heading toward the café at the other end, a place called Bouche. I walk slowly, casting my eyes around my new neighborhood, even though I checked it out before I signed on the dotted line.

Directly across the road from the Aurora is a two-story building with a business on the first floor and what looks like an apartment above. Next door is a locksmith—ha!—a couple of nondescript buildings with who knows what going on inside, then Bouche. On the same side as the Aurora, a long and flat structure houses an auto repair shop and beyond that, about a hundred feet away, is an empty lot. All up, the street has an almost industrial vibe and I love it.

Inside Bouche, I order the all-day breakfast special and a double-shot Americano, then pull out my laptop. Penny for sure will ask for my backstory at drinks this afternoon, so what do I say? I need an explanation for my leisurely lifestyle and if I'm not a high-end thief, then what am I?

I open a text file and type the name of my project at the top—My Normal Life—then stare out the window. A normal life. Is it possible? Yes, because it has to be. I have no clue what went down at my last climbing job, except a detective nearly nabbed me and my best friend and literal partner-in-crime Danni disappeared. Whether her ticket was one-way doesn't matter. She's gonzo. Much like the diamonds that also vanished that same night. She's gone and I have to move on. I push away a curl of grief. No. Most likely, she's living it up somewhere tropical, not a care in the world.

And I've left my old life behind too. I dove in headfirst and became a homeowner. What do you say to that, Doctor Foster? You warned me about avoidant attachment styles leading to future commitment issues, but look at me now. If this isn't a commitment, I don't know what is.

So now I need a cover story. I'm in my thirties, so I should have something of a career. Not having a job would be weird, right? And, as you used to say, Doctor Foster, a person's profession can be their way of finding their place in the world. But being someone's employee doesn't gel with my vision of living a cat's life. No one makes Sol get up at some arbitrary time and go to some random location to be told what to do all day. No. I don't need to slap on a suit and join the corporate commute to keep up my charade. I couldn't do that even if I wanted to because I have a problem with my résumé. I don't know much about living a normie life, but I do know that to get a job, you usually have to submit a résumé. The last legal job I had was bartending and as much as I sucked at it back then, I'm likely to be even worse at it now. So how do I explain a decade-long hole in my career?

Maybe I can say I've been in a coma.

No, too many questions. *OMG you were? What happened? Could you hear people talking to you? What brought you out?*

What if I was a kept woman? I didn't have to work because I had a rich boyfriend. It's not exactly a Hi-Five to feminism, though. Or maybe I was a child bride who's just received a healthy divorce settlement. But then I'd have to make up a spouse, and when lying, the fewer details to remember, the better.

What about some online or influencer-style fortune? I have almost no internet presence, though, and I'm hardly a tech savant. One conversation and a quick internet search and I'm busted. Ooh, what about an inheritance? In truth, I have one parent still hanging on, but so what? I could be an orphan, like Sol. And perhaps the reason I'm not working right now is because I'm taking some time to deal. It's not so far from the truth. I *am* still grieving. For my AWOL best friend and my old life.

My fingers move clumsily across the keyboard as I type out my story—I'm not destined to become a professional typist, that much is clear. But eventually I get there. History rewritten. Gemma Cross, for the past ten-ish years, lazed around with her wealthy boyfriend until her parents tragically died and she inherited a bunch of money. Is that going to fly? I guess I'll find out.

The server arrives with my food, so I pack away my laptop. I'll have to figure out the question of my hobbies later. Really, I should already have one. You don't need to be living a non-criminal life to have a pastime or two. How have I spent the hours until now? It seemed to disappear, what with working out, sleeping in, and planning heists. Time flies when you're stealing stuff.

So what happens when you stop?

5

NICO

DS Nico Davis, surrounded by the bustle of one of Toronto's busiest central police precincts, jiggled her leg and waited. The whirr of something mechanical hummed away in the distance and the familiar smell of burned cheese floated in from the breakroom. Saturday at the station. The Singles Shift. Those working either didn't have a family yet or were en route to divorce-town. The atmosphere was diligent industry—young, ambitious officers hustling toward a promotion—tinged with the distinct whiff of loneliness. Nico knew all too well in which camp her tent was pitched. She'd volunteered to work because she couldn't face tiptoeing her way through the minefield that was her weekend. Painful reminders everywhere she turned. Unexploded grief bombs, just waiting to be triggered.

Nico used to love her weekends. Friday nights had been drinks with the unit, indulging in endless, sometimes pointless reviews of their cases—open or closed—reliving busts and picking through evidence. If she wasn't chasing down a lead or hanging with Izzy, she'd spend Saturday night happily alone. Either a movie and takeout, or cooking dinner, making noodles from scratch while classic Motown serenaded her from the stereo.

But all that was *before*.

A motion near the door drew her gaze, her eyes sharp and hungry, ready to get on with it. Just a couple of uniforms, joking and chatting as they ambled through. She sucked in an irritated breath. Where the hell was this guy? Way to be late on your first day, Detective Jackson.

Her phone beeped. She threw her scratchy mood that way, already knowing who and what. Her sister, demanding Nico join them for dinner tomorrow night. Technically younger, Tatiana was in some ways older. In societal terms, at least, with a husband and three kids and a crippling mortgage. For the past few Sundays, over roast lamb and Tati's famous garden salad, Nico had endured her sister's scrutinizing eyes and incessant questions. All some iteration of: *You sure you're okay?* Yes, she was okay; yes, she was fine. She just needed to get back to normality. Immersing herself in Tati's family and their chaotic energy should be a pleasant distraction. Therapeutic, even. Instead, it made her feel hollow in a way that Tati wouldn't understand. Nico sighed and typed out a reply. **Will confirm tomorrow.**

Unlikely to satisfy her sister, but Nico wasn't ready to tell Tati that she'd returned to active duty. On Wednesday, after three weeks of nothingness, she'd received clearance from the department's psychologist, and Sarge had given her the green light. He couldn't keep one of his best detectives benched, and there was nothing wrong with her. Nico simply needed to get on with things. To get back to work. But not filling out reports, confined to her desk. She needed a case to throw herself into and grind into dust.

"But I'm putting someone new with you," Sarge had said at their meeting. "You can hold each other's hands."

Nico had felt her mouth drop open, the blood rush out of her face.

He'd frowned. "Nico?"

"What?" she'd snapped. "I'm processing."

Because Nico was still waiting for Izzy to stroll up to her desk and say, "What's up, pardner," in the goofy Clint Eastwood voice she used to put on for no reason.

"Not solo, Nico. With a partner, you can get back out there," Sarge had said, his message clear.

"Who?" Her question had come out weird and strangled, but she'd lifted her chin and met Sarge's eyes and they'd both pretended everything was normal.

"He's new to the city," Sarge said. "And you don't have to become besties," he'd added, the young person's word sounding strange in his mouth. "But I think you'll be a good match. He's smart, Nico. Don't underestimate him."

Nico hadn't asked for any more details apart from his name. She hadn't even looked him up, except for his department-issue ID photo. She'd meet him soon enough and find out for herself. So here Nico was, kicking it at the station on a

Saturday afternoon, waiting for the freshly minted Detective Sergeant Jared Jackson to show up and ruin her day.

"Where is he?"

Nico looked up to see DC Patterson hovering by her desk. "Who?"

"Jared," Patterson replied.

Nico frowned.

"DS Jackson," Patterson added.

Nico tilted her head. "You've already met him?"

For a moment he looked almost guilty, then shrugged. "Grabbed a beer last night."

One beer and Patterson is hanging around asking after this guy? What did this apparent man-crush mean for Nico? And what kind of crap had Patterson been feeding Jackson? Nico and Patterson had never been friendly, but since Izzy, their interactions had become even cooler, bordering on hostile. It was clear he blamed Nico. She could almost hear his accusations. *You should have noticed. You should have done something.* And no matter how much she wanted to tell him to fuck off back to the crevice he'd crawled out of, Nico knew Patterson was at least partly right.

She felt a scowl creep across her face. If that little shitter—

Suddenly, her chest was tight. Locked in a vise. She swallowed hard and turned away, trying to breathe normally, panic knotting her shoulders.

"Forget it," Patterson muttered, wandering off.

Nico kept her head down for a moment, eyes closed as she gripped the desk, riding the storm. She forced herself to expand her lower belly as she took a slow breath in through her nose. A full minute passed before she felt ready to lift her gaze again. Damn, that was unpleasant. It had happened a week ago, out of the blue, but she'd dismissed it. The human body was a mysterious beast. It wasn't Nico's job to decipher that particular puzzle and where the hell was this guy? Nico unclipped the gate holding her irritation at bay and let it wash over her; flow freely around her body.

Imbued with a pleasing sense of justified incense, she stalked over to the coffee machine and shoved a cup under the nozzle. She jabbed at the button and sloshed in a dash of milk. Just as she returned to her desk, DS Jared Jackson, the man himself, strolled through the door. Immediately obnoxious, ambling toward Nico all swagger and attitude, as if strutting a catwalk. In the next moment, she realized he was aware of her gaze. And shit, he was enjoying it, her eyes on him. She looked away as he made his approach. Nico was not a gambling woman, but she'd bet money Jackson was going to be a major pain in her ass. And how could she trust anyone after....

He knocked on her desk. "What's up, DS Davis. Nice to meet you. I've heard—"

"Forget what you've heard," Nico barked.

He widened his eyes. "Hey, It wasn't bad."

But then he ruined it by smirking.

She narrowed her gaze, weighing him down with her flinty stare. "Is this it? Is this how it's going to be? You being an asshole and me holding back a slap? Because I'd rather do paperwork for the rest of my life."

"Hey, hey." He leaned back, hands up in a placatory gesture. "No assholes here. I'm all yours and ready to learn."

"Learn?"

Nico's voice sounded gravelly and hard, but so what? The way he'd sauntered in as if he owned the place. Ten minutes late and no apology?

"I'm new to the city," he said easily. "Figured we can cruise around while you give me the rundown on our area."

Nico eyed him for a long moment. It wasn't a terrible idea, but she wanted to say no, anyway.

"I'll drive," he said, waggling his eyebrows.

"You will not." She stood, grabbing her bag and keys.

"It's already past four," he continued as they walked out to the elevator bay. "Any interest in getting food after? Get to know each other."

Nico hit the call button and turned to eye him. Who did this guy think he was?

"No?" he continued. "I'd settle for a beer." He tilted his head, his playful smile dropping as Nico continued to regard him in stony silence.

"I'm heading out either way," he persisted. "Would love some company."

His doggedness was almost inspiring. If he was anything like this as a detective, he would be useful, Nico had to concede. And she didn't need to become his buddy. Sarge had said himself, they didn't have to be friends to work together.

The elevator pinged, and Nico stepped inside. She ignored Jackson's gaze and fixed her eyes on the closing metal doors. "You'll do just fine without me."

6

Penny's apartment is like mine, except I have a small second bedroom. Probably meant to be a home office or even a nursery, it's definitely too large for a cat. But Sol's already claimed it, and I'm not going to argue with him.

"There are only sixteen apartments in the Aurora," Penny says as she shows me around hers. "Bedroom... bathroom..." She nods and points, as if I might not know what they are otherwise. "Four apartments on each floor," she continues, "except for the first and fifth, which have two three-bedrooms. All the oh-ones like yours are one-and-a-half bedrooms, the oh-twos are large bachelors, the oh-threes are singles, and the oh-fours have two bedrooms."

"Huh," I say. "How—"

"I read the building manual and studied the floor plan," she interrupts, anticipating my question.

I've inspected more than my share of blueprints, but it never occurred to me to do so when buying a condo. I cast an appraising glance at Penny. She's obviously ahead of me in the grown-up game and I should stick close to her.

"It was all in the developer's vision," she continues. "Creating beautiful, luxurious homes hidden inside a concrete block. Spacious and high-ceilinged, with whiteware and laundry closets in all. A modern, sumptuous secret."

Is Penny part of their marketing team?

"And we have the waste diversion system in the garbage room, which is a fantastic initiative," she continues. "All of this is the reason these apartments are more expensive than average. In terms of price per square foot."

I nod, even though I'd done zero property market research. And how did Penny afford a fancy apartment on her own? She doesn't look like a high-flying executive or seem like she was born rich.

I follow her back to the kitchen, wondering how to bring up the subject of her job-slash-wealth without being interrogated about my   own situation.

"What do we feel like? Wine or cocktails?" Penny turns and raises her eyebrows.

I hand over the bottle of pinot grigio I'd brought with me. "Happy to drink wine, but whatever," I say, taking in her jeans and floaty tank—classic Penny, it seems—pleased I got my outfit right. Jeans with a sloppy but not scruffy off-the-shoulder cropped shirt. It's not that I don't know how to put together outfits, it's that I have zero experience of what to wear to neighbor drinks.

"You haven't said anything," Penny says suddenly.

Said anything? About what?

She waves her hand from the kitchen to the living room. "What do you think?"

Oh. She wants me to compliment her apartment. Her furniture and her décor. Of course.

"Love it. So elegant."

It's not even a tactful lie. Penny has done a great job. Working with a base of taupe carpet, chrome and stainless-steel appliances, white walls and glossy tiles, she's added floor-length floaty off-white curtains that give *eighties rock ballad* vibes, but in a good way. She's thrown in just the right amount of color to liven up the otherwise neutral tones, with mint, rose and peach pillows and accessories. Her furniture is a combination of sleek—Scandinavian style dining table and chairs—and lush, with overstuffed armchairs, and all up it totally works. How did she do all this in thirty-six hours?

"Seriously, it looks great."

"Oh." A flush of pink crosses Penny's face. "Thanks."

I smile, pleased with myself. I haven't done this female-bonding, friend-making thing much before, because if I wasn't hanging out with Danni, it was with random hotties or criminal world acquaintances, and the less bonding you did with either of them, the better.

As Penny opens the wine, I amble around the living room, wondering what aspects of the décor I can copy without seeming too Single White Female-ish.

"I thought we could sit on the balcony," Penny calls out.

"Sure."

As I walk over to the sliding glass door, I see a sliver of coppery-colored wood on the floor. "Hey, I think you dropped something under the couch," I call out, bending down to get a better look.

Smash.

I jolt upright and spin around. Penny is hurrying over to me, a mess of wine and broken bottle behind her on the kitchen floor.

"What happened?" I ask.

"It's nothing." Her face is bright red as she rummages under the couch. Keeping her back to me, she tucks something under her arm and runs into the bedroom.

I stare after her. "Are you... should I...?"

But she doesn't reply. I look back at the kitchen. Am I supposed to clean it up while she does whatever it is she needs to do? But then she's back, a bright smile fixed on her face and a bottle of spray cleaner in her hand.

"What a clumsy Chloe, right?" She tears off several paper towels from a dispenser on the bench and crouches down.

"Can I help?" I ask, uncertain. The vibe is... off.

"Don't be silly. Go check out the view from the balcony."

"But—"

"Please, Gemma?" She looks up, her eyes wet and fierce.

"Uh, okay."

Penny obviously needs a minute, so I take a seat outside. The spring afternoon is warm and lights from the entertainment district a few miles away are already sparkling, even though the sun is just beginning its descent.

"Here we are," Penny says, pressing a glass of wine into my hand. "Cheers."

I clink my glass against hers, watching as she gulps back a large mouthful. I'm curious, but I'm hardly going to push her to reveal her secrets when I have so many of my own. Instead, I take a sip of wine and settle into my chair. Hanging out and drinking wine is a pretty good kick-off to my Normal Life and I don't want to jeopardize it by being Nancy Nosy Parker.

"So, shall we talk about it?" Penny says, clutching the stem of her wine glass with both hands.

I turn to face her. She wants to talk after all? I wait.

Her lip trembles. "You're still on board, aren't you? Oh, Gemma, please don't back out now."

Right, the mystery planning session. The reason she invited me over.

Her eyes moisten again. I take another sip of wine to stall. Can I wing this without admitting I tuned her out last night? Worth a shot. And does it even matter what this is about? I don't think I can say no to Penny's pixie face.

"Sure. I'm on board."

She immediately brightens. "Fabulous. I thought we could call ourselves The Aurora Crew. Or something." She blushes, fiddling with the ends of her hair. "But we can figure out the name later. And we could put up a poster in the lobby to tell the other residents and give them, I guess, my contact phone number?"

I nod. No way in hell are we posting my number for randos to call me. About what, exactly, I'm still not sure.

"So," I say casually. "What's the, uh, scope of this?"

"Well, like I said, the main idea is to build a community at the Aurora. To have a Neighborhood Watch without the actual patrolling of the streets. That kind of thing. And of course the social aspect. And discussing local events, anything affecting us." Penny's cheeks are pink with excitement. "What do you think? Gemma, I don't have the confidence to do this by myself." Penny locks earnest eyes with me and I find myself, once again, nodding.

It wasn't enough for me to commit to one location, I've bought a condo in a small, not-at-all anonymous building, and now I, ex-criminal Gemma Cross, appear to be a found-ing member of our Neighborhood Watch club.

I guess there's no going back now.

7

When I enter Bar 605 a few hours later, I'm buzzing nicely from drinks with Penny. Only a block away and already familiar to me, 605 is a meat rack, but a classy one. A medium-intensity level of *trendy* with just a dash of *hipster*. The overall vibe is chill. Not sleazy or desperate. Maybe something to do with the overpriced drinks? Whatever the reason, losers don't come here as a last-ditch attempt to hook up. People like me come to meet others with the same goal. Getting laid. Because it has *been a while*. Meeting Tobi earlier today reminded me just how long.

I do a slow sweep of the room, popping into the washroom to check my hair isn't being weird, then settle at the bar two stools down from my target. I spotted him as soon as I walked in, but it's good to know your options before committing to anything. And by commitment, I mean tonight only. Which is the reason I chose a dude. I want an uncomplicated hookup. An entanglement with zero strings. A hot contract that expires after twelve hours. This guy can deliver, I can tell. There's an easy confidence to the way he's sitting, his arms resting on the bar. Big Dick Energy but with none of that alpha male crap. Perfect. And I was a little harsh earlier when I called myself a poor judge of character. More accurately, I let my dopamine-brain make a lot of decisions. I can't even call it decision-making. I just follow my impulses to wherever they lead me. Sometimes it's great, other times not so much. But don't worry, Doctor Foster, I'm pretty good at getting this particular game right.

I glance over at my guy. He's immediately, obviously, good-looking, but that's not what pulls me in. He has that *thing*. An extra layer of allure with no obvious source. His features are relatively nondescript except for his eyes—intense even from a distance. He has a lean, nicely muscled body, perfectly shown off in jeans and a t-shirt, and a good amount of ink. Yes, I have a thing for tattoos. He's not tall, but who cares? It's a definite green light for me. Consider my panties dropped. Or at least, loosened. All he needs now is a half-decent personality, and he's in. Literally.

I lean forward to cast him a cool glance, like I see you, but I don't know if I'm interested... yet, then turn to the bartender. "Vodka martini, please. Dirty. Extra olives. Thank you." I smile, because being nice to servers is the hallmark of being a good human. And this is why, after she's pushed over my drink and moved away to serve my target, I pay attention to how he speaks to her.

"Same again, thank you," he says with a wink.

Normal voice. Polite sounding. Yes, there was a wink, but it wasn't sleazy. Couple of points for you, mister. I arch my back and toss my hair, lifting my chin to expose my neck. The moves are obvious, but that's the point. If I sat in the corner and looked sweet, I'd probably get a phone number and I'm not interested in someone's digits.

At least, not those kinds of digits.

I can tell he's noticed me. I can feel his eyes sliding over my body, but he stays where he is and I sip my martini. Over the next five minutes, two people approach—one after another—because they picked up on my beacon/road flare/air horn. I smile and say I'm waiting for someone. After the second one ambles away, looking annoyed, I turn to find my target leaning against the bar right next to me. The waft of his aftershave mingled with his natural scent makes me want to jump him right there. But I don't. I'm not an animal.

"Are you really waiting for someone?" he asks.

"Yes," I reply. "And here you are."

The rest is a sweaty tangle of pheromones.

But a lady doesn't kiss and tell.

And neither do I.

8

I wake to a banging sound. Ugh. People, it's Sunday morning.

Sol meows, unimpressed. I reach out to scratch his head. "I know, right?"

There it is again.

As my sleep-fog clears, the noise comes into focus. Someone is knocking on my door. Persistently. I grab my phone and try to make my eyes work. Not even eight o'clock, and I got home at three. I'd left my new friend sleeping happily and crept out of his townhouse with my heels in hand like the classic walker-of-shame. Without the shame.

The knocking continues.

Seriously?

I stumble out of bed, pull on my robe, and stagger to the door. Through the peephole I see Penny. Hair done, makeup on, expression anxious.

I sigh. It's like the crack of dawn, Penny. You could take it down a notch.

"Gemma?" she says through the door. "I can hear you."

She can? Either I have been overestimating my stealthiness, or these doors aren't soundproofed. Then again, it is super early and I'm probably breathing like Darth Vader right now.

"Gemma?" she repeats. She has the nerve to sound pissy.

"Yeah, yeah."

I open the door.

"I'm baking for a fundraiser at the hospital," Penny begins, speaking fast, her voice high-pitched. Manic, almost. "And I need one of my boxes from storage. I thought I'd—"

"Penny." I hold up my hand. "It's so early."

She frowns. "It's eight o'clock."

"In the *morning*."

Tears spring into her eyes. "Oh, I... I...."

Oh god, is she going to cry? I've made Penny Pritchard cry.

"Sorry, I'm not a morning person—"

"I know it's stupid, but can you come to the lockers with me?"

I blink. "Huh?"

"I saw something strange."

I yawn. "Call the building manager."

"It's Sunday. It will take Carlos ages to come. I'm not even sure they do call-outs if it's not an emergency."

If it's not an emergency, Penny, why are you at my door?

"Please?" she continues. "I need that box. I don't want to go alone."

I let out a loud, burdened sigh. She makes wide eyes. Yeah, I'm overdoing it, but she needs to understand that this can't become a regular thing.

"Fine."

"Thank you, thank you."

I shuck on my slippers and tighten my robe, then grab my keys and fob.

Penny wrinkles her nose. "Aren't you getting dressed?"

I look down at myself. "I'm fully covered up."

"Yes, but—"

"Do you want me to come or not?" I meet her gaze square on.

She bites her lip and nods. "Um, okay, I guess."

We take the elevator to the first floor and Penny points across the lobby to a door. "Through there are the storage lockers."

We get lockers? They probably said as much in the Aurora building pack, but reading manuals will never make it onto my hobbies list.

As I open the door, a powerful beam of light appears over my shoulder. Penny is holding an actual flashlight. I point at the fluorescent lighting above us, but Penny's gaze stays fixed straight ahead.

"Over there," she says, shining her light at the row of storage lockers lined up against the far wall. Sixteen of them. One for each apartment, obviously. I have no reason to use mine right now, but maybe I will soon. Maybe accumulating enough stuff to need a locker could be one of my goals? It's good to have goals, right Doctor Foster?

Penny nudges me forward. "Look," she whispers, pointing at a locker near the end of the row. The door is ajar with something that looks suspiciously like a shoe poking out. We take a couple of steps closer, creeping forward. Penny clutches my arm as I poke at the locker door. Finally, it swings open.

"Holy shit." I step back, yanking Penny with me. She makes a weird sound and staggers to the side. Crumpled inside the locker, his mottled face covered in plastic, is a dead man.

9

NICO

A small but steady stream of police and crime scene-related people moved from Cannon Street—cluttered with vehicles—through the Aurora's lobby and into the storage locker area. Someone had propped open the door with a plant, and an immediately irritating beep greeted Nico as she approached.

"Key fob access system," Jared said, moving toward the door on the left, also open and beeping.

"I can see that," Nico said. "But thanks, *Detective*."

"No sign of forced entry," Jared continued, not missing a beat.

Nico got the attention of the crime scene analyst who'd just stepped through the door. "You done in there?"

The analyst slipped down her protective mask and nodded. "Not much to process, but you never know."

"Is the building manager here?"

"Think so."

"You got a key fob we can use?" Jared asked.

"No, but...." She gestured at a passing uniform. "They do."

"Thanks." Jared waved them over. "Are you the responding officer?"

"Yes, sir."

"Detectives Jackson and Davis," he said. "We're going to need a fob to get around."

"Of course." She fished in her pocket, then handed it to Jared.

Nico intercepted the pass-off and walked through the door.

"Stay close, we'll talk to you next," Jared said to the officer, then jogged after Nico.

To the right was a bicycle rack, then a row of lockers. To the left, three doors. One labeled *garbage*, another *utilities*, and a third, *equipment*. On the far side was a door leading to the parking garage. Nico walked toward the lockers, numbered from one to sixteen instead of by apartment. She pointed. "We'll have to get the locker assignment list."

They both came to a halt next to the body. Mostly crumpled inside, but with one foot protruding. Plastic wrap covered his face.

"Looks like suffocation. Doesn't seem to be any blood or other injury." Jared tilted his head to get a better look at the body, then cast his eyes around the surrounding area. There were only a few evidence markers. "No signs of a struggle, but you could roller skate in here without leaving a clue. Hard to tell whether this is where it happened."

Nico turned to eye him. "Roller skate?"

Jared shrugged. "I dated a girl who was into it."

Nico cocked one eyebrow. "A girl?"

Jared cast his eyes upward. "You know what I mean. Come on."

"If my new partner says he's dating a *girl* who *roller skates*, I'm asking about it."

Jared grinned. "Aw, you're already calling me your partner."

Nico gritted her teeth and carried on, popping her head into the garbage room, the utilities room, and then the equipment room. Someone had used plastic wedges to prop open each door. Dancing at the entrance to the equipment room, buoyed about by sporadic gusts of air, was a silver wrapper. Nico bent down to look. A protein bar.

"For fuck's sake," she barked. "Who's eating at an active crime scene?" She straightened and glared at the handful of people who'd all stopped in their tracks, frozen. She beckoned to an analyst. "You'd better mark that, just in case."

Shaking her head, Nico started toward the parking garage, vaguely aware of Jared behind her, scrambling to keep up.

Beyond the short set of stairs was the drive-in entrance straight ahead, large enough to permit two-way traffic. The metal grate door was down, barring entry and exit. To the right was a single elevator with a key fob pad next to the call button. Nico noted the one camera in the left-hand corner of the ceiling, positioned to take in the entire small lot. To Jared, she pointed out the key fob access pad on the far side of the garage and the other just inside the door. "You need a fob to get into the building, no matter how you cut it."

"Not to get out, though," Jared added. "Release buttons."

"Yes, as we've already established, I also have the power of sight," Nico said, walking past to look up at the ceiling, checking the corners for more cameras. She saw two. When she turned to Jared to tell him to make a note, he was already writing.

They both stepped back into the lobby, where the responding officer stood waiting.

Jared smiled. "Ready for us?"

The officer tilted her head and patted her hair. "Whenever you are."

Nico rolled her eyes but didn't interrupt. Because Jared had clearly, irritatingly, already established rapport with the officer. When asking people questions, it didn't matter who; you needed their cooperation.

"Any ID on the victim?" Jared asked.

"Nothing in his pockets at all."

"Who found him?"

"Couple of ladies came to get something out of storage this morning at around eight. They both live here, but not together." The officer opened her notepad. "Gemma Cross in four-oh-one and Penny Pritchard in two-oh-three. We took initial statements, then told them to wait in their apartments for you."

"Are you shitting me?" Jared muttered.

Nico took in Jared's clenched jaw and tight expression. "What's up?"

"Was I not supposed to?" the uniform asked, seeming uneasy.

"All good." Jared cleared his throat. "You think the vic is a resident?" he asked Nico.

"He's inside the building. Either he is, or the person who killed him is, or—"

"Someone else with access," Jared finished.

"That might be a long list," the uniform said.

Both Jared and Nico turned to regard her. "Why?" Nico asked.

"The Aurora is brand new. Doors literally just opened. Contractors were probably still on site last week. You didn't see it on the news last month?"

"Only been in the city for two weeks," Jared offered.

Nico said nothing. Toronto born and bred, but last month she'd paid little attention to anything.

"Last year, it was leaked that their building consents weren't up to scratch," the officer explained. "They sorted it out, but it got some media attention. When they announced the opening, it got dredged up again."

"Settlement date was...?" Nico asked.

"Friday, I think."

Jared whistled. "Two days ago."

"Got the name of the development company?" Nico asked. Property was a big deal. Maybe the victim found out something and threatened exposure.

"Boston Works."

"And the building manager?"

"Carlos Santino," she said, pointing toward the other side of the lobby. "He's waiting for you."

Half an hour later they'd learned the doors to the Aurora had officially opened at nine a.m. on Friday. All the keys and fobs, two per apartment, were created last month, with the access and security system activated Thursday night. Friday morning, the Boston Works project manager, Chris Sheffield, had handed keys over to the small group of residents who'd shown up at nine o'clock. He then passed this job to Carlos, who'd given several more sets of keys to owners between ten and twelve o'clock.

Carlos also confirmed that until the end of the day Thursday, several people from Boston Works were still accessing the building for final checks, as were a couple of contractors, and Carlos himself. Carlos would put a complete list together, but one detail had jumped out. The project manager Chris Sheffield had since left the country. He'd gone on vacation to Mexico on Friday night.

"Pretty hasty departure," Jared said.

"And to Mexico, no less," Nico agreed.

"He's gotta be our number one at this point."

But Nico was staring at the list of owners Carlos had just handed over.

"Shit," she said.

"What is it?"

"Check out who owns the top floor."

10

I know you believe in neurochemicals, Doctor Foster, but do you also believe in karma? Because what the hell is this?

I stalk over to the kitchen and grab the cigarettes stowed in the back of my Random Crap drawer. Yes, I already have one of those. And yes, I also have a packet of coffin nails. I'm not really a smoker. I love the buzz, but the wheezy after-effects? Not so much. Now that I've given up professional prowling, maybe that doesn't matter. Maybe *this* could be a new hobby. Some people make smoking their entire personality, so why can't it be my pastime?

I'm trying to distract myself with mindless chatter, but it's not working. I can't forget what I just saw. Not the body in the locker. After that. Fuck. I step out onto the balcony and, with a tremble in my hands, apply flame to cigarette.

That detective is *here*, in my building.

I don't mean Jared, the guy I hooked up with last night—although that he's here too and also a detective is a bit much, really. I'm talking about *her*. The one from *that night*. The detective who nearly caught me the same night Danni disappeared.

Detective Nico Davis.

The responding officer told us to wait in our apartments to be interviewed, but Penny had gone back down to the lobby to snoop, then messaged me excitedly to relay that the male detective onsite was *easy on the eyes*. Restless and curious, I'd gone downstairs to peek through the stairwell door and see for myself. Seeing Jared was enough of a shock, but then DS Davis had strolled into view. I nearly had a heart attack right there.

Maybe it's my fault. Not far from here is the last place I saw Danni and the first place I saw DS Davis. This part of town is obviously her turf, and I'd purchased a condo right smack in the middle of it, like a dumbass.

As I suck on the cigarette, rocking back and forth, already a little dizzy, Sol comes out to investigate. He eyes me warily, then winds himself around my legs, sliding his face against my calves. I pick him up and stroke his head, aiming my cigarette away from his face, but he squirms, so I set him down again. I can't blame him, I'm giving off stressy vibes. Because the night Danni disappeared, the night I'd worked so hard to forget, is coming flooding back.

Neither of us had wanted to take the job. Long overdue for a vacation, both Danni and I had passed on the gig. But Sven had insisted. He'd set it all up, like he'd done a hundred times before. A week prior, we received an encrypted pack of information detailing the targets of the robbery and their ostentatious collection of jewelry. Everyone knew about Michael and Skye Barrington and their glitter, but their decision to move several pieces from a bank downtown to the safe in their high-rise penthouse was less-public knowledge. Sven knew, though. I don't know how. I never did.

Sven wanted to lighten the Barrington's load and Danni and I were the best team out there. Danni's skills run from light hacking to face-to-face scamming, whereas I can climb, crawl and cartwheel my way in and out of any situation. That night, Danni was supposed to get into the building using her con-artistry skills plus a dash of IT wizardry. My job? To access the apartment from the neighboring building and meet Danni inside. We'd finish the job together because you never work alone.

An unexpected traffic snarl had delayed me, but I was only a few minutes late when my phone had vibrated three times. Our code: Danni was in. I'd carried on, picking up my speed to move as fast as I could without risking my butt, and four minutes later I'd landed on the south-facing balcony of the apartment. Another minute passed as I waited for Danni to let me in. I'd pushed away the small curl of worry and assessed the situation. The balcony lock was basic—a mere nod to security for an apartment this high off the ground—so I'd opted to pick it instead of using glass cutters.

A minute later, I stepped inside. The jewelry was in a safe in the main bedroom, so that's where I went. There, my attention was immediately pulled to the large painting hanging above the bed. An ugly, lurid depiction of god knows what. I didn't realize the splashes of red weren't part of the artist's vision until I saw the pool of blood underneath. So red it looked digitally enhanced. My eyes had followed the drops across the room until I found the bodies. The Barringtons. Propped against the door to the closet like gruesome, life-sized dolls. Dolls that had been played with in the worst way.

Fear clawing at my chest, I'd stumbled through the massive apartment in search of Danni. It wasn't until I got to the second living area that I spotted another trail of blood. I followed it out through the open doors and onto their second, north-facing balcony. There, it stopped. Abruptly. I'd started looking for clues, trying to avoid the obvious explanation for this trail to end suddenly, until two things happened. First, I noticed a gray cat cowering under a chair, trembling and terrified, and then I heard someone call out, *police*. I'd lurched into instinctive action, zipping open my top to scoop up the unresisting cat, then hurried toward the balcony railing.

Inside, the door had burst open. I hadn't been fast enough. The spinning of my mind and the now wriggling ten-pound weight had thrown me off my game. Not by much, but enough to make a difference. Just before I disappeared over the edge of the balcony, I made eye contact with an officer. Fleeting but piercing. An eternity within one second. That acrid, visceral moment still rattles around my body. A feeling I can almost reach out and touch.

On the street, trying to gather my wits and calm the mewling cat inside my clothing, I'd again waited too long. Footsteps had sounded, clattering from the alley to my left. She'd called out. Yelled for me to stop. I'd bolted, the last of my adrenaline propelling me forward, and I'd made it. I got out of there and lived to tell the tale. But she'd seen me. As sure as I'd seen her, she'd seen me.

I reached out to all my contacts, tried everything I could think of, but Danni had disappeared. Sven, too. When I tried calling him less than an hour after I got out of that apartment, his phone was no longer in service. He's done that before, disappeared for a while, but never after a job had gone so horribly wrong. Fucker.

That night, Mr. Solomon—named because of his solemn eyes, and I know that doesn't quite make sense, but that's his name so deal with it—had sat with me in my hotel bathroom. Him swaddled in a towel and me still wearing my tools. We'd stared into nothingness until I fell asleep. When I woke up, we were still curled up together. I'd pulled us both off the floor and crawled into bed. We'd slept for another few hours and then woken up to do some more staring into space.

The only thing that got me through those first few days was Sol. He needed food and kitty litter, and not wanting to bring myself to the attention of the hotel staff by ordering weird shit via room service, I'd pulled on a baseball cap and dark glasses and ventured out for supplies. Two days later, I did so again, but this time I stayed out for a few hours. I don't know if it was shock or grief, but I wanted something to drink.

I walked one block to where I found a bar decent enough to eat at but divey enough for people not to pay attention to a woman day-drinking by herself—The Duke. I'd slithered into a corner seat where I could watch the world go by. I pulled my baseball cap low—totally not my style, but that was the point—and hunkered down. When the waitress informed me they offered a bottle of house wine at half price from two until five every day, I said sign me up. Ten minutes later, I was sucking back wine and chowing down fries, and so began my daily ritual.

The days blurred into one. I sat and drank and ate something fried as I watched other people exist. The corner table was officially mine. The waitress even put up a reserved sign. After my mostly liquid lunch, I'd emerge from the bar shielded by unnecessary sunglasses and my lunchtime buzz, and drift the streets aimlessly for a couple of hours. After a while, I remembered there was a movie theater in the mall across the road, and since Sol was doing a lot better and seemed happy lounging around the hotel room, I started staying out longer to catch a movie. I'd go to the VIP session, which meant I could have another glass of wine while I let whatever was playing flicker across my consciousness. I joined the group of regulars who went to movies in the daytime until I almost felt like part of a community. And as strange as that was, it felt good.

Maybe that's why one day after my half-price bottle, I deviated from my normal routine. I took the subway to drift around the area I'd last seen Danni, as if she might still be hanging out nearby. I found myself outside a building with billboards advertising condos for sale. *One week to go! Nearly Sold Out*, it warned. There were a series of photos, including a laughing couple in their forties and an enthusiastic and happy woman in her thirties. Could I become her, I'd wondered? The largest sign said, *This could be your new home. Your new life. Your new community.*

Three days later, I had my condo.

My new life has just begun, and now this. Another dead body and Detective Nico Davis back on the scene. What do you make of that, Dr. Foster? Can't blame this one on dopamine and adrenaline, can we?

I'm totally screwed.
And not in a good way.

11

NICO

Outside the Aurora, Nico disconnected and slid her phone into her pocket.

"What did Sarge say?" Jared asked.

Nico unclenched her jaw. "Work the scene as normal."

"Right." Jared's eyes were heavy on hers, seeming to want more. And there *was* more, but she couldn't. Not yet.

"Is there some backstory I should know about?" He added, still studying her face.

Damn, this guy was good at reading people. A skill likely to help the investigation, but Nico didn't want him sniffing at *her* psyche.

"How do *you* know about Alex Romanov?" she asked to deflect.

He shrugged. "I keep my ears open."

Volk owned the entire top floor of the Aurora, an organiza-
tion associated with a man known to both the city's organized
crime division and to Nico personally. Alex Romanov. At least,
Nico sure as hell knew who *he* was. When Nico had relayed
the news to Sarge that Romanov owned property in a building in which a body had been found, he'd gone silent. She'd
asked if he would hand the case over to organized crime.
After a beat, he'd said no, this was still a homicide. They'd
liaise with org crime, though. Pool resources. Romanov might
be entirely irrelevant, but Nico's gut wouldn't stop churning.

"What does it mean for us?" Jared asked.

Nico pushed away a sudden and unpleasant pinch of
dread. "Nothing. For now."

After a beat, Jared nodded. "Okay, so what are we thinking?
A crime of passion? They killed him right here, panicked, and
shoved him in the locker?"

"Or did someone take advantage of a construction site to
dump a body?" Nico offered. "Motive is always important, but
in this case, access might be the key. The body was either
dumped before the residents moved in at nine a.m. Friday,
or after. Which breaks our suspect list into two groups. New
residents and people associated with Boston Works."

"The Aurora has two motion-activated cameras in the lobby, one in the garage, and another one near the lockers.
When we get the footage, we'll probably have the answer."

"Who knows when we'll get that, or what it'll show," Nico
said. "You wanna take a nap in the meantime?"

Jared grinned. "Work smarter, not harder."

"Right," Nico said dryly. "So what's the *smart* way to work,
DS Jackson?"

He shrugged. "Get the footage now."

"Go right ahead," Nico said, making an *after you* gesture.

Jared gave her a long look, then pulled out his phone and reentered the building. He conferred with Carlos, made a call, and within five minutes was back.

"Did Boston Works agree to send it over immediately?" Nico drawled. "Wait, do you already have it downloaded to your phone? Let's see."

Jared pressed his lips together. "You've dealt with them before. You knew they'd be difficult."

Nico shook her head. "Not them, but enough development and construction companies. They'll be the biggest pain in the ass they can get away with."

Jared took in a slow breath and let it out as a whoosh. "I hear you."

Nico frowned. "Huh?"

He took a moment to find the right words. "You know your shit. I get it. I'm just... I'm settling in. Figuring out who's who. Some detective sergeants, you want to ask who graded their detective's exam, right? Not always the brightest bulbs. But not you, obviously. I guess the rumors are true," he added, muttering under his breath.

"The rumors?" Nico said. Because he wasn't talking about Izzy. He meant her track record. Her undeniable stats in this game.

"With your experience," Jared continued. "I should just let you... lead."

"Was that your idea of a compliment?"

"Pretty much." He held her gaze, lightness in his eyes.

"Okay, let's start with the resident owners," she said, her voice flat.

She would not succumb to his charm.

"There's no point in trying to get a list of people who had access to the building prior to settlement until Boston Works plays ball."

Jared cleared his throat. "When are we talking to the two women who found the body?"

"We've got an initial statement. Let's wait until we know more. We might need to push them on something."

Jared nodded and waved the piece of paper he'd brought back from his brief conference with Carlos. "This is the key pickup sheet. It shows who signed for their keys. It's not everyone, so we'll be able to cross off a few immediately."

Nico nodded. "Good."

She stood next to Jared as they scanned the list. Of the sixteen condos, six were owned by investment companies who had scheduled pickup dates for next week. Next to ten apartment numbers were signatures and Friday's date: apartments 501 and 502 which belonged to Romanov, the two women who'd found the body, Gemma Cross and Penny Pritchard, 401 and 203 respectively, Dr. B. Hobson in 402, Orson Walsh in 302, T. Bollard in 303, C. Pike in 202, George Lee and Marco Esposito in 301, and finally, enigmatically, Mr. and Mrs. Smith in 304.

Nico read the names twice more, committing them to memory.

Was one of these people her killer?

12

I need an alibi.

Normally, that's Sven's department. He'd offer me one of his endless supply of buy-a-buddies. But with both Danni and Sven gone and no one else to vouch for me, I'm swinging in the breeze. And once DS Davis gets a look at me, the first thing she'll do is ask about that night. The Barrington homicide (and their stolen jewels) is still unsolved, which means I have a problem.

I finish the cigarette and glance at my door. How long before they come knocking? Should I pack up and get out while I can? Move to a different country with a fake ID and start again? But I like this place. And what about Sol? Plus, Davis will work it out. If I disappear, she'll think I'm fleeing because I killed that guy. She'll get my name from the condo paperwork, and if she finds a photo of me, she'll realize I'm the woman she saw at the Barrington's.

I don't know how many people you have to kill to get on the country's most wanted list, but I bet three is a good start.

In the bathroom, I wash my hands to get rid of the cigarette stink and eye myself in the mirror. The fastest way off a suspect list is an alibi. I could try finding Sven again, but that could take days. I need something now.

Out of nowhere, a light bulb sparks. Optimism flares. Yes. That will work. And it'll only take an hour. But there are uniforms on both entrances. Not to mention my two friends cruising the lobby. Maybe I could scale the exterior? No. I'm good at my job—whoops, ex-job—but it's broad daylight and even with a climbing outfit that almost exactly matches the color of this building, someone might see. And then I might as well get *Cat Burglar* tattooed on my forehead. What I need is an accomplice, an inside man. Lucky for me, I've already put in the groundwork.

I hurry down the stairs. Through the stairwell door window, I see DS Davis near the front entrance with a phone clamped to her ear. Jared is doing nothing except watching her, his expression twisted with uncertainty.

I open the door an inch. "Hey, Jared," I whisper. He whirls around and recognizes me immediately. I can tell by his wide-eyed *BUSTED* expression.

"Back in a sec," he says to someone to his right, beyond my line of sight. "What the hell are you doing here?" he hisses once he reaches me. His voice is both annoyed and wonderous, as if he'd been so magical in bed I'd tracked him to an actual crime scene. Yes, last night's roll around was good, sure, but let's not go crazy.

"I live here," I say.

"I know." He shakes his head. "I mean down here, right now."

"I need to get something important from the pharmacy."

"Important?" Jared repeats, his jaw slack.

"Very. And if I don't take it soon, you and I will have a huge-ass problem to deal with in nine months. You get my drift?" I raise my eyebrows and wait. I'm counting on Jared not knowing the intricate details of conception and the Plan B window. Fingers crossed.

"Shit. I thought you said... And we used—"

"I am, but I checked my packet this morning and I've missed a couple recently. Distracted with the move, I guess. And rubbers aren't a hundred percent."

Jared's gaze drops to my stomach.

"Ooh, am I already showing?" I say, cupping one hand under my belly.

He rolls his eyes. "Fine. I'll get an officer to run out."

I cock an eyebrow. "To get emergency contraceptives? You thought that through?"

Jared runs a hand through his hair, reconsidering.

"You want to explain any of this?" I press. He swallows and shakes his head. "Neither do I. Let me slip out now, and I can make it so that it never happened."

"Shit. *Shit.* Okay, wait here one sec. I don't want Nico to see you."

Well, duh.

He glances over his shoulder. "Okay, now," he says, pulling at my elbow.

"She's okay to leave," Jared says brusquely to the uniform at the back door. Jared pulls me close as I pass him. "Hey. You'll be okay on your own?" he whispers.

"Of course. But thank you." That was actually kind of sweet.

He nods, then straightens. "Text me when you're ready to come back in." He pushes his card into my hand.

"If you wanted me to have your number, you could have just—"

"Gemma," he hisses. "Go. Now."

"Fine. Look at me, already gone."

On Bright Street, I hail an old school cab and pay cash, so there's no record of my journey.

As soon as I step inside The Duke, I'm greeted by a waft of stale beer and... urine? Nice. I scan the murky interior, looking for my waitress friend from those grief-and-wine-soaked days. There she is. Thank god, she still works here.

"Hey, uh...." Crap, what's her name again?

"Mandy," she offers with a small, wry smile.

"Gemma." I thumb my chest. "How are you? Do you remember me?"

She eyes me, as if wondering whether to admit it, then nods. "Wine of the day." She cocks her head. "Where did you get to, anyway? Here every day, then poof." She snaps her fingers.

"Long story. Listen, I have a favor to ask."

Immediately, resistance appears on her face, which I understand. She doesn't owe me anything.

"I'll pay you," I add.

Her eyes light up.

Ten minutes later, I have my alibi.

13

I get out of the cab at the end of Cannon Street and text Jared as I walk toward the entrance. **Ready for my escort inside.**

I wait for his reply, but there's nothing. Slowing even more on my approach, so I'm not visible to the officers guarding the front door, I spot a familiar figure. On the steps outside the locksmith building across the road is Tobi. Her head is down, doing something on her phone, her short dark hair falling over her face. At her feet is a rucksack, the kind you take for an overnight hike. I guess. I've never gone hiking and I don't plan to start. Climbing, yes. Running, sure. Walking slowly up and down hills? No, thank you.

"Tobi," I say, coming to a stop. "How's it going?"

Her head jerks up. "Oh." She smiles as she straightens to stand. "Gemma."

She's wearing jeans today, low slung on her hips, with a cropped tank and flip-flops that show off purple toenail polish. I glance at my own shoes—converse hi-tops—then back to her mostly bare feet. It's not exactly open-toe-shoe weather, but I'm not complaining. I'm semi into feet.

Tobi, noticing my gaze, wriggles her toes. "When I'm not wearing work or hiking boots, I get these piggies out as much as possible."

"Sure," I say, eventually wrenching my eyes up and away.

She nods at the entrance to the Aurora. A police car and a white van sit out front and two officers stand at the door. "What's going on?"

"You haven't heard? We found an actual dead body."

She blinks. "What?"

"Murdered," I add. "Crazy, right?"

Her mouth drops open. "Holy shit."

"You should still be able to get in, but—"

In my pocket, my phone buzzes. Jared has replied. **In Apt 203. YOU NEXT. Get back to your place ASAP. You're on your own.**

"Hey, I gotta go," I say, jogging across the street. "See you later."

I hope, I don't say. Because I don't want to come off all desperate. Because Tobi is giving off *vibes*, but she's also got a wall up. Invisible but palpable. I want to peek over and see what the situation is, but I have other priorities. At least, I should.

I duck down the side alley that leads to the back entrance. Maybe I'll get lucky and the same uniform will be at the door. I peek around the corner. Nope. Climbing is not an option, so I'll have to bluff my way inside. I'm not a natural sweet-talker, but I've seen Danni do it often enough. Maybe I can channel her. I just have to put them in a position where it's easier to go along with what I'm saying than it is to disagree. And I have to do it with confidence.

I walk up to the door with an easy smile. "Hey there," I say to the uniform. "Thank you so much for letting me pop out for my meds," I say as if we'd arranged this earlier. He frowns. I hold up the bag containing the packet of morning after contraception I'd picked up on the way back. Might as well have a spare pack handy. "Life saver," I add breezily.

He hesitates. "Uh...."

"Detective Davis is interviewing me next. I better get up there so she doesn't give me, or I guess the both of us, a hard time, right?" I give him a knowing smile and try to walk past.

"Wait. What's your name?"

"Gemma Cross. I found the body."

Finally, he nods, relaxing. "Right, yeah. I remember."

"Great."

Tension flooding out of my shoulders, I hurry up the stairs to my apartment. How much time do I have? Should I prepare? But how? I want another cigarette. Wow, it didn't take me long to get addicted, did it? I grab the already crumpled packet from the kitchen drawer and head out to the balcony.

Sol eyes me with an unimpressed expression. "Yeah, yeah," I say. "Drastic times, buddy."

I lean with my back against the railing and look up at the clear blue sky as I suck back noxious chemicals and wait for heady relief to flood my brain.

A rap on the door.

Sol bolts for the bedroom. I wish I could do the same. Because it's them. The police are here. I straighten, ice swarming my shoulders at the same time as something surges in my belly. Excitement. Is Detective Davis going to recognize me? It's awful, but weirdly exhilarating.

I extinguish my cigarette.

Another knock.

I eye the door. To walk over and let them inside, to suddenly be two feet away without a buffer, seems impossible. I need to do this slowly. Step one, they open the door. Step two, they walk inside. Step three, I come in from the balcony. They edge closer; I edge closer. No sudden moves. Everything will be fine.

"Come in," I call out. "It's open," I add, trying to sound relaxed.

The moment the door swings open, I realize my mistake.

Detective Davis enters my apartment, sees me standing on the balcony, and freezes. We stare at each other; the moment suspended in time. Disbelief at my stupidity thunders through my head, making me giddy.

Look at me, recreating the night we saw each other, like a dumbass.

It had been almost exactly like this—me on the balcony; her coming through the door—when our eyes had locked.

As I take a step backward, she lunges forward. "Don't move a fucking muscle."

14

I shift in the cold, hard seat and rub my wrists where the handcuffs cut into my skin. The harsh fluorescent lights bear down from above, making Detective Davis, sitting across from me, look even more menacing.

The door to the interview room opens and Jared hurries inside. His eyes flick to my cuffed hands, then to her. "Nico—"

"Shut up," she barks.

My shoulder throbs from when she'd wrenched my arm behind my back. She's not fucking around, but I'm not going down without a fight.

I lift my chin and eye her. "What am I doing here?" I ask. "I'm no legal eagle, but I'm pretty sure you're not supposed to randomly handcuff people." I turn to Jared, obviously the sane one in this detective duo.

"Don't look at him," she growls. "Look at me. I'm the one you should be worried about. If you had any sense at all, you'd know."

"But I want *him* to interview me," I say, unable to resist adding a pout and a flirtatious smile for Jared.

He shoots me a warning look, but a bloom of red washes over his neck.

"Why did a dead body show up in your building?" Detective Davis asks.

"Beats me. Will it devalue the property, do you think?"

"Don't be a smartass. This is serious. You found him."

"Technically, Penny did."

She leans forward suddenly, her eyes drilling into mine. "Where were you the night of March second?"

Jared clears his throat. "Davis, I—"

She cuts him off with her hand.

"Are you kidding?" I say. "That's more than a month ago."

"Don't play dumb with me, you—" She stops and takes another breath. "Where were you?"

"Nico," Jared says, his voice a soft warning.

"Shut up," she growls.

I widen my eyes. "Is this how she talks to you?" I say to Jared. "Partner abuse, seems like."

His lips press into a line. "Answer the question, please, Gemma."

I flick annoyed eyes in his direction. Take her side, why don't you?

"Fine." I cast my eyes upward and bite my lower lip as if trying to remember, but I, of course, already know. The Barrington murder. The gig that sent me into retirement. The night she'd seen me on their balcony. Not according to Mandy from the Duke, though. You better come through for me, Mandy. I'm counting on you.

"A Saturday night, if that helps," Jared says, looking up from his phone. Interesting. He's going along with her questions, but he doesn't know the significance of the date.

"Oh, it does. Thanks, babe," I say, smiling.

Jared shoots a panicked look at Davis, but her eyes are fixed on me.

"Well?" she says.

I snap my fingers. "That's right, I was at a bar. The Duke on Yonge. I was going through a phase." I roll my eyes. "They have this great special—"

"I'm not interested in the fucking specials. Who can corroborate this?"

"What does corro-bor-ate mean?" I ask sweetly, tilting my head to one side.

"Were you with anyone?" Jared offers.

"Thanks, babe. No, not technically, but the waitress, Mandy, will remember me. I'm a regular," I add with a smile. "At least, I used to be."

"You can sit there smirking and grinning all you like," Davis growls, "but I'll check, and when I find out you're lying, you're going down."

I frown. "What is your problem?"

Her eyes widen. "Who the fuck do you think you're talking to?"

Jared moves closer, his expression uncertain.

"Do you need to get laid or something?" I ask. "You should, you know. You'll thank me later." I glance at Jared, watching me with horror. "I could try hooking you up?" I continue. "What are you into?"

"Shut. Up," she hisses.

I snort. "Hit a nerve, have I?"

In a flash, she's on her feet, leaning forward, her face furious and her eyes blazing.

I clench my jaw. "Being a cop doesn't give you permission to be a total bitch. I have rights."

She lurches across the table.

15

NICO

Nico sucked in short, panting breaths. The room felt like a vacuum.

"Nico?"

Jared's hand gripped her shoulder. As much as Nico hated him invading her personal space, she needed that hand. Its strength and warmth; the reassurance. She took another breath, trying to slow her racing heart.

"You're okay, you're fine." His grip tightened. Another pulse of support. As the tension slipped from her muscles, she relaxed her jaw and took a slow inhale. She was calming, but part of her wanted to hold on to the anger. Because damn, it felt good.

"What the hell was that?"

Sarge's voice. From somewhere behind her. Nico looked up, taking in her surroundings. Still in the interview room, but

Gemma had gone. Jared and Sarge were staring at her with questioning eyes. Four spheres of unblinking doubt.

"I'm fine." Nico straightened and held up both hands. "I'm fine."

"My office," Sarge said, striding out of the room. Nico watched him go.

Shit.

When she turned back, Jared's eyes were locked on hers. "You sure you're good?"

Nico nodded.

"There's obviously some history there, and I'd like to hear it, but I think Sarge means now." Jared gestured to the door. "Talk about it over a beer after work?" he added.

Nico was suddenly exhausted. Adrenaline seeping from her muscles and leaving her limbs like lead. "Whatever," she whispered.

In his office, Sarge sat behind his desk, his fingers pressed together, one eyelid twitching. His face read *unimpressed*, and his eyes were full of doubt. She was close to getting yanked off the first case she'd been assigned in weeks. But she wasn't out of the game yet.

"She's involved in the Barrington homicide, Sarge, I'm sure of it."

"What?" he hissed.

She knew that would get his attention. The Barrington double-homicide had been one of the city's most high-profile murders of late.

"What do you have?" he asked.

Nico took a breath. "I saw her that night. Gemma Cross. I saw her face at the crime scene. I chased her, but she got away and then.... But I'm sure it was her."

Sarge's eyebrows lifted. "That was the same night—"

"I know what you're thinking, and maybe you're right, but it doesn't mean we shouldn't take a look at her."

"There's a big difference between looking and detaining someone without reading them their rights. If she complains, there will be fallout, Nico."

Nico let out a short laugh. "She won't complain."

"You could have compromised the case." He leaned forward. "This isn't like you, Nico. I've never had to warn you about this before."

She dropped her gaze to study her hands. "I know."

Nico felt weirdly detached from what happened in the interview room. But she didn't know how to explain that without making things worse. Making it sound as if she was out of control.

"Here's what's going to happen," Sarge said. "You can check her alibi for the night of the Barrington murder. If she's clear, you drop it. Okay? The same goes for the locker body. Do the legwork, but tread carefully. Take Jackson with you. Especially for any situations requiring actual contact."

"Sarge—"

"This isn't a negotiation, Davis. You either do it my way or don't do it at all."

After a beat, Nico stood. "Yes, boss."

"I don't want to have—"

"Understood."

Nico didn't stop as she walked past Jared's desk. "You mentioned a beer?"

"Yeah?"

"Meet you at the Pig & Parrot in an hour."

16

I step out of the shower, exhausted and raw. I did my best to scrub away my time at the police station, but I still feel dirty. And not in a good way.

A knock at my door.

I inspect my aching shoulder in the mirror. Yep, there it is, a bruise already forming. What do you think about that, Doctor Foster? You once said *the police are just doing their jobs*. But that's not always true, is it?

I press at the tender skin, wincing. I'm used to getting knocked around a bit—climbing up means sometimes falling down—but Detective Davis had really wrenched my arm. And my nose aches from colliding with her elbow in the interview room. *Sorry*, she'd said in a singsong voice, her eyes glinting with malice. Definitely not an accident. I thought she might be excited when she saw me. I didn't expect her to act like *that*. If Jared hadn't been there—

"Gemma?" Penny's voice floats through the door.

I sigh. I don't know if I have the energy for a Penny visit, but I pull on a robe and let her in.

She looks surprised by my wet hair, as if there's only one time of day to take a shower and this isn't it. And now that we've had cocktails and discovered a dead body together, she doesn't bother waiting for an invitation to bustle into my apartment.

"We should get together with the others in the building," she says.

I make a noncommittal noise.

"Soon," she adds firmly, lifting her chin and pressing her lips as if we've been arguing, and this is her last word on the matter. "Maybe tomorrow? A pre-dinner drink?"

"Do we have to?"

"This is a big deal, Gemma. An *actual corpse*," she whispers theatrically. "I think it's the perfect time to meet the others." She examines my face, as if only now noticing I don't look so great. "How did your interview go? I think he's rather nice. Don't you?" Penny blushes and fiddles with her hair.

"My interview was...not so great."

"Oh." Penny looks confused, as if spending time with the police is usually a blast.

"Long story. Maybe tell you later," I say.

But I can't, can I?

How is my new life already so complicated?

"Great," Penny says, either not picking up on my unenthusiastic tone or ignoring it outright. "I'm going to do some door-knocking and tell the others to meet at my place tomorrow at six."

I sigh. "Sure." Maybe this is exactly what I need. Something to distract me from thinking about Detective Nico Davis and what she might do next.

"You could come with—?" Penny starts.

"See you tomorrow." I shut the door.

I walk over to the couch, patting at my nose. Not broken and not even swollen, somehow, but it still hurts. Based on Jared's reaction to Nico's behavior, he thought she'd been heavy-handed too. I probably have grounds for laying a complaint. But that would mean more cops asking me questions and someone else snooping around in my life. The opposite of what I want. The sensible thing to do is to lie low and wait for this to blow over. Because I've done nothing wrong. Well, I have, but not the wrong things they're investigating. And if I leave *it* alone, then Nico might leave *me* alone, right? She'll be assigned other cases and eventually stop sniffing at me like a jackal at a carcass. Right?

17

NICO

The Pig & Parrot was a mishmash of students, suits, civilians, and a few chronic barflies—the lost souls trying to disappear into the ether. There wasn't another law enforcement professional in sight; exactly what Nico wanted. She couldn't face the claustrophobic throb of a cop bar. The probing looks, the whispered questions.

Did you hear she flipped out on a suspect?

"Free booth," Jared said, pointing to a spot near the back. Nico nodded. When the waitress came over, Jared ordered a lager. Nico asked for the same. Jared absent-mindedly picked up the menu. "They've got a ribs special," he said, more to himself.

Nico wanted to be at home eating noodles and staring into space. But she needed to be here talking it out, she knew. Because she was on the edge of losing it all.

"You went somewhere," Jared said.

Nico looked up. "I wanted to check her alibi."

"From a month ago? Yeah, we'll get to that, but I meant in the interview room. Where did you go?"

Nico took a breath and eyed Jared, still undecided. She'd known him all of two minutes. But how else was she going to explain her behavior? What if he thought that was normal for her? He'd think she was out of control. Or just plain corrupt.

"You're stronger than you look," Jared said into the silence.

Nico scowled and looked away. The waitress arrived with their beers. With a smile for Jared, she nodded at the menu.

"See anything you like?"

"Maybe." Jared grinned back, his eyes lingering. "Still thinking about options."

Nico glared at Jared. He somehow loaded normal words with innuendo. As if by 'options', he was deciding which sexual position they might try later. The waitress, as if to confirm Nico's interpretation, pushed her breasts in Jared's direction and tilted her head. Nico reached for her bag. No way would she sit here and watch them eye-bang each other all night. But Jared held up his hand to stop her.

"I'll let you know if we want to order something," he said to the waitress. "Thank you."

"No worries." The waitress ambled off, clearly disappointed.

"You sure I'm not cramping your style?" Nico said, her voice loud and hard.

Jared held her gaze. "I want to talk to you. Are you going to give me the backstory?"

Nico set her mouth.

"Come on," Jared continued. "You owe me an explanation for—"

"I don't owe you anything."

"Nico."

She sighed. "Fine. You heard about the Barrington double homicide?"

Jared nodded. "We've got nothing, right?"

"Three separate 911 calls. Two from residents, hearing a scream. One anonymous caller who must have been inside because they knew there were two bodies. I happened to be killing time at the station when the call came in. I met the uniforms onsite and when we busted in, we found a bloodbath. Motive was obvious. The safe was open and empty."

"Right." Jared took a sip of beer, waiting for the rest of the story.

"*She* was there."

Jared spluttered, spilling his drink. He grabbed a napkin to wipe his mouth and then the table. "Gemma Cross was at the Barrington homicide?"

"On the balcony, making her escape. I saw her before she disappeared over the edge."

"The edge of the *balcony*? Of a high rise?"

Nico waved this off. "I got downstairs as quickly as I could, and almost caught up to her on the street. Almost."

For a long moment, Jared said nothing.

Nico spread her hands. "There it is," she said, even though there was more.

"You sure?" he asked. "Really sure it was her?"

Nico lifted her head, regarded the ceiling. "Listen, I know memory plays tricks. Things can change in the brain after the fact. So no, I'm not one hundred percent sure. Let's say I'm at ninety, okay? Which is a lot."

"Then what?"

"I had no clue who she was. No name. No fingerprints."

"Professional job?"

"Exactly. It was as if a ghost hit that place. No leads, nothing. Until now."

His eyes had more questions. "Earlier, you checked her alibi for that night."

Nico nodded. "The Duke on Yonge. The waitress confirmed her story."

"Solid?"

Nico shrugged. "Gemma was a regular there for a while. Most nights, boozing it up. Mandy remembers that night in particular because there was some sort of altercation between Gemma and someone else."

"Anything on paper?"

"Nope."

"The waitress reliable?"

"She has a sheet. Small, inconsequential, mostly from years ago, but...."

"With nothing else on Gemma, it's a dead end," Jared finished.

Nico didn't reply.

"And that's it?" Jared said, a frown wrinkling his forehead. "That's all? Because the way you were in that interview room...." He raised his eyebrows.

Out of nowhere, a fist gripped Nico's heart, constricting her chest and flooding her head with panic. She dropped her gaze and took a slow breath, trying to calm herself as she focused on the tiny bubbles fizzing in the amber lager. How much did Jared know about Izzy? Gossip traveled like wildfire in the station and she'd be amazed if he hadn't picked up something. Was he going to ask her what everyone else did?

Did you know? Did you suspect? Izzy was your partner.

No, of course I didn't, Nico thought, a bitter taste filling her mouth. She took another slow breath and lifted her beer. When she raised her gaze, she met Jared's watchful eyes.

"There's more, but—" She shook her head.

He nodded, seeming to understand. "Soon, though?"

She looked away, pressure behind her eyes.

After a while, as the tension dissipated, Jared asked, "So… you got a girlfriend?"

Nico turned back to roll her eyes. "A woman doesn't show overt interest in you, doesn't drop at your feet panting for it, then she's gay? Your ego is unreal."

Jared laughed easily. "It's not about me. I'm just curious. You're hard to read."

"There's nothing to read."

"Gotcha."

She studied his face. Did he? Did he *get her*? She'd known this guy less than a day, but maybe he did. As she shook off this intrusive but weirdly reassuring thought, Jared's phone buzzed. He took another swig of beer as he read the message. A small grin played at the corner of his mouth as he texted back.

"Setting up a hookup for tonight?"

Jared shrugged, then grinned. "It goes both ways, Nico. You don't get the dirty on me without giving up something on yourself."

Nico held his eyes for a moment. Jared lifted his shoulders again, as if to say, *your rules.*

"Careful, Jackson." A uniformed officer said, appearing out of nowhere. Damn. She thought cops didn't come to this bar.

"She's a tiger, this one," the uniform continued, wearing a smirk, "just not in the way—"

"Quit it," Jared growled, rising to stand. "Way I see it, she's your superior. In more ways than one."

"Easy," the uniform said, raising his hands. He nodded at Nico. Something of an apology.

Nico watched as Jared dropped back to his seat and returned his attention to his phone. *Interesting.* The popular choice would have been to respond with something neutral. To hedge his bets until he knew how things were going to play out with her. But Jared had made his loyalties clear. Nico continued to watch him as he chuckled to himself, returning another text.

Could she trust him?

18

Penny bustles around her apartment, making sure everyone has a drink, a napkin, and one of the cute little snacky things she made. From scratch, apparently. She's a natural at this. Does she do it... professionally? Like, a party planner? We didn't talk about jobs when we had drinks, and now that I think about it, that's kind of weird. We talked about being single because Penny is divorced and considering a dating app. I told her I did my hunting the old-school way, at bars, which Penny seemed appalled by. Wait until you try the apps, Penny.

I lean against the kitchen counter and eye the small group of people sprinkled around Penny's living room. On the couch, clutching a soda, is Cassie. She's mid to late twenties, with large, pretty brown eyes and long hair piled on top of her head. She introduced herself as Cassandra, then urged me to please call her Cassie. As if I'd be doing her a favor. Cassie seems to be made up entirely of scarves and other patterned floaty material, and has barely said anything. She clearly prefers to observe rather than make conversation.

Someone else not interested in chatting is a guy a few feet away from Cassie, oblivious to everyone and everything except his phone. I'd guess he's in his thirties, has *Computer Nerd* written on his t-shirt, and is either making a bold choice with his hair or didn't look in a mirror before he left his apartment.

Huddled on the balcony are Marco Esposito and George Lee, who I met on the way in. They're speaking in urgent whispers and slipping in and out of Spanish, clearly arguing. I watch them for a moment, curious. Is the fight to do with the obvious age gap? Even I can see this one. Marco is in his early fifties, I think, and George is maybe twenty years younger. Suddenly, they both turn to stare straight at me. Whoops.

"Penny, hey." I grab her arm as she passes. "Did you invite Tobi?"

Penny tilts her head. "Tobi?"

"Tallish. Black hair. I met her on Saturday. Pretty sure she's a resident."

Penny shakes her head. "No, I don't think so. Stuffed artichoke?" she adds, holding out a platter.

"Uh, sure." I take one and watch as Penny scuttles away, cheeks flushed and eyes bright. She's having a pretty good time at this dead-body party, considering she almost fainted when we found it.

"Welcome, everyone," Penny says suddenly. "Let's get started." She waves George and Marco inside. "Thanks for coming. I wanted us to get together anyway, but because of what happened yesterday," Penny widens her eyes, "I thought it even more important."

"You mean the dead dude," Computer Nerd says, finally looking up from his phone. Was that a British accent?

"Yes," Penny replies stiffly. "Thank you, Orson."

Orson? Who names their kid Orson? Maybe I'm not the only one with sucky parents.

"Let's do a round of introductions," Penny says earnestly. "Like an icebreaker kind of thing."

Ew, Penny. *Ew.* The last time I had to do icebreakers was at a youth therapy group. Remember that one, Doctor Foster? It ended in a fistfight. But we have wine and snacks this time, and none of us are (still) delinquents. I don't think.

"Let's start with you, Cassie," Penny says with a smile.

"Um, okay." Cassie looks around the room, seeming nervous. "I'm an author."

"You are?" Penny seems delighted. "I'm a total bookworm. I was even thinking of starting a book club here at the Aurora. Have you written anything I might have read?"

Cassie lifts one shoulder shyly. "It depends on what genres you like. I write as C. B. Breaker."

Penny gasps. "The Steampunk Detective? I adore that series."

Cassie blushes. "Thank you."

"Steampunk?" I say.

Penny taps at her phone, then holds it up for me to see. It's a book cover. A woman wears an old-fashioned dress and aviator style goggles on her head and carries a rifle. C. B. Breaker is printed in bold across the bottom.

"The first in the series was a bestseller," Penny adds excitedly. Cassie nods, pleased by Penny's ongoing enthusiasm.

"Looks cool," I say. I'm not so much an avid reader as an avid magazine skimmer, but I'm turning over a new leaf. Maybe reading can be one of my things.

"Yes." George snaps his fingers. "I saw you on that break-fast show," he adds definitively, as if he's just provided the answer. As if we need him to confirm Cassie's author status.

"I hate doing interviews." Cassie fiddles with the bottom of her scarf. "But I have to. My agent makes me."

"*Makes* you?" I repeat.

"Yes," she replies glumly.

"Where did you live before here, Cassie?" Marco asks.

"With my mother. She... uh, she, uh...."

We all wait.

"She needed looking after," Cassie finally finishes, clearly uncomfortable.

"Is she dead now?" Orson asks. Everyone turns to look at him. "What? Just asking," he mumbles.

Penny tsks at Orson's bluntness. "Sorry, Cassie. You don't have to explain."

"It's fine. She's alive, but she, uh. I can pay for professional help now, so.... What about you two?" she blurts, turning toward George and Marco.

"Sales and law," George replies, not clarifying which of them does what.

"And where did you move from?" Penny asks, as if she's doing a survey.

"We're both locals to the city, but this is our first place together," George replies.

"Do you mean first time buying, or living together?" Penny asks.

"Both," George says, his voice clipped.

"We decided to go for it. Took the plunge," Marco adds with a funny expression. "We've only been together for a year, but it was *time*, apparently," he says. As George looks away, the atmosphere suddenly becomes heavier.

"Right." Penny turns to Orson, "You're up, Orson."

Orson announces that he's originally from Leeds, England, but has lived here for eight-ish years. And he, as his shirt explains, is in IT. He works from home and doesn't get out much. He seems proud of this, proof of his dedication to his Gamer Guy brand. At his last place he had a roommate named Spencer, and he bought this place because he wants to live closer to downtown. Why, exactly, he doesn't say.

"And last but not least...Gemma," Penny says brightly.

Immediately, my whole backstory traitorously flies out of my head. *Shit.* Am I supposed to be a Youtuber or independently wealthy or.... Crap.

It takes me a moment, but I finally get it together and explain awkwardly that I usually work in sales but I'm in between jobs. And the moment this leaves my mouth, I remember the inheritance story I came up with. Damn. There's a reason Danni had been in charge of sweet-talking her way into places while I crawled around behind the scenes.

"Right then," Penny claps her hands once. "As I told each of you earlier, I'm eager to set up a committee to keep this place in tip-top shape, and to make it feel like a community. But before we get into ideas for that side of things, we should talk about what happened."

The room falls silent. Even Orson sets down his phone to listen.

"Sunday morning, Gemma and I saw something sticking out of a locker. When we got closer, we realized it was a foot. And when we opened the door, we found him."

I listen, confused. Penny is tweaking this story, but why? Sure, we both found the body. But only after she saw the foot and came to get me. Probably embarrassed that she was too scared to check it out on her own. Maybe she's one of those people who thinks they have to appear invincible. Danni was like that. I catch myself. Danni *is* like that. She's still like that, just somewhere else.

"Did the police talk to each of you?" Penny asks the group.

"Yeah. Angry Cop and Hot Cop," George says, getting a chuckle from the room.

"Who was the dead guy? Does anyone know?" Marco asks.

"No," Penny says. "No identification on him."

"Is he an owner?" Cassie asks.

Orson makes an irritated sound. "How would they know?"

"Sorry, I.... Maybe someone recognized him."

"And we don't know when it happened except it was between Friday and Sunday, correct?" George says, seeming to want the group's attention back on him. "So, who visited the lockers this weekend?"

"I did," Penny says, her voice tight. "Several times. But that doesn't mean—"

"And you saw nothing?" George interrupts.

"Of course not." Penny replies, setting her mouth in a line. "Did you, George? You were there too, remember?"

George looks taken aback. "But I didn't go to the lockers."

"We haven't yet decided what's going to storage and what is staying in our apartment," Marco adds loudly. "And I haven't been down there at all since we moved in."

Penny keeps her gaze on George for a moment, looking thoughtful, then turns to Cassie. "You moved in on Saturday afternoon?"

"Around four, yes. But I haven't unpacked yet," Cassie says, sounding nervous.

Penny nods officiously. "Gemma, you arrived at around lunchtime on Friday," she continues. "And Orson, you picked up your keys on Friday, but moved your belongings on Saturday, right? Same for the couple in three-oh-four, but we haven't met them yet."

Does Penny have CCTV set up? How does she know so much about this?

"I invited them tonight, but they weren't home," Penny added.

Or didn't answer when they saw Penny's earnest—*the reason I'm here is going to inconvenience you*—expression through the peephole.

"Why are you asking us all these questions, Penny?" George says, his voice cutting across the room.

"Oh, uh." Penny blushes. "Just curious."

"You need a fob to get in," Orson says. Everyone turns to him. "His killer could be an owner."

Silence falls, tension immediately rippling through the air. Orson has a point, and we all know it.

"So whose locker was he in?" Orson continues.

Penny's eyes land on me. I stare back, waiting. If anyone knows, it's Penny.

She raises her eyebrows. I raise mine too. "Well?" I say. "Whose was it?"

"Gemma," she says softly.

"Penny," I reply.

"You can admit it."

"Can I?" I say, something unpleasant gripping my chest. "Admit what?"

"It was your locker."

"Wait, what?" I lurch up. "That body was in *my* locker?"

What the actual fuck.

19

NICO

Nico, seated in one of the larger booths at the back of Shaolin Kung-Fu Noodle house, looked up as the waitress approached. They gave her this primo spot and let her stay for hours, churning through her case notes, because she ate there at least three times a week and the owners liked having a police presence. For Nico, it was a great place to work without distraction.

"Hand-cut sour lamb noodle soup for Detective Davis," the waitress said, depositing a steaming bowl in front of Nico. And then there were the noodles. Best in the city, in her opinion.

"Thank you."

Nico took a slim-line container from her bag and retrieved a pair of chopsticks. She hated the cheap wooden or plastic ones, so she carried her own. Few knew about this quirk, but

Izzy had. She'd known almost everything about her. Pity Nico couldn't say the same. As a painful lump surged in her throat, Nico closed her eyes and rode the wave, taking slow breaths until it passed.

For the next while, Nico slurped noodles and let her brain wander nowhere in particular, then picked up her phone and went to her sister's Facebook account. She liked a few posts and commented on several others, so Tati wouldn't complain.

When she finished her food, she sat back, allowing a wave of fatigue to crest and pass, then pulled out a crumpled list from her bag. Excluding the six investment properties who could be discounted because they didn't have access to the building, there were ten Aurora owners who'd signed for their keys on Friday.

202 Cassandra Pike
203 Penny Pritchard
301 Marco Esposito and George Lee
302 Orson Walsh
303 Tom Bollard
304 Mr. & Mrs. Smith
401 Gemma Cross
402 Dr. B. Hobson
501 and 502: Volk. Co (Alex Romanov)

Her eyes lingered on Romanov's name. It made her want to fold in on herself, to crumple up into a ball and disappear. She couldn't ignore his presence in the building, but she needed more intel and more time before she faced him.

Who knew what he might say? She wasn't ready for that conversation.

And then there was Gemma Cross.

A shadow appeared at the table and Nico, assuming it was the waitress, muttered her thanks and pushed her empty bowl to the edge of the table.

"Not sure what you want me to do with that."

Nico looked up and scowled. DS Jackson leaned against the edge of the booth with an indulgent smile. As if there was something cute or amusing about Nico eating.

"What are you doing here?" Nico asked, her voice hard.

Jared slid into the seat opposite.

"I didn't ask you to join me," she growled.

"Just checking in, partner."

Nico glared at him, her jaw tight. "Did Jill tell you where I was?"

The Staff Sergeant's assistant had always been on the nosy side, but since Izzy, she'd been watching Nico like a hawk.

He ignored the question and gestured at Nico's list. "A working dinner? Where was my invitation?"

She narrowed her eyes.

"Any updates?" he added.

She sighed. "Since you're here, what happened in your initial interview with Penny Pritchard?"

"You were there."

"Not for all of it."

She'd been delayed on a call and had joined halfway through. Upon entering Penny's condo, she'd thought the atmosphere felt weird.

He shrugged. "She seemed shocked."

"Anything else?"

"She was pretty interested in whether we'd identified the body." Jared nodded, thoughtful. "You think that's something? She's kind of high-strung," he added. "Probably worried about security. But I'll follow it up. Give her a nudge. Make sure it's nothing more. I'll also see if I can get hold of the residents we haven't interviewed yet."

"Great, you go do that and leave me in peace."

Jared rose from the table, pulling out his phone to check the display as he moved away. Nico couldn't deny he had a graceful way about him. She understood his attractiveness on a theoretical level, but his charm wouldn't work on her.

"Jackson?"

He turned. "Yeah?"

"Don't come here again."

He smiled and sauntered away.

"He bugging you?" The waitress asked, appearing at the table.

Nico pursed her lips. "I'm not sure."

The waitress picked up the empty bowl and watched him exit the restaurant. "He can bug me if he likes."

Nico rolled her eyes and opened a new search on her phone. She had an alert set up for the Barringtons in case the media got hold of something before they did. Nothing new. She took a slow breath, trying to calm her skittering mind and racing heart. Gemma had an alibi for the night of the Barrington homicide. Nico had promised Sarge she'd let it go, but, dammit, *Gemma had been there that night.* She didn't care what that waitress said about Gemma being at the Duke. It was Gemma who Nico had chased down, wasting precious minutes. Gemma was the reason.... Nico's eyes started to sting. She blinked away tears and looked down. She needed to focus on the locker murder.

They still had no ID on the body, but she could look up photos of each owner to see who matched their John Doe. Because the obvious reason for him being stuffed in the locker was that he owned one of the apartments. Another was that his murderer did. Stupid to dump your victim on your own doorstep, but maybe they had no other option.

Her phone beeped with a notification. An email from Carlos Santino with the locker assignments. She scanned the list with feverish eyes, then slammed her hand on the table, startling the waitress as she passed.

"I fucking knew it."

Got you, Gemma Cross.

20

"How could you not know?" George says, making it clear he doesn't believe me. I look around the room. All the eyes on me—everyone except Orson, who's gone back to his phone—are dubious.

"You haven't used your locker?" George continues.

"Obviously not. I think I might have noticed a dead guy."

"Where's all your stuff?"

"I don't have much, okay? This is my first place."

George pursed his lips. "Really?"

"What? It's not that strange."

"How old are you?" Orson asks, looking up.

"It doesn't fucking matter how old I am. I had no stuff to put in storage, so I didn't." I stalk to the door. "And because you're all obviously wondering, I didn't kill him, you assholes."

I stomp back to my apartment, throwing my keys onto the kitchen counter, earning an unimpressed glare from Sol who I'd clearly woken up from a nap.

Was Penny some sort of passive-aggressive stealth bully? Had she gathered everyone at her place just so she could blame me in front of an audience?

"Not cool, Penny," I hiss. Sol growls. "Sorry," I say to him. "But that was so unfair."

I wear out my living room carpet for a few minutes, letting my anger spit and fizz, but it's not enough. I need to be outside. Because I'm suddenly feeling trapped inside this beautiful, spacious apartment. I grab my keys and run down the stairs, gathering momentum until I barrel out of the building as if it's on fire.

But   outside is worse.

Across the road, almost as if she'd been waiting for me to come flying out, is Detective Davis. She walks right up to me, her eyes blazing, and jabs a finger in my face.

"You're going down for this."

"For what? Existing in public?" I retort. My voice sounds confident, but my heart is a jackhammer in my chest.

"The dead man was found in *your* locker." Nico throws the words at me like knives.

"Yeah, so I heard," I mutter, waving it off as if it's no big deal. Wait.

If the lead detective on this case only just found out it's my locker, how did Penny already know?

"Fingerprint analysis is underway." Nico lifts her chin, her eyes flashing with triumph.

"Well, they won't find mine," I say.

Because I'm a trained professional and I don't leave those lying around. But I can't say that.

"I didn't step foot in that room until Sunday morning and even then I touched nothing. If you want to take me down, you're going to need more. I recommend actual evidence."

Something flickers across her face. What was that? A flash of pain? But it's gone now, replaced by anger.

"You're done, Gemma Cross," she hisses. "You'll pay for that night. I promise."

She stalks back to her car, parked illegally on the sidewalk. A moment later, with a squeal of tires, she's gone.

I stare after her. I'll pay for *that night?* She has to be talking about the Barrington heist. But why does it seem so personal? Why is she so angry? Waiting in that hotel room, I'd set up an online alert for Danni's name, but otherwise stayed off the internet. What am I missing?

I pull my phone from my pocket and open a search engine. I type in DS Nico Davis along with the date of our first run-in. *That night.* It's the first result to come up, and the information hits like a punch to the stomach.

"Oh, shit," I whisper. I now know the reason she's so hellfire and fury around me. Why she's determined to put me away.

Her partner died.

And finally, I understand. It's so obvious it's as if she said it to my face. This isn't about dead locker guy. It's about her dead partner. I was at the Barrington's, yes, but there can't be any evidence tying me to the crime scene, because I'd be locked up by now. Nico clearly blames me for her partner's death, but she can't get justice for that.

She's going to put me away for the body in my building instead.

21

I take my coffee out to the balcony and let the morning sun warm my back. The caffeine hit is good, but it's not enough. My eyes land on my Random Crap drawer. I want a cigarette. I lift my gaze to the exterior of the building. Or maybe it's a climb I'm jonesing for. Yes, itch identified. I want to be scaling a wall, looking for an entry point, breath catching and stomach fluttering. Not from fear, but from excitement. The risk of getting caught. The thrill of the chase. But guess what, Doctor Foster, you don't get the same rush from being hassled by a cop with a bug up her ass. I'm at risk, sure, but it's not a thrill at all. It sucks.

I now know why Nico is out to get me, and as reasons go, it's pretty good. The irony is, we both lost our partners that night. Weirdly, I want to tell her. But I can't. Obviously. Because any admission about that night would set me on a direct path to prison. Is this what happens when you put down roots and try to live a normal life? You find a dead body and get a dog-with-a-bone detective riding your ass?

Gaze still latched on that drawer, I drain my coffee, curse under my breath, and head into the kitchen. I can give up smoking another day. When my new life isn't crumbling at my feet. I grab one cigarette and the lighter and return to the balcony. I light up and inhale deeply, letting the smoke drift out of my mouth in a satisfying stream, when a voice floats up from below.

"Those will kill you."

I look down. In the middle of the garden, directly below my apartment, stands Tobi. She's wearing a cheeky smile, a white tank, an actual tool belt, and *look at my thighs* shorts. Her arms are glistening with sweat and I can see the muscles in her legs moving. She's definitely got my attention. I lick my lips and take another drag.

"Something has to, right?" I call back. "Kill me?"

"I'm going for old age," she replies.

An optimist. A cute one. I watch as she pulls a pair of shears from her tool belt and swings them around her fingers, then glances up at me. Okay, that was definitely for my benefit.

"So you don't live here? You're our gardener?" I ask.

"Landscape artiste, thanks very much." She grins.

I smile and lean farther over the railing, warming up. "Well, thanks for tending my patch."

She raises one eyebrow. "Did you actually just say *tending your patch*?"

My stomach does an excited flip. "That's what I said."

"Get a room, you two," someone says from below, his voice breaking the spell.

George Lee in 301. He's totally cockblocking me, but at least he doesn't seem mad that I called him an asshole last night.

"Hi Tobi with an I," George calls down.

"Hey, George. How's it?"

"Not bad."

"And what about you, Gemma?" Tobi adds. "Staying out of trouble?"

I tilt my head. "Wouldn't you like to know?" With a coy smile and a cute hair toss, I stub out the cigarette and sashay back inside. Tobi is adorable, yes, but I've got my hands full. And isn't there a saying about shitting where you eat? It's a gross expression, but it gets the message across. I can't have a hook-up hanging around where I live. Or, I guess, another one. I need to focus.

From my bag, I pull the pretty rose and mint notebook I'd purchased this morning. Because if I'm going to solve a murder, I'm going to need to write stuff down. Yes, I could use my phone, but Penny uses a notebook. If I'm going to figure out how a dead guy ended up in my locker before Nico can put me away, copying Penny's adulting seems like a smart move. You used to have a notebook, too, Doctor Foster, do you remember? Large and leather-encased, the holder of all my secrets. I fantasized a few times about leaping over the coffee table and yanking it out of your hands. Or breaking in at night to liberate it from your filing cabinet. Ha. Maybe that was my criminal awakening.

As the sound of George and Tobi chatting floats in from outside, I push away my FOMO and settle in the large arm-chair near the window. On the first page, I write *The Locker*

Body. Here I'll record all my clues and questions. But this notebook has two purposes. I flip to the back and scrawl: *Hobbies*. Obviously, here I'll decide what to do with my free time. Assuming I won't soon be locked up with prison-mandated hobbies. I return to the front. Once they identify the body, the detectives will be back to question us some more. At which point I'll find out his identity. Until that happens, all I can do is write down what I know. I tap my pen against the paper. We found the body at eight on Sunday morning, stuffed into my locker. Who is he? Why was he killed? And why my locker?

Wait. Is *my* locker the relevant bit? Is this related to my past? Danni and I mostly stayed away from the crooked underbelly, keeping to ourselves and dealing with our handler Sven only as needed. I've met a few people I most definitely don't want to come across in a dark alley, though. And my most recent job, the retirement shitshow, for sure could have stirred up something from society's dark depths. Crap. Is this about the Barrington diamonds? Is Nico actually inadvertently right on the money connecting me with these two cases? I suck in a breath. Fuck, am I now on the radar of the wrong people? But if this dead body is a message, then what is it? If it's nuanced enough to escape me, then it can't be from them. Criminals tend to go for a slap-you-in-the-face communication style. Cut off a few fingers to get the message across, vibes.

I sigh. I'm not getting very far with this chaotic and, yes, panicky thinking. Because I don't have enough information to make proper progress. But I know someone with an unhealthy amount of intel about this building and the people in it. Including when everyone moved in, which could be important. Penny. Plus, she has that kind of gung-ho, use-a-notebook, get-things-done attitude I can only muster if there's some sort of treat at the end. And no, avoiding prison doesn't count, it just doesn't. It's a dopamine thing. Right, Doctor Foster? You explained it all to me once. Something about how I'm only motivated by the possibility of pleasure instead of the threat of pain. Because pain doesn't stop me from doing much.

I nod to myself. Yes, getting Penny always-a-step-ahead Pritchard involved is clearly the best way to figure out what happened to this guy. I pick up my phone.

22

Penny opens her door and fixes me with a frosty smile. Oof, I should have worn a scarf for this kind of chill. I attempt a charming smile. "Hey."

She lifts her chin and presses her lips together. She's madder than expected. Not a fan of being called an asshole, I guess. Can't blame her, really. But in my defense, she started it. She organized that shindig, then turned it into a *let's call Gemma a killer* session. But, as Danni says, these are the cards I've been dealt. It's up to me to play the hand as best I can.

"I'm sorry for cussing you out," I say to Penny's tight expression, "but it was like all of you were accusing me. Of *murder*." I present my bottle of wine peace offering and raise my eyebrows.

She hesitates, then visibly relaxes. "We shouldn't have ganged up on you."

A minute later, I'm settled on the couch and Penny is opening the wine. There's a new peach throw draped on the couch, which I'm kind of into. I make a mental note.

"What happened after I left?" I ask as she hands me a glass.

"Not much." She gives me a pointed look, as if I'm to blame.

"The reason I got so offended about the whole locker thing is because," I start, still searching for the best angle, "the detective is trying to pin the murder on me."

"What?" Penny looks shocked. "Why would he do that?"

"Not Jared, uh, Detective Jackson. I mean the other one, Detective Davis." I pause, and Penny waits.

I want to tell her that Nico and I have crossed paths before, but how can I? Oh, yeah, we met last month when I was rappelling away from a crime scene.

"I don't know why, but she has a problem with me," I say finally. "I think I'm going to have to solve the murder myself."

"What?" Penny whispers, her face going gray.

I frown. "I have to solve—"

"Yes, I heard you, I just...." She raises one hand to her mouth.

This whispery shock is a bit much given she held a dead-body party yesterday.

"Just?" I prompt.

"I heard it was something to do with the construction company," she says.

"Like, his body was dumped before we even moved in?"

She nods. "It makes sense."

"But it could also be someone in the building," I press. "Which is pretty freaky."

She leans forward, eyes wide. "Why do you think the murderer is a resident?"

I frown. "Because he was found inside the building. In a locker."

"Your locker."

"Yes, I'm aware," I say, frustration bubbling. "It wasn't me, okay? But it could have—"

"No." She shakes her head. "We should leave it alone. Let the detectives do their jobs."

"But—"

"But nothing." She sits up straighter. "It's none of our business," she says primly.

Is she kidding? Where's the woman who knocks on doors at the crack of dawn?

An irritated sound flies from the back of my throat before I can stop it and Penny gives me a *look*.

"How about we try again with a rooftop get-together?" she says brightly.

"Rooftop drinks?"

She nods.

"Yeah, okay."

Because what better way to get the dirt on my new neighbors than after some lip-loosening booze? I have to divert Nico's attention away from me, and the most obvious way is to direct it somewhere else.

"Great!" Penny picks up her notebook and pen from the coffee table. "We have eight resident-occupied apartments in the building at the moment."

"Only eight?"

"I know." Penny shakes her head. "I'm not impressed either. They advertised this place as a community, but clearly some are investor condos." She sniffs. "They won't become Airbnbs on my watch."

"Cassie, Orson, George and Marco, you and me," I count them off. "Who are the others?"

Penny consults her notebook. "Your neighbor in four-oh-two is Doctor Beatrice Hobson. She's retired. I met her when she popped in on Friday to pick up her keys before she went on vacation. A cruise. Not back for six weeks, I think. Good to have a doctor in the building, right?"

I sit up straighter. "What if Doctor Beatrice killed him, then skipped the country!"

"Gemma," Penny cautions me.

"Fine. Okay, who else?"

"The man in three-oh-three is called Tom, but I, uh, haven't seen him yet. There's the couple in three-oh-four who I know are there because I've seen lights on, but they're never home when I knock," she finishes, seeming annoyed. "I mean, it's just plain courtesy."

"People don't have to be friendly with their neighbors," I say gently. "It's not compulsory."

"No, I suppose not, but...."

She checks her notebook again, then rattles off apartment numbers and investment company names. As I listen, I wonder again how she's getting all this information. Some of it from snooping around the building, maybe. But what about the other stuff?

I snap my fingers. "The Aurora has security cameras. What about the footage?"

Penny frowns. "I said I didn't want to discuss that anymore, and I meant it."

"But maybe we could—"

"Gemma." Her voice is flint and her eyes are steel. "It's a matter for the police."

"Fine."

I take a slow sip of wine, eyeing her over the rim of the glass. Penny and her harmless pixie persuasion is a powerful tool that I need to make use of. So how can I get her to play ball? And why the reluctance? What's changed? The difference between nosy neighbor Penny and this *let's all mind our own business* version is striking.

If I had brought my notebook with me, I'd be writing: *What is Penny's deal?*

23

NICO

N ico was not surprised to learn the victim was the owner of apartment 303. Tom Bollard. They hadn't been able to get hold of him and his demographics were a match: Caucasian, male, 42-years old. Tom was five eight and 167 pounds, with an appendix scar but no other identifying features. Cause of death hadn't come in yet but was likely to be asphyxiation. Tom had sustained a blow to his head shortly before he died, but it didn't break the skin, so the lack of blood at the lockers didn't mean he wasn't killed there. Tom had been dead for about two days when they found him on Sunday. They didn't know where he'd been killed or how long he'd been in that locker, though. The coroner hadn't yet released an official time of death.

The previous address listed on Tom's apartment paperwork turned out to be a hotel, which was interesting. His will bequeathed his assets to Alcoholics Anonymous, and while he had no children, he had been married. Alice Thornston now lived with her second husband and their two children half an hour from the Aurora. Nico found her phone number and dialed. Straight to voicemail. A recorded message explained Alice was away helping with a school event and would have limited cellphone access. Nico left a message, then returned to the basic profile she'd put together from a general internet and police database search. Tom, trained as an accountant but most recently working as a financial consultant, had two arrests on record. A drunk driving charge and a drunk and disorderly, both from around nine years ago. About the same time he left a top accountancy firm he'd been with for six years. Did he quit or was he fired? His marriage had also broken up at some point. Was it then or later? Did everything go wrong for Tom all at once? Nico could almost see his life unraveling. And given his will, he was almost certainly in AA. So was the drinking an after-effect, or the cause? Nico had a lot of questions, but at the top of the list was whether she could connect Tom Bollard to Gemma Cross.

An hour later, she leaned away from her computer screen. At a superficial level, she couldn't link them. But part of the problem was Gemma had no ties to anyone. She was a ghost in the justice system. The same went for social media. The reason was obvious to Nico—she was a criminal. Gemma was either an assassin for hire, or she'd been in the Barrington's apartment for the jewelry. But Nico couldn't prove anything. Yet.

Her phone rang. She eyed the display. Her sister, Tatiana. She sent it to voicemail. Nico wasn't interested in an interrogation right now, even a sisterly one.

She rubbed her tired eyes and refocused her gaze on the screen. If she couldn't come up with a link between Tom and Gemma, then....

Jared ambled up to her desk. "I've got news."

"Something good?"

"It's interesting. The Aurora's security cameras were scheduled to be activated at midnight on Thursday."

Nico eyed him warily. "And?"

He dropped into a nearby chair and wheeled himself closer. "Well, for one, there's a problem getting access."

Nico narrowed her eyes. "What kind of problem?"

"It's a question of who can grant it."

"Why not Boston Works?"

"They're supposed to be handing everything over to the Aurora condo board, but it hasn't been set up yet."

"For fuck's sake, this is a murder investigation. Who's being difficult?"

"Hard to tell. Carlos didn't want to get into trouble for doing the wrong thing, so he's shunted the problem upward. It's tricky because they're in the middle of handover."

"Don't they have acting presidents or people who can decide stuff until the condo board is officially formed?"

"Yeah, but guess who the proxy president is."

Nico held Jared's gaze. "Not our AWOL project manager? Chris Sheffield?" She shook her head. "What a joke. Pick the guy who's leaving for vacation, why don't you?"

"They didn't know someone would be murdered."

Nico widened her eyes. "Or did they? Maybe his vacation was less about needing a break and more about being unavailable for questioning."

"You think he's the killer? Or that he had to leave because of what he knows?"

Nico shrugged. "Either way."

Jared nodded. "I'll follow up and find out when he booked his leave. And his flights. See what kind of reaction I get from Boston."

"Let me know how difficult they make things for you. Maybe it's coming from higher up in the food chain. Maybe all of this is bigger than Tom Bollard."

Nico dropped her gaze to write: *Bigger than Bollard? Boston Works covering something up?*

"There's more," Jared said, leaning back, scratching the stubble on his jaw.

"Yeah?"

"The Aurora security cameras were *scheduled* to be activated on Thursday at midnight," Jared said, "but I have a feeling we're going to find out they weren't switched on."

Nico sighed. "Really?"

"Reading between the lines, yeah. They're stalling, hiding behind the access issue. But if I was a gambling man...."

"Are you?" Nico asked.

Jared tilted her head, something of a smile at his mouth. "Nope. Never saw the appeal."

"Neither." She looked down again. Why had she asked him that? She wasn't supposed to be getting to know him, merely tolerating his presence for as long as Sarge told her she had to.

She cleared her throat. "Maybe that's why Boston is being difficult. They breached protocol."

"So they sent Sheffield away until they could cover themselves legally."

"We won't know for sure until someone at Boston talks." Nico stood up. "Meantime, I'm heading to the Aurora to check out Tom Bollard's apartment."

"What about crime scene analysts? They're booked for later today."

"Just a look-see. I'll be careful."

Jared rose too. "We can also check on the elusive Anne and David Smith from apartment three-oh-four."

"Good idea. It's strange we haven't talked to them yet."

"What about Romanov?" Jared added.

Nico went still. "What about him?"

"Someone from the criminal world buys the entire top floor of an apartment building in which a dead body is found?" Jared sucked his teeth. "We gotta give him some attention."

"We've got that guy from organized crime. Mike. He'll deal with Romanov."

"So we're totally hands off?" Jared eyed her for a moment. "You had any prior contact with Romanov?" he added casually.

Anger surged. Why was he picking at her like this?

"Nico?"

She shook her head. "Never met him."

"No history?" Jared pressed.

Heat flooded her cheeks. "What are you getting at? I know as much as you do."

"Fine, fine." Jared nodded, then met her eyes again.

"If you're desperate to talk to him, then go right ahead. We're not attached at the hip."

He raised his hands. "All good."

As she shrugged on her jacket, she could feel Jared's eyes on her. "What?" she hissed.

"Nothing. I'll drive."

Carlos met them outside the Aurora and took them up to level three. He unlocked the door to 303, then stepped back without opening the door.

"Superstitious?" Nico guessed. "Don't want to enter a dead man's apartment?"

Carlos gave a nervous laugh.

"Did you meet him?" Jared asked.

"Who?" Carlos's voice was too loud.

Jared glanced at Nico to raise one eyebrow. "Our man Tom? You see him at all?"

"He picked up his keys from Chris Sheffield, so no. But he emailed to ask if I could receive his furniture deliveries."

"Why wouldn't he be here himself?"

Carlos raised his arm to wipe away the sweat forming on his forehead and shook his head. "Didn't say." He cleared his throat.

Nico and Jared locked eyes again.

"You'll have to keep any other deliveries that arrive for him," Jackson said. "This is a crime scene."

Carlos nodded.

"And we're going to need to see all correspondence between you and Tom," Nico added.

"Of course."

"Carlos?" Jared said, turning to face him. "You're holding something back. Let me guess, he made it worth your while?" Carlos didn't reply. "It's not illegal for someone to give you a gift for helping them out," Jared added, his voice gentle.

"Fine." Carlos sighed. "It was a hundred bucks to be here for his furniture deliveries."

Nico stored this information away. There wasn't anything inherently suspicious about this arrangement. In a homicide investigation, however, anything could be relevant. You needed every piece of the puzzle, otherwise it wasn't complete.

Nico and Jared pulled on gloves and shoe protectors, then stepped inside.

"Don't touch or move anything," Nico said.

"No shit," Jared muttered.

Nico stayed near the door for a moment to cast her eyes around the virtually empty open-plan kitchen, dining and living room. Tom had begun moving in, but hadn't gotten very far. Sitting right next to the door was a medium-sized red suitcase.

"Jackson, we have another suitcase in the evidence log, right?"

"A large black canvas bag in the garbage room. Empty."

"They're checking for trace?"

Jared nodded. "Another day or two."

If Tom wasn't killed downstairs, then someone had to get his body there somehow. A large bag was as good a way as any. She resumed surveying the room. Next to the suitcase was a cardboard box which contained only Styrofoam.

Jared gestured at it. "You know what normally comes with boxes like that?" he said.

"Plastic wrap," Nico replied.

The forensic report had listed this as the likely culprit in Tom's asphyxiation. Whatever happened to Tom probably did so at the Aurora. But right here, in his condo? The space felt too calm. Undisturbed. Crime scenes often had the echo of trauma. A trace of violence lingering in the air. Unquantifiable but palpable. Nico believed in concrete evidence and hard science, but she also knew science couldn't explain everything.

Nico's attention latched onto a yellow package on the breakfast bar. She moved closer to read the label. Addressed to Tom and unopened. Interesting. She returned her gaze to the rest of the room. The TV from the box sat atop an ugly glass TV stand. There was a still-boxed IKEA bookshelf, but where was everything else? All the detritus that comes with being a human being? Wait. What was that? Lying on the ground near the TV. The remote? As she got closer, she realized two things. First, a measuring tape lay there as well, almost invisible against the pale carpet. Second, the item that had brought her over wasn't a remote. It was a phone.

"Check it out," she said, allowing a pulse of excitement as she pointed it out to Jared.

"Nice."

They grinned at each other. Phones always yielded clues. Who the victim called recently, his frequent call list, what websites he'd visited and even what apps he had.

"Anything in the bedroom?" she asked, moving over to the door.

"A bunch of clothes dumped next to the closet and a few small pieces. A lamp, a few books. Nothing at all in the bathroom. Not even a toothbrush."

"Based on this half-assed unpacking situation, I'd say it's likely he was killed Friday morning. Maybe within an hour of him getting his keys."

Nico turned back to the package on the kitchen counter. Who unpacks and sets up their TV but leaves an envelope sitting on the bench, unopened. This was a clue. She could feel it.

24

"It's so pretty up here, isn't it?" Penny coos as we step out onto the rooftop. We're not up high enough for a panorama, but it's still beautiful with the twinkling city stretching out to the water beyond. Large outdoor plants are dotted around the space, with four small tables and chairs clustered in the middle and a few extra stools on the far side. There are even a couple of sun loungers, which I will definitely be using. Someone (my money is on Penny) has created festive vibes by putting fairy lights in the larger plants. All up, it's perfect for a neighborly get together-slash-interrogation because I'm determined to gather intel tonight. I didn't bring my notebook—that would look weird—but I can jot down any clues in my phone.

The drinks are BYO, so Penny brought a bottle of chardonnay in an ice bucket—already added to my To Buy list. I opted for pinot grigio, with two bottles on standby downstairs. I want everyone's tongues as loose as possible, just not for the normal reason. I need secrets to be spilled.

"Look at you two, nice and early." Penny says, scuttling over to where Marco and George are perched on stools, holding cocktails. George gives me a wary glance, but Marco waves so I wave back, staying near the tables to pour myself a glass of wine. Just as I do, Cassie steps through the door.

"Hey, Cassie."

"Hi," she says, seeming nervous. She has something behind her back, looking like a kid with a secret.

I hold up my bottle. "Join me?"

"I, uh...."

"Oh, you don't drink," I say, remembering she had a soda at Penny's.

"No, I do, I just...." She wrinkles her nose and presents a carton of pulpy organic orange juice. "I wasn't sure what to bring."

"Up to you." I point at the goblets on the table. "I brought extra glasses."

"Okay, yes please," she says with a shy smile.

Cassie seems like the kind of girl who, as a teenager, read books instead of going to parties, and I'm guessing this behavior stuck. She's now twenty-six, Penny told me earlier, and this is the first time she's lived on her own. My path was different—leaving home at seventeen and never looking back—but maybe Cassie and I have ended up in the same place. New at adulting and trying to figure out our new lives.

"How's the writing going?" I say as we settle at the table. "Are you working on a new book?"

Immediately, Cassie recoils. As if I asked her to reveal her darkest childhood trauma. "Oh, um...."

Her phone buzzes. She reads the message, raising one hand to her mouth to cover a half-thrilled, half-terrified smile.

I know that expression.

"Hot date?" I ask.

She blinks and nods. "We planned to go for drinks, but then Penny—"

"We have drinks right here," I say, waving at the table.

Her eyebrows lift. "Should I invite him?"

"Definitely."

"If you think so." She fixes her large eyes on me for a moment, almost as if she's giving me a chance to change my mind. Nope. I may not be a Penny-grade Nosy Parker, but I do like to be involved in romantic entanglements.

Cassie drops her gaze to type out a reply. "There." She looks pleased. "I told him to come over."

"How long have you been dating?"

"We've only been out once."

I try not to let my eyes bug out.

"Oh." Cassie raises her hands to her face. "Is it too soon to bring him to a get-together? I don't have any experience with this."

"Dating?"

She nods. "I've never really...." She lifts one shoulder. "You know."

"Never dated?"

Her eyes widen. She looks almost panicked.

"It's no big deal," I add quickly, but wow, am I looking at a virgin?

"Mom, she...." Cassie twists her hands. "She was strict, and then she got, uh, sick, and caring for her took up all my time. I never had a chance to... and then with writing. It's all-consuming, you know? And solitary, so I—"

"You don't need to explain," I say.

"It's too soon though, isn't it?" Cassie repeats, fixing her stricken expression on me. "For him to come here."

I glance over Cassie's shoulder, trying to get eyes on Penny. This seems like a Penny sort of situation. What would I know about being an adult virgin?

"This is just a relaxed hang," I say, failing to get Penny's attention. "Low pressure."

Cassie nods. "And he's super outgoing. He won't have a problem meeting a bunch of other people."

"It'll be fine."

As Cassie drops her worried gaze to her phone, Orson-the-IT-nerd ambles through the rooftop door, scratching his stomach. He's carrying a large tumbler of something dark-colored, and comes straight over to us. He plonks himself at the table, then looks at me expectantly. Like, *I'm here. Your move.*

"Orson," I say. "What's up?"

"Hey." He turns to Cassie and nods.

"Nice evening," she says.

He glances up at the sky as if to check. "I guess."

As Cassie's eyes return to her phone, Orson's gaze drifts to me. When I don't speak, because I have no clue what to say to this guy, he nods to himself and pulls out his own phone.

If everyone else is scrolling, maybe now's the time to think about questions to ask my neighbors. I could write a list. Or maybe I should just ask Cassie and Orson straight out. *Hey, either of you a murderer?*

But then the door to the roof swings open again and it's none other than Tobi, the hot gardener. She's holding a sixer of beer, wearing a pair of mid-thigh bicycle shorts, work boots and a cropped t-shirt that offers a tantalizing glimpse of the ink on her side. I swallow. The only way I can stick to my rules and keep up sensible decision-making is when temptation doesn't appear twenty feet away.

"Leighton will be here in five minutes," Cassie whispers to me. She's gripping her wineglass so tightly I'm worried it might break. Bringing my favorite goblets up here might have been a mistake.

"How do I look?" she asks.

Like a high school art teacher, I want to say, but don't. She's paired a floaty scarf with a peasant-style skirt and she looks nice, but not *sexy*. But that's okay. People don't always have to look sexy.

"Great," I say. "Very nice."

She gives me a nervous smile. "I better go let him in downstairs."

"Good luck."

"Gemma!" Penny says breathlessly, dragging Tobi over to the table. I stand to meet them. Orson stays put, engrossed in his phone.

"Did you meet our landscaper yet?" Penny says. "She's putting in a vegetable patch!"

"Wow, vegetables, really?"

Tobi lifts one eyebrow. "Not much of a green thumb, huh? Or is it veggies you're not into?"

"Vegetables, I'll allow with a good sauce. Gardening?" I shrug.

Tobi takes my hands and inspects them, stroking the calloused skin on my palms and fingers. She looks up at me, head cocked, eyes interested. Shivers run up my arm.

"Not the soft princess hands you were expecting, huh?" I say.

She smiles, clearly waiting for me to explain, but how can I?

"I basically murder plants," I say into the silence, pulling away. "You don't even want to know."

"Don't I?" Tobi says.

The moment hangs until Penny hurls a series of gardening questions at Tobi. She answers them, throwing me an occasional *save-me* expression. This, I ignore. I have to. Because saving her will definitely involve flirting and probably hooking up, and I've already decided that's a bad idea. The new Gemma doesn't make crappy decisions. Not anymore.

When the roof door opens again and Cassie steps through with her date, I make my excuses and hurry over. I'm not ready to test how much willpower the new Gemma has.

Cassie's cheeks are flushed. "Gemma, this is Leighton."

"Nice to meet you," he says, his lip curling as he gives me an obvious once-over.

Not a great start, Leighton.

"Hey," I say neutrally.

I guess you could call him good-looking in an Advertising Bro kind of way. I glance at Cassie. She's gazing at him as if he's some sort of miracle. I want to say, *this dude, really?* But I can't because she seems smitten. And maybe the sex will be good. Leighton looks as if he gets around. I would know.

"Where'd you two meet?" I ask.

"At the café on the corner," Cassie says.

"Bouche." I nod. "Love that place."

"We both ordered a green tea latte and there was a bit of a mix-up," Leighton says with a condescending smile, seeming to imply Cassie's some sort of dimwit who can't remember her own drink order.

Cassie giggles and tucks her hair. "I honestly thought they called my name."

"Hey, Gemma?" Leighton says, pointing. "Someone's trying to get your attention."

I turn to see George waving urgently.

"I better go see what he wants."

When I reach them, George pulls at my arm. "Who's the new arrival?" he whispers excitedly, dropping his sulk with me now that I've got the inside scoop.

"Is that why you called me over?" I say. "You could have been less obvious about it."

George lifts his shoulders as if he doesn't care. "Is he with the mousy writer?"

"Don't call her that," Marco cautions him. "Cassie's lovely."

"Yes, but her style is... that." He waves his hand. "And it's obviously on purpose." He eyes me. "Well?"

"His name is Leighton and they've just started dating," I say.

"How long do you give it?" George smirks.

At this, I shrug. He's being kind of bitchy, but he has a point. They don't look like a couple.

George drains his drink and rattles the ice. "Bummer."

"I guess that's us," Marco says, lifting his also-empty glass.

"Already?" I say. I haven't even talked to them yet. I've been too busy involving myself in new relationships and hot gardeners.

"Do you two like white wine?" I ask. "I was about to grab another bottle of pinot grigio."

Marco opens his mouth, but before he can speak, George says, "We'd love a glass."

"Okay, one sec."

Inside my apartment, Sol is curled up on the armchair. He raises his head to glare at me, as if I've got some nerve interrupting him when he's supposed to have the place to himself. "Sorry, bud," I say.

I use the washroom, fluff my hair and reapply my lip gloss—I'm not taking questions on the reason—then tuck both bottles of pinot grigio from the fridge under one arm. I then grab four of the plastic goblets I'd bought specifically for this kind of outdoor drinking situation.

"See you later," I call to Sol as the door clicks shut behind me.

Just as I get to the top of the stairs, I hear voices.

"Tell me," someone says from the other side. His voice is low and urgent, and it sounds like Marco.

"It's done. Move on," George hisses.

"How can you say that?"

"I'm not doing this again. Drop it."

Silence.

I wait, but there's nothing else. They must have been passing the door. But as I'm about to reach for the handle, it bursts open. Marco comes barreling out, his face set in an angry expression. He pauses briefly to cast an apologetic smile in my direction before hurrying down the stairs. When I turn back, George stands in the doorway, looking worried.

"Everything okay?"

"I guess," he murmurs.

I nod my head toward the bottles under my arm. "Still interested?"

"Definitely." George reaches out to take them from me and we both return to the tables. Before I can get the intel about their fight, Cassie and Leighton, then Penny and Tobi join us. Orson looks up, bewildered at the activity, then lumbers to stand as well.

As I pour wine, Leighton says loudly, "Hi guys, I'm Leighton."

Cassie blushes. "Sorry, I was going to—"

"No worries, babe," Leighton says.

"I'm Penny," she says, nodding eagerly. "And that's Tobi, Gemma, George, and Orson."

Orson, suddenly more alert, puffs out his chest and steps forward to shake Leighton's hand. "Did Cassie tell you about the dead dude?" he asks. "A classic whodunit."

"A what?" Tobi says, her dark brows creased.

"A group of people in one location and then a dead body shows up," Orson says. "We were all here the weekend the guy was killed."

"Not everyone here is a resident," Tobi says, her voice flat.

"You're the gardener," Orson replies. "You've got keys."

Tobi jerks back, as if insulted. "Only so I can store tools in the equipment room."

"Is that true?" George says, excited. "You have your own key fob?"

"Sure, but...." Tobi trails off.

"The body was found in the locker room," George says. "Which means—"

"Yeah, yeah, we get it," Tobi mutters, seeming pissed. "But I'm not dumb enough to kill someone then put the body right next to where...." She doesn't finish, her mouth in a line.

"Everyone is capable of murder." Orson nods. "I read that on Reddit."

"Even *landscape* gardeners," George adds.

"Give it a rest," Tobi says, her jaw working.

"Yeah, George," I say, annoyed on Tobi's behalf. "Let it go."

Tobi tosses me a grateful smile, but there's something dark and worried behind her eyes.

"This can't be everyone?" Leighton asks, gesturing at our group. "All the residents?"

"We haven't met Anne and David Smith yet," Penny says. "The couple in three-oh-four."

I eye Penny. How does she know their names?

"It's creepy," Cassie says, tugging at the end of her scarf. "When you think about it."

"You write about murders," George says.

"Not like this. And even if I did, it's fiction. It's not in my building. Not right downstairs." She shudders.

"Their name is *Smith*?" Orson says, ignoring the conversational drift. "Sounds suspicious. Like an alias."

"A pretty elaborate alias to buy an apartment with that name," Penny says.

"Not if they used a company to purchase," George replies. "The apartment could be listed under the company name and then they could tell us their names were whatever they wanted."

That means everyone could be lying about their names. Also, why didn't I think of that? Using a fake name would mean Detective Davis couldn't.... No. I've turned over a new leaf and I'm making progress with my new life. So far, tonight is going great.

The roof door opens again, and the smile falls off my face.

Detectives Davis and Jackson are here.

25

NICO

Nico and Jared paused by the roof door to take stock. Seven people stood in a huddle by a table, all eyeing them with wariness. Nico kept her gaze on the group as a whole, trying to ignore the specific individuals. Gemma, in particular. Despite her efforts, Nico's eyes found Gemma's face. Her expression was blank, but Nico could see a skittering mind behind that calm facade.

Yeah, you should be worried.

"Evening, all," Jared said as they strolled over. "Nice night for it."

"Detectives," Penny replied, stepping forward as if in charge. "How can we help you?"

There was a wobble to her voice, Nico noted. Was Penny naturally anxious, or did she have something to hide?

"A few follow-up questions," Jared said. "We've identified the victim."

Someone gasped. Nico scanned the group, trying to get eyes on the source.

"We'll talk to you one by one," Jared continued, then nodded at George Lee, closest to them. "You're with me," he said, leading George across the rooftop.

"Penny, over here please," Nico said, pointing. "Don't go anywhere," she said to the others. "We need to talk to all of you."

Nico could hear that her voice sounded stiff and strange, but it was the best she could do with Gemma fucking Cross standing less than five feet away.

"Shouldn't take long," Jared added over his shoulder. "Just take a seat and relax."

Nico pulled out her notepad and the picture of Tom Bollard they'd copied from his driver's license. She held it out to Penny, who took it, eyes wide.

"His name was Tom Bollard. Do you know him? His name mean anything to you?"

"No." Penny gulped. "Was he an owner?"

Nico nodded. "What about this?" She showed her a photo of the black bag that had been left in the garbage room. Trace had come back with a match to Tom. Which likely meant either the bag belonged to him, or it was used to carry his body.

Penny blinked, then shook her head, almost as if trying to dislodge something.

"You alright?" Nico asked, watching her.

"Fine, just...." She raised one hand to press it against her temple. "A headache."

"What were your movements over the weekend?" Nico asked, pen poised.

"I already told you."

"Once again, please," Nico said firmly. It had been clear from her original interview that Penny paid attention to the building comings and goings. Would her account differ this time? Or contradict someone else's?

As Penny ran through her weekend, Nico made notes, keeping her head down until she mentioned the lockers.

"So you went down on Saturday, but you didn't see the body."

"N-no."

Nico studied her for a moment. She was nervous, but innocent people sometimes were even with routine questions. And Penny was definitely the type.

Forensics had confirmed Tom could have been hidden inside the locker all weekend. Natural processes like gravity and decomposition could have moved Tom's leg, making it pop out of the locker on Sunday morning.

Suddenly, Penny looked flustered. "But you should ask George Lee and Orson Walsh. They were both there, too."

"When?"

"I saw George near the lockers on Friday at around three o'clock."

Nico glanced at Jared, still talking to George. They would compare notes later.

"What was George doing?" Nico asked.

"Looking around, as far as I could tell."

"He wasn't putting something into storage?"

"No, but he could have before I got there." Penny nodded to herself.

"What about Orson?"

"Technically, I saw him in the lobby, but he appeared to be taking things through to the lockers."

"Do you remember what, exactly?"

Penny frowned.

"Bags? Boxes?"

"Sorry."

"What time was this?"

"Oh, gosh." Penny bit her lip. "It was after I saw George and before I popped out. Gemma came over at five and I was home for at least half an hour before she arrived, so...." She thought for a moment. "It must have been about three-thirty."

"Gemma was with you on Saturday?" Nico said, trying to keep her voice neutral. She risked a look. Gemma sat at the table drinking wine with an amused expression. Seemingly not a care in the world, but her leg was jiggling hard enough to make the table wobble. Nico smiled to herself. Her serenity was a charade, and Gemma was obviously practiced at keeping cool.

"We met on Friday night," Penny continued. "I knocked on her door to introduce myself and invite her to come over for drinks the following day."

"Was Gemma alone?" Nico asked.

"Friday? Yes. Or she was at around nine." Penny looked uncertain. "Although it was hard to tell because she barely opened the door."

"She didn't let you inside?"

Penny shook her head.

Nico swallowed. Had Gemma been hiding something inside her apartment? Tom Bollard's dead body, perhaps?

"Did you see Gemma at the storage lockers?"

"I didn't see her moving her things at all."

"Anything else worth noting?"

Penny shook her head.

Jared appeared. "How are we doing over here, ladies?" he said, winking at Penny.

Penny blushed and tucked her hair behind her ear. "Just fine, thank you."

"Contact me if you think of anything else." Nico handed Penny her card.

As Penny moved away, Jared said, "There used to be seven people up here."

Nico looked back at the cluster near the table. "What the fuck?"

"Cassandra with her date, Leighton," Jared said, counting off the remaining people. "Orson, Penny, George and Gemma."

"Who left the party?"

"Tobi the gardener."

"Huh. Access to the building?"

Jared nodded. "Apparently so."

"Make a note to follow up."

"Will do."

"I'll take Orson, you talk to Cassandra," Nico said. "Without her date, okay? Your *skills* won't be as effective with him there."

Jared grinned.

At Nico's beckoning, Orson walked unhurriedly over and fixed her with a blank stare. "Yes?"

"Do you know Tom Bollard?" Nico held out the photo.

Orson inspected it. "No."

"You didn't see him during the weekend at all?"

He shook his head.

"His condo is on your floor."

Orson shrugged. "Don't know what to tell you. I didn't see the dude."

"What about your neighbors, Anne and David Smith? Have you seen them yet?"

Once again, he shook his head. The Smiths were the only residents they hadn't spoken to. Where were they?

"I understand you took some stuff into storage on Saturday," Nico continued. "Did that include a large black canvas bag?"

"Maybe. Details like that elude me."

Nico frowned. Was he being evasive on purpose?

"Even moving house? Your own belongings?" she pressed.

Orson grinned. "It doesn't stick."

Nico held out another photo. "This look familiar?"

"It's a black bag."

Nico bit back a sarcastic *no shit, Sherlock*, and pushed on. "Go over the timeline of your weekend."

"It's kind of a blur."

Nico gritted her teeth. "Can you try? Start with Friday morning."

As Orson churned his way through his activities, umming and ahhing and making Nico wonder whether there was even any point in taking notes, she glanced across the rooftop. Jared had finished talking to Cassandra and now stood with Gemma, who was tilting her head and touching Jared's arm. Unbelievable. And Jared wasn't stopping her. He was leaning closer. As Gemma squeezed his forearm and threw her head back to laugh, Nico abandoned Orson mid-sentence and marched over.

Nico yanked at Jared's elbow, dragging him a few feet away. "You need a professionalism check about now?" she said in a low voice.

Jared widened his eyes. "Do you?"

She took a long breath. Unclenched her jaw. Tried to focus.

"There's more than one way to ask a question, Nico."

"I bet," she said, glaring at him.

"Are we done?" Gemma called over.

"Yes," Jared said. "Thanks."

"Are we?" Nico said, tension gripping her shoulders. Something surged up from her stomach. Fast and hot. She blinked and swallowed. Took a slow breath through her nose. She couldn't lose her shit again. Not here.

Jared dropped his voice. "You're on thin ice with Sarge. You want to turn this into another situation?"

Nico kept her eyes on Jared for a moment, then shook her head.

"Come on," he said. "Let's get out of here."

26

NICO

It was getting late, but Nico was happy to be at the station, combing through the case details. It felt good and natural and normal. Even if it was with Jared-unchecked libido-Jackson. Because festering at home would be a mistake. The kind that led to other, career-ending mistakes.

"Guess who has a record," Jared said, tilting his laptop so Nico could see. "October Hart. Otherwise known as Tobi the gardener."

"I was expecting as much," Nico said.

"We can bring her in tomorrow."

After a moment, Nico shook her head. "I'll talk to her somewhere neutral. She'll clam up in a police station."

"Alone?" He raised one eyebrow.

She shifted her gaze to him, leaning back casually but confidently in his chair. "Not everyone is susceptible to your charms, Jackson. Some will take one look at you and put up barricades."

"Rarely," Jared said easily. "I'm a people person and you know it."

"You also look like a guy who did some bullying in high school."

After a beat, Jared said, "The opposite, actually."

Nico nodded. "I believe you. But you don't give that impression now."

Jared didn't reply at first.

"Would you count spaghetti as a noodle fix?" he said finally.

Nico frowned. "Noodle fix?"

"Nico loves noodles." He grinned. "I pay attention." He patted his stomach. "It's a good time to call it a night and I'm starving. There's an Italian place on College. House red wine is decent and their food is great."

No. Nico's stomach clenched. *Too soon.*

She lurched up. A jerky motion. Almost as if unable to control her own body.

"What are we, dating?" she said.

"Nico—"

"You're right about calling it a night, though." She picked up her bag. "Good work today," she called over her shoulder. Something of a consolation prize.

As she walked out to the elevator bay, she acknowledged the ping of regret humming in her chest. Eating alone had its perks, but it wasn't always what she preferred.

Still, she was smiling as she rode down to the lobby. Team Davis and Jackson might just make it after all.

27

I twist and turn and churn my way through the night, the messiness of my entanglement with two of Toronto's finest crawling through my mind like fire ants. Itchy and insistent.

Body heavy and brain like slush, I stay in bed well into the afternoon, scrolling and dozing and thinking about both Jared and Nico—in very different ways. Also, Tom Bollard, whoever the hell he turns out to be.

When Sol gives me one of his famous side-eyes and meows loudly, I get up and make us both breakfast. Or I guess, lunch. Sol gets the same old sloppy crap—he loves it—and I eat the rest of the pizza I ordered last night after our rooftop drinks-turned-police interrogation.

Sated but restless—my need for an adrenaline fix is a siren song I won't be able to resist for much longer—I take my coffee out to the balcony. I turn my back to the sun, letting it kiss my skin. The dead guy was a condo owner. Does this make it more likely someone in our building killed him? The idea is kind of thrilling. A dysfunctional reaction, yes, but no surprises there. Right, Doctor Foster? Totally on brand.

As I turn to get rays on my face, there's a movement in the trees. I raise my hand to shield my eyes and in the next moment, all logical thoughts disappear. My hot gardener Tobi is attached to a harness and hanging from a tree. She's wearing what are basically hotpants and holding what looks like a weed whacker. There's a guy underneath spotting her, but who cares about him? I watch her expertly lopping off branches, deftly swinging and balancing and wielding that machine. Her muscles move and glisten in the sun, and a pulse of heat rockets through my body. Wow. Tobi likes to dangle from things, I like to dangle from things. Are we meant to be?

I keep eyes on her for another minute, all sweaty and athletic, then get an idea. Two can play at this game.

I dart inside and change into my smallest workout shorts and a top that's barely a bra. I take my yoga mat out to the balcony. Yes, Doctor Foster, I do yoga sometimes. It's relaxing. Plus, I'm pretty sure it cancels out the smoking.

Pretending I haven't noticed Tobi, I start stretching. After I've waved my arms about a bit to make sure she sees me, I do a sun salutation, reaching back into downward dog. Then, some cat-and-cows, arching my back to push my butt higher in the air.

"Hey," Tobi calls finally. "Gemma."

I straighten, playing at surprise. "Oh, hi," I say, sitting back on my heels. "I didn't see you there."

"You didn't?" she says wryly, already smiling.

I gesture at her, hanging in the tree. "You know, some might call this kinda desperate." I grin. "You could have just knocked on my door."

Tobi chuckles. "It might be hard for you to believe, but all this," she indicates her harness, "isn't about you."

"You're not watching me?" I fake a pout.

Tobi purses her lips. "Can't I do both?"

"Not if I'm doing this properly," I say, going back to the cat-cow motion and pushing my butt up even more. "You shouldn't be able to concentrate at all."

There's a knock at the door.

I stop, jolted out of the moment.

What am I doing?

I've already decided this is a bad idea, but here I am, diving in anyway. This is why being a grownup is difficult. Tough decisions and tests of willpower at every turn.

"Sorry, gotta go," I call.

I abandon my yoga mat, which Sol is now approaching with interest, deciding whether he wants to claim this as yet another chill out/sunbathing space, and run inside. Another knock. I need a cold shower, but that will have to wait. I have whoever this is (my money is on Penny), to thank for pulling me out of my lusty fog.

It's not Penny.

Detective Jared Jackson leans with one arm up against the doorjamb, exposing both the muscle of his biceps and his washboard stomach above his belt. Oh shit. He jerks upright at the sight of me, his face becoming vacant and slack-jawed as his eyes move down my body, taking in my light glow of perspiration, my cleavage-revealing bra, my tiny shorts and the rise and fall of my chest.

Neither of us have a chance.

I step up, loop my finger into his belt buckle and pull myself so that I'm right up against his body. I graze his lips with mine, pausing before I lightly run my tongue along his lower lip. He sucks in a breath and grips the edge of the door, as if trying to stop himself from being dragged into my vortex, but then makes a low sound in the back of his throat, winds his arm around my waist and pulls me even closer. No space for light or air; it feels incredible. He leans down and kisses me urgently with a sighing noise that would have dropped me to my knees if he wasn't gripping my body against his.

"Why are you here?" I whisper as he dips his head to my neck. But instead of waiting for him to answer, I unzip his fly.

I'm sure you know how the rest goes, Doctor Foster.

28

In a tangle on the bed, I prop myself up on one elbow. "Did you come over for this... or official reasons?"

His sheepish expression tells me the answer. I grin.

In a flash of gray, Mr. Solomon appears at the edge of the doorway, his curious eyes peeking around to assess the situation. He lets out a small growl of disapproval, then slinks away. This kind of activity is new to him. Or I guess, us. He's not a fan.

Jared shakes his head. "Gemma, this wasn't... I'm not—"

"Supposed to screw witnesses in a murder case?"

"I should be questioning you."

"Pretty sure I said *yes, oh, yes,* a few times, if that helps."

He disentangles from me and scrambles out of bed. "Shit."

"You can still interview me."

"Detective Davis is here too."

"She is?" I look around with wide eyes, hamming it up. "Prefers to watch, does she?"

"Here in the building," he says, his voice low.

"Nico could literally catch you with your pants down." I smirk.

Nico's obsession with me is a problem, sure, but one for future Gemma. Because right now I want to enjoy watching Jared hop around my bedroom, pulling up his trousers.

"Detective Davis to you," he says over his shoulder.

I make a face. I guess I know where his loyalties lie, even if all of his body parts don't agree.

Finally, dressed and professional again, he puts his hands on his hips. "Put on some clothes and we'll talk in the living room."

"Sure, *officer.*"

I pull on my robe and follow him out.

"Can I get you a beverage?" I ask. "There's wine open."

"I'm on duty, remember?"

"This is you on duty? Maybe I should become a cop. I'd be great at it."

"Gemma, please." He sighs. "Is this what you're wearing?"

My robe is not the full-length, fluffy variety. It barely covers my ass.

"I'm about to take a shower," I say. "Why isn't Nico here, by the way? Why isn't *she* the one doing the follow-up interview?" His brow furrows. "Because she's not allowed, right? Because she has a problem with her temper." I watch his face.

"If you would get changed, I would appreciate it."

"Fine." I flounce into the bedroom and pull on a pair of light sweats and a cropped, sleeveless tank. My ensemble does not include a bra. "Happy?" I say, returning to the living room.

His eyes flick over me, pausing on my chest, then settle on his notepad. I catch a hint of a smile.

"What does the name Tom Bollard mean to you?"

"You already asked me this."

"Not properly." He holds up a photo and fixes a serious expression on me.

He's pretty cute in work mode. I don't know how good a detective he is—he obviously shouldn't be having sex with a suspect in a murder case—but he seems to care about his job. And even though he's been the enemy my whole life, it's weirdly endearing.

I take the photo I've already seen and inspect it again. Non-descript white guy, fortyish, squarish face. So who wanted him dead?

I hand it back. "Nope."

"You've never heard of him, never met him before?"

"Since he's an owner, he could have let his murderer inside, right?"

Jared doesn't reply.

"Complicates things, doesn't it? What about security footage?"

Jared opens his mouth, then shuts it again. "You know I can't tell you this stuff." His phone buzzes. "I have to go meet Nico, uh, Detective Davis. Before I go...." He gestures to the bedroom. "That shouldn't have happened."

I pout. "Regrets?"

Jared makes a face. "It's better for both of us if we don't—"

"Yeah, yeah, I get it."

He stands up, and I do too. He leans forward slightly, instinctively, as if to kiss me goodbye, but then pulls back. "If you think of anything else, call." He gives me his card.

"I already got one of these, remember?"

Jared slides it into his pocket. "Gemma, please believe me, it's better if you tell us things before we find them out ourselves."

Yeah, right.

"Gotcha," I say.

I lock the door after him and take a shower, then pour myself a glass of the pinot grigio Jared rejected. I pad over to the leather armchair next to the window and tuck up my legs. Jared is probably right. While breaking the rules makes things much hotter, screwing a cop will make my life too complicated.

I set down my wine and pick up my laptop. Sol comes to join me, clearly pleased I have ejected the strange man from our home. As I open a browser, he settles on the armrest to supervise. One of my favorite things to do—after climbing, cat-burgling and sex—is to have a glass of wine and play online. Sol seems to like it too and tonight, we're shopping for clothes. Lucky for me and my aversion to trying things on, I have a relatively well-proportioned body, so stuff usually fits. And now I have a new persona—a normal, non-criminal who hangs out with her neighbors—I need a new wardrobe. Obviously.

Sol approves a bunch of new outfits, then I switch to more general surfing: hotties, incredible travel spots, and funny animal clips (Sol's favorite). By the time I call it a night, I'm following a couple of new crushes, I have a few deliveries to look forward to, and there are three new destinations on my Dream Vacation list.

I fall asleep immediately, but wake less than an hour later.

Someone is in my apartment.

29

Sol's tense little body is aimed at the living room. Ears forward; eyes like lasers. Heart thumping, I peel back the covers and move silently toward the ajar bedroom door. My intruder is quiet, but stealth is my game. I peer around the corner. Immediately, I see one foot. What is it with me and unexpected feet? The foot wiggles. An improvement, at least. This one is still alive. Wait. Leather loafer, no socks. My shoulders drop. I know this foot; this person.

I stalk into the living room, slamming on the light and cursing myself as the brightness burns my eyeballs.

"This is a no shoes apartment," I bark. "What the hell, Sven," I add as a more general complaint.

"Gemma. How nice of you to join me," he says as if I'd finally shown up to his dinner party.

"Join you?" I screech. "You disappeared after that night, then nothing. *Nothing*. And *now* you show up in my apartment and scare the crap out of me?"

Sven Karlsson—hailing from Norway but with a murky origin story—job booker and narcissist extraordinaire. Narcissist is maybe too strong—I'd have to get your expert opinion on the situation, Doctor Foster. Self-serving, for sure. It's all about Sven, all the time. You just have to hope you want the same things as him. Ten years ago, Danni introduced me to him, her boss. And when he offered me a job, I didn't hesitate. I'd needed something to pull myself out of the less-than-amazing existence I'd been festering in. After only six months of learning the game—literally, the ropes—I was playing the game.

As anger bubbles, I start to pace, my steps short and sharp.

"Darling, relax," Sven purrs, watching me with an amused smile. "You'll wear out the carpet. Although...." He wrinkles his nose as he waves at the floor. "This color is—"

"Beautiful." I scowl. "What would you know?"

His long limbs are permanently clad in black, which isn't a fashion statement. At least, not entirely. He's color blind. He has no business commenting on the color of anything.

His eyes flick to me and I catch the warning. The icy promise of retribution if I push too hard.

"Gemma, come now." In one graceful movement, he slides out an old-fashioned silver cigarette case.

"You can't smoke in here. Penny would have a fit and Sol—"

He strolls over to open the balcony door and waves his hand, like, *happy now?*

"Goodness, Gemma." He smirks, lighting his cigarette. "It didn't take long to domesticate you, did it?" He holds up my lighter. "Where do you think I got this from?"

I clench my jaw. "What do you want? Why are you here?"

Sven tilts his head. "Am I to assume this *settling down*," his voice carries more than a hint of disgust, "means you are officially out of my employ?"

"Are you kidding? I couldn't get hold of you to save my life. Almost literally. I had to make a new one."

"Still, some sort of courtesy communication would have been the polite thing to do." Sven pouts.

"How? You changed your number and *disappeared*," I yell. "So, yeah. I am officially *out of your employ*." I use air quotes in case he doesn't pick up on the sarcasm. It's heavy, but Sven can be oblivious. Not sure whether it's the language thing or the narcissism thing.

"Do you know who was here today?" I hiss. "Detective Nico Davis. The cop who nearly busted me at the Barrington's. She chased me down a fucking alley, Sven. She definitely saw me."

Sven takes a drag and waves one languid hand, telling me to get to the point.

"She's sniffing around because there was a murder in this building, and who does she bump into? Me." I let the story tumble out. "And guess who's the number one suspect?" I angrily thumb my chest. "This girl."

Sven eyes me coolly, losing patience, but I can't seem to stop myself.

"And where the fuck is Danni?" I say, planting my hands on my hips and widening my stance before realizing this makes my robe gape open at the front. Sven has never shown any interest in the contents of my robe. Even so, I adjust the tie and fold my arms across my chest. "She wouldn't just disappear," I finish.

"She would if she didn't have a choice."

"That doesn't answer my question. Where is she?"

"You know where Danni is," he says. "You just haven't ac-cepted it."

My stomach roils.

"Damn you, Sven, why—"

His eyes turn to slits, and I close my mouth. Sven can be charming if you're in his good books. Or he wants something from you. He can even be fun. But he has another side. He has to, doing the job he does. I've only seen Sven turn ugly once. When a fence went back on his word. And once is more than enough. He most definitely has the bad stuff inside to bring out if the situation needs it.

"Why are you here?" I ask again.

He takes another drag, watching me carefully. I check the smoke detector on the ceiling.

"If the alarm goes off, people will come running," I warn.

"Gemma, you've become so borrrrring," he says, rolling his eyes and flicking the cigarette onto the balcony. I grit my teeth and stalk over to make sure it's extinguished, then pick up the butt and dump it in the trash.

"Sven. What are you doing here?" I ask once more. But I already know. There's nothing else it could be. No other reason for him to show up like this.

"The diamonds," he says finally.

"Sven, I told you what happened that night. I left as soon as I saw the bodies and then the police—"

"Gemma." His voice is a warning.

I throw down my hands. "I don't know what to tell you, Sven. Maybe I should ask you where the Barrington jewels are. Because where did you go that night? Why did you disappear when everything turned to shit?"

Sven is quiet for a moment, examining his hand. "DNA is such an interesting thing, isn't it?"

I stare at him. "What?"

"So hard to explain away these days."

I swallow.

"Especially when found under someone's fingernails."

Ice washes over my shoulders. "Someone? Someone like who?"

He smiles. "Tom Bollard."

"You wouldn't. You couldn't."

But he could. He would. I'm even more screwed than I thought.

And not in a good way.

30

NICO

The morning was sunny and sharp, seeming to mock Nico's sluggish mood. She'd dreamed about Gemma and Izzy and Jared last night. A murky, nonsensical nightmare that left her stomach churning and her body heavy with dread. In the light of day, it seemed ridiculous, but Nico knew what her subconscious was saying. Don't lose focus. The only way to get past this was to keep moving forward. To work the case like the home-run detective she'd always been.

"Nico?" Sarge's assistant Jill waved at her. "Sarge wants to see you."

"Yeah?" she paused, halfway between Jill's desk and her own.

Jill nodded and pointed, meaning Nico should go in. Nico couldn't help the nervous squall that rushed through her in response. But everything was fine. No reason to worry.

As soon as Nico stepped inside Sarge's office, he gestured at the chair opposite, then steepled his fingers. "How's it going?" he asked, his gaze weighty.

"Great." Her voice was tight.

"You and Jackson working out okay?" he added.

Nico took a deep breath.

He frowned. "No?"

"Actually, against expectations, quite well." She gave him a wry smile.

He looked pleased. "I thought you'd be a good fit. Opposites attract and all that."

"Attract?" Nico made a face.

"You know what I mean." He pushed over a file. "And since you're doing so well, I've got something else for you."

"Another homicide? We have a team, sure, but—"

"Missing person. Very possible she'll turn up alive and well, but we're getting pressure."

She opened the file. Kimberly Dallant, a fairly high-profile model-slash-influencer, was reported missing a few days ago. There was no evidence of foul play, but people don't just disappear without telling anyone.

"Why us?" Nico asked.

Sarge hesitated. In the silence, Nico tried to read his expression.

"Every chance it will be nothing. She travels a lot," he continued. "But I have to be seen putting good detectives to work."

Nico let out a slow breath. "Because I solved the Minnie Madison case."

"You sure did."

For a while, Nico had been high profile herself. Minnie Madison was an actress whose disappearance was at first presumed a publicity stunt because of similarities to the movie she was promoting. But Nico had always believed it was a real abduction, and she'd been correct. She'd found Minnie in the nick of time and saved her life.

"That was years ago, Sarge."

"People still talk about it. Take Jackson, though. He'll be useful."

So Sarge had noticed Jackson's effect on people, too. Was that the reason he'd put them together? Because Nico didn't have any charm herself? She saw the patterns and generated leads and Jackson followed along, smoothing away the jagged edges she created as she sawed her way through?

"Questioning models? He'll be so upset," she said.

Sarge chuckled, then nodded at the door, indicating they were done.

Nico left his office unsure how she felt about being assigned this case. Did it mean he trusted her, or was this the first step toward taking her off the Tom Bollard homicide?

Jill snapped her fingers as Nico passed her desk, holding her phone away from her ear. "Wait."

"Where's Jackson?" Nico asked.

Jill glared at her, waving the receiver. "I'm on a call, Nico. Alice Thornston. Apparently you left a message? She's at home and has time this morning if someone wants to ask her questions."

Nico immediately hurried over to pick up her bag and keys.

"Nico!" Jill waved the receiver again. "She's on the line now."

"Tell her I'm on my way. I have the address."

31

NICO

When Alice Thornston opened the door to Nico, her expression was somewhere between practiced pleasantness and wariness. She looked like a soccer mom, a homemaker, a wife. Someone who'd been handed a manual on *How To Be A Woman Of Value* and had devoured the rules without question. Nico had been a teenager when she realized she herself wouldn't be following this set of instructions. That she would walk a different path than most. Things had changed now, though. Nico could see her sister's daughters growing up with a new set of rules. Or at least, a wider variety of options. For this, Nico was grateful.

"Come in," Alice said, beckoning Nico inside.

When Nico told Alice her ex-husband was dead, her expression didn't change, but she excused herself to make coffee.

A few minutes later, she was back. "Here you go." Alice handed Nico a cup of what looked and smelled like good, strong coffee.

Nico, who wasn't yet fully caffeinated, took a sip and smiled. "This is great, thank you."

Alice sighed as she sat down with her own cup. "Poor Tom."

"I have to say, you don't seem surprised."

"Things weren't easy for him."

"You divorced eight years ago?"

"Closer to seven, actually."

"Because...?"

Alice looked affronted. "That's rather personal."

"Sorry, but we need to understand why he was murdered."

Alice's eyes widened. "Murdered?" she whispered.

Nico nodded. "You assumed he died from...?"

Alice let out a heavy breath. "A drunk-driving accident, I guess. Or even an overdose, I suppose. He got himself into a bad way after we divorced. Well...the signs were there for years before I properly realized."

"Signs of?"

"A substance problem. And gambling, I found out later."

"But this wasn't the reason you left him?"

"Not entirely. A factor, of course, but it was more that...." She sipped coffee. "He withdrew. Became a liar. I discovered he'd lost his job. Which was surprising because he was very good at what he did. A whizz with numbers. I still don't know what went wrong. He completely shut down. No more talking, no more... anything. I suppose it sounds cliché, but it's what happened." She gave a helpless shrug. "The drinking got worse, then I found out about the gambling. And then he went back on the promise of children. I wasn't getting any younger, so I gave him an ultimatum." Alice lifted her chin.

Did Alice still hold guilt about this decision? It maybe wasn't in the *Perfect Wife, Perfect Life* handbook.

"His toxicology report was clean," Nico said into the silence. "In case that matters."

Alice nodded. "I'm glad. Even if...." She swallowed.

"Cute kids," Nico gestured to the two smiling faces in a photograph on the wall. "From the new marriage, obviously."

"Yes. Matthew and Margaret. Six years old. Twins."

Alice got straight back on the horse, it seemed.

"I know what you're thinking," Alice said, her voice sharp. "I can see you doing the math in your head. No, I didn't leave Tom for Craig. But, as I mentioned, our marriage had completely deteriorated by the time we divorced. I met Craig shortly after we separated, and I was ready to move on. Already thirty-five and I wanted kids   . Craig did too and so... things moved quickly."

"What line of work is Craig in?"

"He's a lawyer."

"They get on? Craig and Tom?"

"They only met once when Tom showed up here last Christmas Eve, drunk."

"Aggressive?"

"No," Alice shook her head. "More maudlin than angry." She nodded. "He called in January and said he was back in AA. He was clean and he was sorry."

"And yet you weren't surprised when you heard he was dead."

"Well, it's easier said than done, isn't it?"

The moment hung. They both sipped their coffee.

Nico set down her cup. "No other recent contact?"

"I called him in February for his birthday. To reassure my-self he was okay. And he seemed to be. Mostly."

"Mostly?"

"He seemed down. I asked him why, and he mumbled something vague and referred to something *never going away*. I assumed he meant his addiction issues, but now you've told me he was, uh, murdered. I wonder...."

Nico wrote this down with a hitch of excitement. "You've no idea what he meant about something never going away?"

Alice shook her head.

"Tom was living in a hotel last month. Any idea why?"

"When I spoke to him in February, he was still in that apartment on the other side of town. He didn't mention moving out and I don't know the address, sorry. He only mentioned it in passing. Referred to a neighbor he was friendly with. I remember because I felt better knowing he had someone close by."

Nico made another note. "His name?"

"Sorry."

"Any other friends worth mentioning?"

"He fell out of most of his friendships when the drinking got bad." She shrugged. "I have no idea about more recent ones."

"And his work situation?"

"He was working. Financial consultancy."

"Got the name of the company?"

"He did tell me." Alice's forehead wrinkled with the effort of remembering, but then she said, "Oh. I have it written somewhere. Craig asked me to."

"Why?"

"Worried, I think. He wanted to check Tom wasn't lying to me. Since I was still in contact with him."

Or to make sure Tom didn't have any ideas about reuniting with his ex-wife, Nico speculated.

"And?"

"Craig called the number, spoke to a receptionist, and was put through to Tom. I think he hung up before he actually talked to Tom, satisfied he'd told the truth about his job." She shrugged.

"Could you find the number for me?" Nico pressed.

"Oh yes, of course. One moment."

As Alice disappeared down the hall, Nico wrote: *Did Craig have a problem with Tom?* She tapped her pen against her lip. As motives went, it was bog-standard. But often the reasons behind murder were just that.

Alice returned with a piece of paper. "Here you go." She handed it to Nico. Under the words, *Five Star Finance,* was a phone number.

"I guess I have no need for it now." Her eyes moistened and her lower lip trembled. "Gosh, it's the little things that make you realize."

"Indeed."

Nico hadn't yet deleted Izzy's number from her phone.

A sudden tightness gripped her chest. She'd almost forgotten about this sensation, distracted as she'd been. But here it was again. Out of nowhere. A visceral reminder. Of what, though? Nico dropped her gaze, pretending to write in her own notebook as the vice around her lungs got tighter. She tried to swallow, to push away the panic. Alice was speaking, but all Nico could hear was the roaring in her ears.

Finally, it passed. Nico blinked twice, one hand still gripping her knee, and forced her eyes to focus on her notes. "So," she said, making her voice sound even. "The last time you spoke to him was February. He was clean but seemed bothered by something hanging over his head, to paraphrase, and you don't know why he was living in a hotel."

Alice nodded, still looking sad. "It's a shame. He wasn't a bad man at all. Just troubled."

32

Last night, I told Sven he could search my apartment as thoroughly as he liked. But I'd never be so dumb as to stash stolen diamonds where I live, and we both know it. Before he left he said, "I'll be back," which would have been comical—with his accent he totally sounds like The Terminator—except it's not funny at all. Because if it wasn't bad enough with Nico on my case, I now also have Sven nipping at my heels. And since Sven hasn't threatened violence (yet), they're both offering the extremely unattractive possibility of going to jail. So who's more likely to deliver? I don't know how good a cop Nico is—or bad, for that matter. Is she capable of pulling the trigger on a frame-up? Sven sure is, and he's only given me a week to cough up the glitter.

"Gemma?" Penny says, her head bobbing into my line of vision.

"Huh?"

"Was that a yes to a gin and tonic?"

"Definitely."

For a moment I watch her bustle around the kitchen, slicing up both lemon and lime and pulling glasses from the cupboard. Penny is a proper grownup and I feel like a teenager cosplaying one. She's got a few years on me, but how many? Maybe I just have to wait until the magical age when life no longer feels as if you're scrambling around putting out fires.

"How old are you?" I blurt.

Penny jerks upright. "Pardon?"

"Sorry. Can't figure it out."

"I'm forty-two," she says after a moment. "And you're in your early thirties?"

I nod. "Is it true what they say about your forties? Everything comes together?"

A sudden flash of pain crosses Penny's face, but she shakes her head and forces a smile. "Not in my case."

"Are you—"

"Let's go out to the balcony."

"Uh, sure."

I guess Penny isn't interested in telling me how to sashay elegantly into my next decade. She probably also doesn't have any advice on how to sidestep biased detectives or unreasonable Norwegians, either. But being here is better than being in my apartment, which still feels contaminated by Sven. Sol gave me extra cuddles today, seeming to be aware I needed them, but Sol never offers me gin and tonics, so Penny has him beat there.

When I step through to the balcony, I see two figures across the road. Mouths suctioned, arms wrapped, pelvises locked. One of them is Cassie, and the other is her rooftop date, Leighton.

"Wow, check it out," I call out to Penny.

"What is it?" She comes to stand next to me and follows my gaze. "Oh."

They pull apart, and Leighton lets them inside the building. A moment later, they're visible again as they walk past the upstairs window.

"Maybe he's cooking her dinner?" Penny says.

"Or maybe they're starting with *dessert*." I air quote.

"It's only six-thirty," Penny says, as if that's too early for sex.

I shrug and point. From here I can see I was right about that second floor being an apartment. Because there's a bed in that room and that's where they're going. Seems like Cassie is diving straight into the deep end of her new sex life. No water wings for this one.

"He's probably just giving her a tour," Penny adds.

"A tour of his penis?"

"Gemma!"

"Seriously, though, a tour of what?" My eyes drop to the signage outside the building. *Tiles & Textures*. "His job is selling *tiles*?"

Penny nods. "Tiles."

Is this what normies do? They spend all day trying to sell other people *tiles*? That cannot be remotely interesting and I cannot for one second imagine it being my life.

"What do you do?" I ask. "For work?"

"Oh, uh...." Her eyes dart to the side. For a moment, she seems almost panicked at the question. I frown.

"I do consultancy work here and there," she says, her voice tight.

A consultant, huh. Maybe I can be a consultant in something.

"What do you consult on?"

"Oh, is that my phone?" Penny says, turning away.

"I didn't hear anything."

"One second."

She hurries inside, and I watch her go. Did her phone actually ring or is she avoiding talking about her job? Because 'consultant' sounds a lot like 'sales', which is my cover story. Do Penny and I have more in common than I thought?

When she returns, it's with a bowl of mini pretzels. "So, what's up?" she asks conversationally. "You said you wanted to chat?"

"Yeah."

I'd reached out to Penny earlier today, not only to talk to someone who isn't trying to screw me over, but because I have to figure out what happened to Tom Bollard. I have to find a way to make Penny help me.

"We know who the dead guy is now. I was wondering if you met him? His place is right above yours."

"No, no." Penny fiddles with her cup. "We must have missed each other."

"Hang on." I straighten. "That's kind of weird, right? You saw everyone else, but you didn't see him at all?"

"Him or the couple in three-oh-four." Something flickers across her face. "I have an idea," she says brightly. "Let's invite the others to join us. Our rooftop drinks were interrupted, after all."

I look at the sky. "It's supposed to rain tonight." Being a cat burglar means having weather alerts set up, and I like my daily notifications about the day ahead.

"I can host." Penny is already typing a message. She looks up with a smile. "George and Marco are in. They were about to have a cocktail, anyway." She drops her eyes to her phone again. "Cassie hasn't read it yet."

"Well, duh." I waggle my eyebrows and gesture across the road.

"What about Orson?" Penny asks.

I make a face. "It's hard to imagine Orson having cocktails with us."

"Excluding him would be mean," Penny says. "I'll message him too." After a minute, she sets down her phone and jumps up. "I'll just pop out and put a note under three-oh-four's door."

"Penny, I think they—"

"Back soon."

When Penny returns, Marco and George are with her. I leave the balcony and join them in the living room.

"Orson didn't reply, and no one answered at three-oh-four," Penny says. "Even though I knocked *twice*."

They're probably out getting a restraining order.

"Gemma, nice to see you." Marco kisses me on the cheek. George only nods his greeting.

"A round of gin and tonics, or do we want wine?" Penny says.

"Another gin and tonic, please," I say, lifting my glass.

"Sounds good," Marco agrees.

"I was telling someone yesterday that we have neighbor drinks and they were so jealous about our community," George says.

"Isn't it great?" Penny beams.

"You didn't mention the dead body?" I mutter. Only Marco seems to hear, casting me an uncertain look.

Am I the only one treating this situation with any sort of seriousness? Why aren't they more curious? Or worried? But maybe if I didn't have two excellent reasons to figure it out, I'd be pretending it never happened as well.

"But then I realized I don't know much about you, Gemma," George continues, turning to me suddenly. Almost like an accusation.

"Uh, what?"

"You said you're in sales...?"

He eyes me expectantly, and my stomach clenches unpleasantly. Am I about to be busted for lying? Already? And why is his expression so doubtful? Why *can't* I work in sales? What is it about me that's so un-salesy, anyway?

"But what about your love life?" he finishes.

My shoulders drop with relief. "I do okay," I say. George frowns. "I'm single," I add. "If that's what you're asking. Happily single."

"Never married?"

"No, I...." What's my cover story supposed to be again? That my ex had paid for everything, but now we're donezo.

"I recently ended a long-term relationship," I say. "Finally figured out being a kept woman isn't worth it." I attempt a *You Live You Learn* expression.

GEMMA AND THE ACE DETECTIVE

George's face lights up. "A kept woman? You had a sugar daddy?" he breathes, clearly thrilled. "Or was it a sugar mommy?"

"I didn't have to work, so I guess so," I say, one eyebrow cocked, intentionally not answering his question. The less detail I have to remember, the better.

"Interesting," George says, nodding. I can almost see him ferreting this away for future use. I pull out my phone to make a note. This version might differ from the one I wrote last week.

"Oh, and Penny?" George turns toward the kitchen, where Penny is making more drinks. I'm out of the hot seat, at least for now. "I ran into someone yesterday who knows you," George continues.

Penny startles. "Y-yes? Who?"

"Miranda Otis? She volunteers with you at the hospital."

Volunteering. Huh. Is that something I could do?

"And she mentioned you used to live in Bayview Village," George says. "I've always loved that area."

Penny shakes her head. "No, no. I didn't live there."

"I'm pretty sure—"

"No, I said. No. She must be mistaken." The smile on her face is set in concrete. Suddenly, she claps her hands. "Nibbles. We need nibbles," she shouts, closing then opening the fridge door.

"Uh, I'll help," Marco says, casting a worried look at Penny as he hurries into the kitchen.

I lean closer to George. "What was all that about?"

George leans in too. "She's lying," he says in a low voice.

"About what?" I whisper.

"She did live in Bayview, because I saw her name and address attached to a legal case related to the one I'm working on at the moment. A wrongful death suit."

"What happened?"

He clamps shut his mouth; eyes wide. "I shouldn't have told you. It's confidential."

"Then why did you tell me anything at all?" I say, annoyed. "Now I want to know." I drop my voice again. "What wrongful death?"

George holds up his hands and shakes his head. "I can't say anything more."

I sit back, disappointed. But George has basically confirmed that Penny is lying. I know why *I am*, but what does Penny have hidden in her past?

Another dead body?

33

NICO

With Jared at a HR seminar for newcomers to the department, Nico would ride solo today. She'd follow up the leads that didn't involve the risk of bumping into a certain someone at the Aurora. Because Gemma Cross could still fuck with Nico's head and, potentially, her career.

As Nico finished her coffee, she flicked through Tom's file. Why had his life taken that turn? What was he never getting away from? The A4 package in his apartment had contained a contract from Five Star Finance and a yet to be unlocked password-protected flash drive. Likely an irrelevant document from Tom's work, but Nico still had to check it out. She picked up the piece of paper Alice Thornston had given her with the company phone number. Who chose that name? Nico wondered as she dialed. It sounded like a shady operation at best.

A few minutes later, Nico disconnected. Five Star Finance offered a type of middle-man consultancy service that didn't have employees, but organized financial consultants and accountants on request, taking a fee for this arrangement. It had no physical office, just a website and a call center, and yes, the flash drive and paperwork was Tom's next job. He hadn't accepted it within the set timeframe, so they'd reassigned it. They didn't seem to care at all that one of their consultants had been murdered. Even one who'd been with them for over five years. Harsh, but ultimately not suspicious. Something of a dead end, but they had given Nico, without hesitation, Tom's previous address.

Nico picked up her bag and headed out, waving to Jill and DC Singh as she stepped into the elevator. What would it be like to work for a company that didn't exist outside the digital space? No office or colleagues. No one to complain about, or with, over food or drinks. Many would love it, working in their pajamas, taking naps, and hanging out with their pets. But Nico suspected Tom had probably lost himself in that environment. Because some need structure and other people to normalize and stabilize. Was Nico herself one? Maybe, she conceded. Maybe.

En route to the midtown apartment building, she stopped at the hotel Tom had stayed at in the weeks before his move to the Aurora. A three-star operation that needed to update their lobby furniture. The desk clerk had started off helpful, confirming to Nico that Tom had been scheduled to check out on Friday, April 5th, and that he'd done so using the key drop box and the automatic checkout. But he clammed up as soon as the duty manager appeared. Nico knew her luck had run out by this man's expression alone, but tried asking for the lobby security footage, anyway.

"Certainly, once you provide us with a warrant."

Nico gave him a tight smile and promised to be back. "To be clear," she said as she left. "If the footage goes missing in the meantime, there's going to be a problem. I'll hold you personally responsible and charge you with obstruction."

Tom's previous residence was a twenty-story apartment building. As nondescript as they come. She parked in one of the visitor parking spaces and called the superintendent's number.

"Did you know him?" Nico asked the serious-looking woman as they rode up to the tenth floor.

"I spoke to him once or twice," she replied. "Seemed nice enough."

"He didn't give you any trouble?"

"Not at all."

"And the work you mentioned they're doing in his apartment. It isn't because…. He wasn't running a meth lab?"

"Just a standard paint job."

Nico nodded. She wouldn't gain much from looking at this apartment, but the super had assumed she wanted to see it. And this way, Nico might find the neighbor Tom's ex-wife had mentioned.

"Do you know why he moved out?"

"The owner asked him to leave." The super sniffed.

"The building owner? These are apartments, right? Not condos? All owned by the same company?"

She nodded. "Nothing to do with me."

Nico, noting the unusual phrasing of the response, waited for more. But the super closed her mouth and strode ahead. A moment later, she gestured to a door.

"Here we are." She unlocked it to let Nico inside, but remained near the doorway as Nico wandered around the one-bedroom space. Couch, coffee table, shelf. There wasn't much to see.

"Are all the apartments in the building furnished?"

"About fifty-fifty."

There was something kind of awful about a 42-year-old divorcee renting a furnished apartment, Nico thought. Did he really only have a few bags and one box to show for his life? Maybe it was a choice. Maybe he'd given up the clutter of materialism. Or maybe moving to the Aurora was a completely fresh start; he was still rebuilding his life.

Nico stepped back out into the hall. "I'd like to ask his neighbors a couple of questions."

"Fine by me, but I have to get back downstairs."

"No problem. I'll see myself out when I'm done."

Nico knocked on the door directly to the right of Tom's old apartment. No answer. She leaned closer to listen. No sounds came from within. Before she could try the apartment on the other side, her phone rang. Her sister. Again. Nico eyed the display for a long moment, then answered the call.

"Hey, Tati."

"What are you doing?"

Nico sighed. "About to talk to someone about a case."

Silence.

Nico rolled her eyes. "You got something to say about that?"

"Honey—"

"Don't call me honey. You know I don't like it."

"Yeah, yeah."

Their mama used to call them honey, and the first time her sister did it, right after the funeral, Nico had slapped her. Tati had cracked her right back, and they'd ended up in a tear-soaked hug. But every so often, Tati would use this term, usually when she was being maternal. Which bugged Nico because Tati was younger.

"Should you be working?"

"I can't just sit around my apartment. That's worse."

"There are a million things you could do instead of—"

"I need this, alright?"

Tatiana sighed. "Are you coming for Sunday dinner?"

"Gotta go. Talk later," Nico said, disconnecting, because a man now stood in the doorway of the apartment to the left.

"Hi there." He had a folded newspaper under his arm. Several years off retirement age, probably, but seemingly not in the middle of a workday. "What can I do for you?" he added with a smile. "I heard you talking out here."

"DS Davis." Nico held up her ID. "Did you know Tom Bollard?"

"Yes, what's this about?"

"Your name please, sir?"

"Franek Novak." The smile dropped off his face. "Wait. *Did* I know Tom? Past tense?"

Nico nodded somberly. "Can I come in for a moment?"

"Shucks, that's a shame," Franek said after Nico had delivered the bad news. He settled himself into one of the two lazy-boy armchairs facing a wide-screen TV in the living room. Nico remained standing. Her father had had one just like it and she already knew there was no professional way to extract oneself from those cushy depths.

"I wondered why I hadn't heard from him," he continued. "I called to ask about his new place, and it went straight to voicemail. He never got back to me. Thought it was strange, but then I remembered his vacation."

Nico forced herself not to smile. Finally, someone who knew about Tom's current life.

"A real shame," he repeated, looking out into the distance.

"You two were friends?"

"Sure were. Both divorcees. You know how it is." He flicked his eyes to her. "Well, maybe you don't, but when he moved in, he'd cleaned up his act, but was still hurting. And I could relate."

"He stayed clean while he was here?"

"For the most part." Franek made a face. "Is that what got him? I worried about him moving into a place with no one to look out for him. To keep him in check."

Nico shook her head. "No, he was murdered."

Franek's eyes widened. "Who did it?"

Nico suppressed a smile. "If I knew that.... The investigation is ongoing. You don't know anyone who might wish ill of him? Any issues he had?"

Franek nodded slowly. "You know what? There was. From his past. He wouldn't talk about it. But something dark. He was a mess for a while." Franek held up his hands. "His words. But yeah, a weight on his shoulders for sure."

There it was again. Tom's past hanging over his head. Did it get him killed?

"Did Tom have any other friends?"

Franek thought for a moment. "Didn't meet anyone." He shook his head sadly. "He was doing so well, but then the business with the owners...."

"Which was?"

"Some sort of frame-up, if you ask me. One minute everything is fine, the next they want Tom out. No reason given."

"Do you have the owner's contact details?"

"Sure." Franek eased himself out of his chair with surprising grace, then walked over to the fridge to pull a business card from under a magnet.

"Thanks." Nico took a photo of it and handed it back. "So you never found out why Tom had to leave?"

"At first Tom was angry, but when I asked him a day or two later, he seemed to have let it go. Dropped it quickly in the end. Maybe he learned the reason, and it was good enough for him? Maybe because he got that new place. I wondered where the cash for fancy digs like that came from, but I never asked. It didn't seem right. I was going to visit him when he got back from vacation."

"Vacation to...?"

"New York." Franek chuckled, as if this was an inside joke.

"Thanks." Nico noted this down. Tom's trip was likely the reason he asked Carlos to receive his furniture deliveries. But Chris Sheffield, the AWOL project manager, was also on vacation right now. Were those two connected?

"Vacationing on his own?" Nico asked.

"Far as I know."

"Thank you." She handed him her card. "If you think of anything else...."

Franek nodded. "Will do."

"I'll let myself out," she said, already at the door.

To Nico, it seemed as if someone might have manipulated Tom by dangling an ugly secret from his past. But why? Who gained from him moving out? Who was doing the dangling, and what had Tom done?

34

I set the grocery bags on the kitchen counter. Yes, Doctor Foster, actual groceries. You used to go on about gut microbiomes and mood and at the time I thought you were making stuff up. But look at me now. There are vegetables in here. What I do with them is a problem for Future Gemma.

Sol, understanding that these bags mean food, comes to wind his way around my legs, purring and meowing and giving me his cutest eyes. I glance at the time. Nearly five. "Okay, Sol." He'll definitely forget this ever happened and try to convince me at eight o'clock that he's literally starving to death, but whatever. Life is short, and he's been through a lot. I won't withhold treats from him. If I don't do it for myself, how can I?

I spoon out some of his favorite globby meaty crap, then wash my hands and take the coffee I'd brought back over to the armchair. My sleuthing operation is half-assed, at best. Spluttering along in fits and starts. I haven't even looked up Tom Bollard yet. My internet skills aren't anywhere near professional level—that was Danni's department—but I can still do a decent dive. I pull my laptop over and open up a new search tab.

Fifteen minutes later, I know more about Tom but have zero clues why someone would want him dead. He had one of the random finance jobs that so many do, and according to his Facebook account, he's the most generic man alive. Born here, went to U of T, got married (and divorced), no kids, likes various ball sports. Leans to the right. Likes to post incredibly boring things about the economy. It's so, so bland. Too bland, almost. Like, is this some sort of cover story? Where's the drama, Tom? Because there must be drama, otherwise you wouldn't have ended up stuffed in a locker.

From where I left it by the door, my bag emits a muffled wail. I frown. What the.... Oh. A phone call. I hurry over and check the display: *Cassie 202.*

"Hey, Cassie," I say, trying to keep the surprise out of my voice. Penny made us all exchange numbers at rooftop drinks, but I didn't expect anyone else to use them.

"Hi Gemma, how are you?"

"Not bad. What's up?"

"Um." She clears her throat, sounding nervous. "I was wondering if... if you're not too busy... do you want to get dinner? Tonight? You're probably busy, though. Right? That's okay, we—"

"No, tonight's good." My stomach growls to confirm. "Food sounds great."

Tom Bollard can wait a few hours, because it's clearly time for an update on the Leighton situation. And from what I saw igniting over at Tiles & Textures, Cassie will have stuff to spill. I will always make time to talk about sex.

"How do you feel about takeout, though?" Cassie continues. "I don't want to go out. Or cook."

"All good with me."

Since I don't have a dining table and I do have an illegal cat, I suggest we hang at Cassie's. I'll show up around six o'clock because Cassie likes to eat early and I'm hungry right now. It works out perfectly.

I'm kind of excited to visit Cassie's apartment, to see what she's done with her space. Perhaps I'm a nosy neighbor in the making. Maybe I can pick up where Penny left off. Because who knows what's going on with her. She's ignored all my attempts at getting her involved in my amateur investigation, which is totally off brand. And what about that wrongful death thing?

When I knock on Cassie's door a little after six, she opens it immediately.

"Hey," she says with a shy smile. "Thanks for coming."

"No worries."

Her apartment is a 'Bachelor', which means a studio: no separate bedroom. But this is nothing like the ones I've been in before. It's airy and spacious and gives *New York Loft* rather than cramped and awkward and *am I standing in your bedroom?* vibes. Cassie's bed is visible in the corner, but she's set up a screen that keeps it mostly hidden. And even though the fixtures are modern, she's chosen retro furniture, and it somehow works. She has a purple velvet loveseat and accent chair, a dark blue teal fifties-style couch, also velvet, and then another kind of oversized, high-backed armchair in a dusty pink. They clearly aren't a set, but they look great together. There's not much other furniture, apart from a huge bookshelf across one wall. Plants dominate the space, and I immediately want the same large, green leafy additions to my place.

"This is really cool," I say.

She nods, pleased. "My agent Liz helped me. She's got an eye for this stuff."

"Can you message me where you got these plants?"

"Of course."

"And your furniture?"

"Sure."

I amble over to the large windows.

"No balcony, but that's okay," Cassie says. "I'm not an out-doors person, anyway."

I turn back to face Cassie. For a moment, we stand awkwardly in the living room area.

"What do you want to eat?" she asks, blinking expectantly.

I shrug. "Not fussy."

"Neither."

The silence hangs.

Cassie bites her lip and fixes her gaze on me. "I honestly don't know if I can make a decision right now." Suddenly her eyes are wet.

Yikes. I study her face. Am I supposed to ask what's up? But instead I say, "Mexican?" and she nods gratefully. I wave my phone. "I know a place. I'll order online for delivery." I scroll through the menu, then pause. "What about Penny?"

"What about her?"

"You didn't invite her?"

"Oh." Cassie fiddles with her hair. "No, I...."

Is Cassie also suspicious of Penny? Maybe we all should be. Maybe Penny's pixie hair and pointy chin are the harmless façade of an evil mastermind.

"I wanted to get your advice on something," she continues. "Just you."

"Yeah?" I'm weirdly pleased, as if I've been chosen first for a school team.

"It's about dating and, uh, things like that. I thought you're probably—"

"More experienced?" I anticipate.

She looks down. "I don't want to offend you."

"No offense at all. I *do* have experience. With sex, at least. Relationships, not so much, but I'm in. Just give me one sec." I confirm the selection of tacos and burritos, as well as the obligatory side of corn chips and guac, then slide my phone into my pocket.

"Is this a conversation to have over wine?" I say.

Cassie beams. "I thought you might say that, so I bought a couple of bottles of the kind you had at rooftop drinks."

"Perfect."

If nothing else, Cassie's a quick study.

"Hey, what did you say your job was again?" Cassie asks once we're settled on the couch.

"Uh...."

This is a normal question, I know, but it feels so intrusive. Loaded, almost. And it's all anyone seems to ask. What's so important about having a job, anyway?

"I'm in between things at the moment," I say.

She nods slowly. "But what's your profession? Or, I suppose, your career?"

I frown. "I thought you wanted to talk about Leighton?"

"Right." She gives me a nervous smile. "I do."

"So what's up?"

She rubs her temples. "Maybe it's because I've been so stressed recently, with the move and finishing my book and then dating Leighton and the things he expects."

"First up." I hold up my hand. "You don't have to do anything with Leighton you don't want to do, okay? I don't care what he *expects*."

She nods. "I do want to do the things, though. I'm just nervous."

"Good. But don't let him get kinky if you're not into it." I nod firmly and take a sip of wine, relaxing into the conversation. Could I be... good at this? Is professional sex mentoring a thing? Sex therapists are, so why not? This could be something for me. I should have brought my notebook.

"Gemma?"

"Yes?" I clear my throat and lean forward. "Sorry, can you repeat?"

"So, Leighton and I...." She bites her lip.

"Had sex." I say, because she doesn't seem able to.

She nods, fiddling with her scarf. "It's kind of embarrassing."

I take in her expression. "Your first time?"

"No." Cassie looks away.

"But near enough?"

She hesitates, then nods.

"And?"

She grimaces. "It didn't go very well."

"The first few times often don't."

"I was so awkward and self-conscious and he...."

I wait, curious. What's Leighton like in bed? He's probably good at landing women. He's confident enough. But what about his actual prowess?

"He almost seemed annoyed with me. At least at first, and then I got the sense he was, uh, laughing at me. Not overtly, but mentally. I felt as if I was doing it wrong."

Wow. Leighton sounds like a total dick. And not in a good way.

"Did you tell him you haven't done this much before?"

Her eyes go wide. "Oh, god no. I couldn't."

"Sometimes you don't gel with a person sexually. With more experience, you'll figure this out before you get to the bedroom stage. Although not always. Sexual chemistry is weird. Intense attraction can come out of nowhere and fail to appear when you're sure it will." I nod encouragingly. "Don't beat yourself up. You two might not be compatible, or maybe he's terrible in bed. Either way, you shouldn't feel embarrassed or bad."

She looks uncertain. "It's hard not to feel as if I've failed."

"I get that." I pat her hand. "Do you want to keep seeing him?"

She nods.

Ugh, okay. I guess she has to see this through to completion. I just hope it doesn't turn ugly.

"But I don't know if *he* does," she adds.

"Well, you can't make him, but you can reach out and ask for another date."

"I can?"

"Of course."

"What if he says no?"

"Then he's not for you and you move on."

Cassie makes a face. "And if he says yes?"

"Try to relax. If it helps, think of it as practice. Like a learning opportunity. Then, when someone better comes along, you won't be as nervous."

"Someone better than Leighton?" Her eyes go wide again.

"Yes."

Leighton is definitely *not* the end goal. But I don't say that.

"Okay. I'll try not to stress about it and go with the flow more." She nods to herself and takes a sip of wine. "It's been messing with my head. And I was already stressed out with a book deadline. I keep forgetting things. I even...." She breaks off with a shaky laugh. "I completely forgot a conversation I had with my editor."

I take in Cassie's worried expression. "If you get comfortable with sex, it can help with stress."

"It can?"

"Yup. For sure." For a moment I'm lost in the memory of Jared, then shake my head to push him out of my mind. He's a cop, I'm a criminal. I mean, ex-criminal. And he's made it clear that his job and his partner, Nico, are important to him.

"I also wanted to ask you something kind of weird," Cassie continues.

"I like weird," I say happily.

"Why are you here, Gemma? Really?"

"What?" I swallow. "What do you mean?" I stammer.

She tilts her head. "Here at the Aurora. It just feels strange. Like, off somehow."

"I... I...."

I'm paralyzed. Almost literally. As if she's tied me up and grabbed my throat so she can hiss these accusations at me.

"You're like a ghost online. It's almost as if you don't exist, or if you have another identity or something." She tilts her head and leans forward. "Who are you really, Gemma Cross?"

WTF. Ambush.

35

NICO

When Nico got back to her desk, Jared was there. In one hand he held her pocket-sized puzzle book—it helped distract her busy mind—and in the other, the small, framed photograph of Nico and her mother. She snatched them away. "What are you doing? That's private."

"But it's right here for anyone to see." Jared raised his hands. "And it's sweet. You look like your mom."

Her mother had passed years ago now, but his comment felt too personal.

"Sorry if I overstepped," he said after a moment, then took a seat.

"So where have you been?" Nico asked. "The seminar got out at five."

He eyed her warily. "Why?"

"Just wondering."

"I don't need a hand-holding service."

Nico almost laughed. When Sarge had put them together, he'd said *you can hold each other's hands.*

"We're supposed to work together," Jared added. "Which means trusting each other. Do you want me asking where you've been every five seconds?"

Nico sighed. "No."

The moment hung, then passed.

"I made progress on Romanov," Jared said, his eyes heavy on hers. "I figured involving you might complicate the situation."

He was right, and she knew it. "Fair," she said finally, the only word she could muster.

"And it's pretty good," Jared continued. "The same legal firm that handled the purchase of Romanov's two apartments also handled Tom Bollard's."

Nico's stomach clenched. "Shit, really?"

"Is it enough to get a warrant to search them? For signs Tom was there?"

She shook her head. "That firm likely deals with thousands of property sales. And they'll be as slippery as hell."

Jared eyed her for a moment, as if deciding whether to say something.

She lifted her chin. "What?"

"There's more."

"You've got my attention."

"I didn't just get intel about Romanov, I saw him."

Nico swallowed the hard ball in her throat. "Was that a good idea?"

"If you're asking whether I ran it by org crime? Yes, I did. And Sarge. I didn't go alone. I'm not an idiot."

"Just checking."

"We didn't get very far," Jared said. "We walked into the restaurant and as soon as Romanov saw Mike, he immediately said *talk to my lawyer*. But before we left, I landed one question."

"Yeah?"

"I asked how he liked his new apartments. He smiled and said he's never been near the place. His assistant picked up the keys. I bluffed and said we had security footage so we'd find out for ourselves. Just to see how he'd react. Why not, right? And here's the interesting part."

Nico leaned forward.

"He gave me this shit-eating grin and said, *really*? As in, he knew we couldn't check."

Nico sucked in a breath.

"I figure he's either got someone on the inside, telling him how this case is going, or knows because he disabled the cameras himself."

"We don't know for sure they weren't working. Not yet."

"Sure, but I can't see us getting lucky."

"Let's say you're right. Romanov gets the system shut off so there's no record of something he's doing that weekend. On Friday, Tom is unlucky enough to bear witness to whatever this is. Romanov, or someone who works for him, chases him down. Hits him over the head and wraps his face in plastic that's lying around, then takes him down to the locker."

Jared nodded. "It's decent."

"But what about Sheffield and Boston Works? They had full access until Friday morning. They could have pretended Tom got his keys and made it look like he'd started moving in. Hell, they could be working with Romanov."

Jared sighed. "With the evasive shit they pulled and with Sheffield going on vacation, which no one will give me a straight answer about, it's possible."

"Having two possibilities is better than none," Nico said. And that wasn't even counting Gemma Cross. Because she was still a player. At least, she was in Nico's mind.

"I'm gonna dig deeper into Chris Sheffield," Jared said. "He's clean on paper, but guys like him often are."

"Good idea. We still have so many unanswered questions."

"What about the ex-wife?"

"No red flags," Nico began. "She was away when he died, and they divorced years ago. No anger. And no motive, as far as I can tell. Tom's spiral into drugs and alcohol abuse had nothing to do with their relationship, it seemed."

"She had to watch it happen from the outside."

"But she did drop an interesting nugget about Tom's recent life."

"They were still in contact?"

"A little. A couple of months ago, he mentioned never getting away."

"Those exact words? Like, he wasn't able to leave?"

Nico pulled out her notebook. "Something *not ever going away*," she read out.

"So Tom had a ghost." Jared smiled. "That, Detective Davis, is another lead."

She found herself smiling back. "I agree. Because I also checked Tom's previous address and talked to his neighbor. He and Tom spent some time together, it sounds like. And he also mentioned Tom being troubled. And Tom's departure from that building was kind of hasty."

"Yeah?"

"An issue with the building owner. It's why he had to stay at a hotel for a few weeks before he moved to the Aurora. I've got Singh looking into it."

"We need to know more about what was haunting Tom," Jared said.

"I agree."

Jared's phone buzzed. He immediately dropped his gaze, a smile appearing.

A social text, Nico thought. From a hookup? A girlfriend? She was curious about the kind of woman he went for. He flirted with everyone and probably wasn't picky when it came to casual sex. But who would he settle down with? Part of Nico wanted to get to know him as a person, she realized. As a potential friend. Maybe she shouldn't fight it. Maybe this was progress.

Jared dropped his phone. "You know what's bugging me? Anne and David Smith. They didn't answer when I knocked on their door yesterday and they're not picking up on the number Carlos gave us. You haven't spoken to them, right?"

"Not a word. I asked Carlos the same question, and he hasn't seen them since they got their keys on Friday, just before midday."

"You know what I'm starting to wonder?"

"What?"

"What if we've got a multiple homicide on our hands and we don't even know it?"

Nico sat back in her chair, letting it swivel for a moment. "That's something we need to determine sooner rather than later. I'll get Carlos to meet us at the building."

36

NICO

As Jared pulled up outside the Aurora, Nico checked her phone. "Carlos is five minutes away."

"He pissed?"

"Probably, it's nearly eight."

If Anne and David Smith didn't answer the door, Carlos had agreed they could use his master key. This was a murder investigation, after all. That literally no one had seen two of the supposed new residents was a good enough reason to enter the premises.

Jared cleared his throat. "Hey, what happened with Tobi Hart yesterday?"

Nico watched him. Was that a hint of color grazing his cheeks?

"Lucky she was here working in the garden," he added. "A nice neutral place. But did she talk?"

Nico made a face. "Tobi was not what I'd call chatty," she admitted.

"You got attitude from her, too." Jared grinned as if he'd won a bet.

"She's had some rough treatment from our colleagues in the past, so I let it slide," Nico said. "Really, I don't blame her. Once I acknowledged that and assured her I wasn't interested in using her as a scapegoat, she relaxed."

"And?"

"She had access to the Aurora in the two months leading up to the opening and she's contracted to work on the garden through summer. Zero ties to Tom Bollard, though."

"Here's Carlos." Jared pointed at the entrance. They got out of the car and followed a stony-faced Carlos inside.

Outside apartment 304, they paused. "You smelling this?" Nico asked Jared.

"Sure am."

The odor was hard to pin down. It didn't smell like a dead body exactly, but it didn't *not* smell like one.

Carlos knocked and waited, listening. Nothing. He turned to give Nico and Jared an uncertain smile, then rapped again. "Mr. and Mrs. Smith? Are you there?"

"How long has it smelled like this?" Nico asked Carlos.

Carlos shook his head. "Haven't been on this floor the last few days."

Nico raised her hand to bang on the door. "Hello? DS Davis and DS Jackson here. We need to talk to you."

Silence. Nico and Jared exchanged glances.

"I'll check with Orson," Jared said, walking over to apartment 302.

As soon as Jared knocked, Orson appeared, clutching a sandwich. "Hey." He leaned forward to eye Nico and Carlos standing across the hall, then returned his gaze to Jared. "What's up?"

"When did you first notice the smell?"

"What smell?" Orson's face was blank.

Jared raised his eyebrows. "Really?"

Orson shrugged. "Bad sense of smell. How's the investigation going?"

"You talked to your neighbors?" Jared thumbed over his shoulder at apartment 304.

Orson shook his head. "Never seen them."

"At all?"

"Not even once."

"Have you heard them?"

"Not a peep."

"Okay." Jared crossed the hall back to Nico. "Let's go in."

"I don't know about this," Carlos said, his expression uncertain.

"We've got probable cause," Nico said, making her voice hard. "We can break down the door and give you a headache, or you can let us in."

Carlos flicked anxious eyes from Jared to Nico, then got out his keys.

"Police," Nico called out, banging once more. "We're coming in." She turned to Jared. "Ready?" He nodded and Carlos turned the lock. Every muscle tensed, Nico pushed open the door.

Inside, perched anxiously on two beanbags, a man and a woman sat holding hands, blinking wide, scared eyes.

"Anne and David Smith?" Jared asked. They nodded slowly, almost in unison. Jared took another step. Nico trained her ears toward the closed door beyond the couch.

"Anyone else here?" Nico asked. Together, they shook their heads, still staring, not speaking. "You sure?" Nico added, frowning, taking a few more steps into the space. Their fear, their body language... it was as if they were being held hostage. Nico flicked her eyes to Jared. His gaze met hers. She nodded at the door behind the couple. He dropped his chin once to confirm and jogged lightly over. He waited a beat, then opened the door and stepped inside. Thirty seconds later, he was back. "Clear."

Nico took a few steps toward the bathroom. She used her foot to push open the door, then peered inside.

"Clear," she said to Jared, letting out a breath as she returned to the living room.

Her fight-or-flight senses no longer on high alert, Nico became acutely aware of the smell. The smell they'd detected in the hall, but ten times stronger. On the kitchen counter, Nico saw a pulpy mess that could be the main olfactory offender. She could also detect the distinct aroma of body odor. Finally, a garbage bag sat on the floor in the corner, well overdue for a trip downstairs. On the coffee table, three incense burners emitted a sickly sweet smell; an attempt at damage control, but actually somehow fusing the smells into one mutant stink.

Nico gestured at the pulp on the kitchen counter. "What's that?"

"Durian," Anne said.

Nico waited.

"Fruit."

"What's in here?" Jared stood at the trash bag.

"Garbage. Normally we'd take it down by now," Anne said nervously, "but since that body was found...."

"We don't like to go out," David added.

Jared nodded. "Ever consider cracking a window?"

They started laughing in the elevator and didn't stop until they reached the main doors.

"What now?" Jared said as they emerged onto the street.

The evening was balmy; the sun starting to set.

"You mentioned something about a good pasta place?" Nico said.

37

NICO

Jared raised his glass of red wine. "Good, right?"

"Yeah, yeah." Nico pushed away her empty plate. She wanted to ask for more bread to mop up the last of the sauce. But Jared was already too puffed up at his successful choice.

As Jared finished his spaghetti, Nico leaned back and cast her eyes around the restaurant. Jared had taken the conversational lead, entertaining Nico with stories from his last precinct and his family. Single mother, epic uncle, one sensible older sister and a hot mess of a younger one. Jared, in no surprise to Nico, had grown up surrounded by women and was the wildcard middle child. Nico shared a few family classics featuring her sister Tati, then a couple of old cases she always got asked about by those new to their department.

"Listen, I know you think there isn't much more to me than the first layer," Jared said out of nowhere, "but there is." He looked down. "I've lost people too. I know what it's like." He glanced up at her, seeming to gauge her reaction. "It's okay to let me in. You could give me a chance."

"Why do you care what I think?"

"Because you're more than a good detective. A great one."

Nico took a sip of wine to hide her smile.

After a beat, Jared asked, "Are you ever going to tell me what happened?"

Nico sighed. He was asking about DC Isobel Stevens. Izzy. About her partner who'd died six weeks ago. He would have heard some of it already, but probably a warped version. She should set him right, at least. For Izzy's sake. And maybe her own.

"Izzy was my best friend. She was kind... the *kindest*. Smart. Non-judgmental." Nico picked up the napkin next to her plate. "But she fell in love with the wrong person."

Jared nodded, his eyes trained on Nico's.

"The night it happened we'd separated for dinner—she was eating with *him*. When the call came in about a possible homicide at the Barrington place, I'd been at the station filling out paperwork. I volunteered and went straight to the apartment. Izzy called me right as we were going in, but I didn't pick up. I missed two more calls while chasing Gemma down that alley. When I checked my messages.... Izzy sent her final SOS from some random address, only a ten-minute drive away. I got there as fast as I could, but...."

"She was...?"

"Nearly." Nico swallowed. "She died soon after."

Jared shook his head. "I'm sorry."

"At first, it looked like she'd stumbled into something and gotten caught in the crossfire. But it turned out it wasn't random, or an accident. She'd been lured there and shot."

"The guy she fell in love with?"

"Crime family." Nico gritted her teeth.

"When they found out...."

Nico nodded.

When Nico had arrived on the scene, she'd taken it at face value—stray bullets—but in the following days, Nico had uncovered the truth. If the timeline she'd pieced together was correct, Izzy's secret relationship with her informant had progressed from an acquaintanceship into a head-over-heels love affair incredibly quickly. Izzy had gotten snared in a notorious crime family, and Nico didn't even know if she'd tried to get herself out. Finding out Izzy might have been corrupt—she'd certainly crossed lines—was almost as traumatic as watching her die, making awful gurgling sounds as she took her last breath. To say Nico felt betrayed didn't even come close. That Izzy had willingly risked it all as well as lied to her face on so many occasions made her sick to her stomach.

And then there was the grief.

Nico took a large gulp of wine. After a few moments of silence, Jared asked gently, "This crime family, would it be Romanov?"

Nico nodded.

"Not Alex himself?"

"His nephew." She looked down.

"Nico." Jared waited until she met his gaze. "I'm sorry. About Izzy. That's rough. And thank you for telling me. I appreciate it."

Nico gave him a small smile as the waiter came bustling over to clear their plates.

Jared took a long pull of wine. "I understand why you've stayed away from Romanov so far. And he's still a question mark." He looked thoughtful. "But maybe he'll go down for this and we'll have one less scumbag on the street."

They clinked glasses and let silence fall. Comfortable, despite the subject matter. With this ease, Nico realized how much tension she'd been carrying. She hadn't thought about Gemma Cross once throughout dinner. Unlike every forced social event she'd attended recently, Nico wasn't in a rush to leave. This was due, in part, to Jared, she had to admit. Chewing through the case with him reminded her of working with Izzy.

And even tinged with grief, it felt good.

38

S weat drips down my back, pooling at my butt crack. I slow to an easy pace as I turn into a side street, trying to calm my breathing. In no surprise to anyone, I'm out of shape. I went from working out every day to lazing around (grieving/recovering), existing on wine and fried food. But that weird conversational turn with Cassie earlier tonight triggered me enough to propel me into my first run in weeks.

I'd wondered whether I could live a normal life. But, as I've now realized, that's not quite it. It's bigger than that. A disturbance pushing up from underneath. A rumbling, threatening tremor. As if the ground I'm standing on is unstable, about to tip me off balance. Different from the looming threat of going to jail. In a way, worse.

What if I don't belong anywhere?

Cassie and I got past the awkwardness and made it through dinner, but as soon as I left her place, I headed out again. I had no plan except to follow my nose, and my nose turns out to be a stupid bitch because she leads me to the Barrington's neighborhood. If Nico is still interested in me as a suspect for that double homicide, and I'm sure she is, then it's possible she has eyes on me. And how would I explain being in the same alley where she nearly caught me that night? Because yes, that's what I'm doing, standing here like a dumbass.

What do you make of that, Doctor Foster? You always said I was smarter than people gave me credit for. But maybe you're not as smart as you're supposed to be.

I turn around and start back, casting my eyes left and right to check whether I have a tail, but it looks clear. Still, the uneasiness won't leave me and when I reach my block, I'm still trying to get rid of this awful rattling, curling dread.

Maybe that literal jog down memory lane was to remind myself of who I am. Or who I used to be. Because at least the old Gemma was someone. A criminal, yes, but she had people and purpose and a life. The new version of me has Sol and a notebook with an empty *Hobbies* section.

I stop at the edge of Cannon Street. I guess this is what they call an identity crisis. Why else would Cassie's words affect me so much? Her intuition is right on the money. The Aurora *is* a weird place for me. But having it thrown in my face like that was a bit much. Too close to an uncomfortable possibility. That now I've given up my criminal ways, I'm adrift in the world. Untethered. But not in a good way.

To Cassie's question, I'd stammered a lame response about not liking social media. Cassie, seeing my reaction, had apologized. She'd blamed it on her inquisitive writer's brain and I'd let it slide. Maybe that's all it is. Or maybe I've been underestimating Cassie. She's naïve in the romance department, but that doesn't mean she's not someone to be wary of.

Oh my god, speak of the devil. Sort of. Across the road, Leighton is outside Bouche. He's greeting a woman who has just emerged from a cab. I step back into the shadow of a building and continue to watch. They hug and kiss each other on the cheek. Is this a date? It's hard to tell. And the woman looks familiar. Her shoes and coat are incredible and her hair looks expensive. Is she a celebrity? Is that how I know her? And what could Leighton offer someone like her? Maybe I'm missing something. Maybe the world of Tiles & Textures is more exciting than it seems. And Leighton and Cassie have only just started seeing each other, so maybe they've agreed to keep it light. Would Cassie really be comfortable with a casual sex arrangement, though? I sigh.

This is none of my business and I've got other things to worry about.

Inside my apartment my eyes land on the armchair Sven sat in last night and my stomach roils. Damn you, Sven. How do I shed you? And why should I do *anything* for you? As thanks for screwing up my life? For getting my best friend disappeared? No. His visit was just more motivation to figure out who murdered Tom. Because then I can ditch both him and Nico and get on with my life. Whatever that ends up looking like.

After a shower, I settle in my armchair with my notebook. The last thing I wrote jumps out at me. *What is Penny hiding?*

It's hard to believe pixie face Penny Pritchard could be a murderer. But what would I know? I've met several killers and I never twigged until Sven told me afterward. George mentioned a wrongful death suit and Penny was clearly lying about where she lived before the Aurora. And that *consultant* bullshit. I know a fake cover story when I hear one.

I open Facebook. She friend-requested me that first day we hung out, so I have full access to her busy-looking page. Her profile name is Penny Penny, and since mine is also cryptic—Gemma Amsterdam—it seems like more evidence that she's hiding stuff.

After a bit of scrolling to warm up, I put on my scuba gear and dive deeper. I can't find her previous address and I don't know if George is right about that wrongful death suit, but I do learn she attended U of T and she was born Penelope Millerhouse. Pritchard is her married name. She's divorced but hasn't changed it back.

Wait.

U of T. That's where Tom Bollard went. I sit up straighter. And Penny and Tom are both 42. My breath catching, I type his name and then Penny Millerhouse into the search bar.

Holy shit.

The connection isn't U of T; they went to high school together. *Penny knew Tom.* That's what she's been hiding. That Penny seems sweet and kind and not at all murdery doesn't matter. It can't. Because maybe the first thing I learned—thanks Mom and Dad—is you have to look after yourself. Because no one else will. No one else has my back, so I have to watch my own.

39

NICO

Nico disconnected. Where the hell was Jackson? He'd left straight after the morning briefing without a word, and now he wasn't picking up? This was important. Tom's phone was fully charged and unlocked and waiting to be explored. She also had his call log. They finally had something to work with, but Jared had gone AWOL.

"Tough luck, Jackson," she muttered, grabbing the printout. She went straight to Tom's most recent calls and immediately saw that he'd dialed 911 at 2:27 a.m. on Friday morning.

"Singh," she called out.

"Yes?" DC Singh replied, walking over to Nico's desk.

"Can you look into this 911 call?" She pointed. "It barely registered, Tom hung up almost immediately, but if you listen to the recording, there might be something."

"Sure."

"And go through the rest of them. We're looking for connections to anyone on our list. Residents or Boston Works. You know the drill."

"On it." Singh nodded, her eyes bright.

Feeling the weight of someone's gaze, Nico looked up, expecting to catch Jill eyeballing her with an unreadable expression—that woman was an enigma. But it was DC Patterson projecting a dirty look across the room. Nico turned away. Jared had been giving him the inside track, but Nico wouldn't do the same. Tough shit, Patterson, because your best buddy isn't here right now and you should have tried kissing my ass more.

Tom had called emergency services. Was this an indication of time of death? Or at least the start of events leading to his murder? But she shouldn't get ahead of herself. Maybe he'd dialed it by accident and hung up as soon as he realized. Nico picked up Tom's phone and tapped the email icon. Tom's bank statements hadn't come through yet, but they should give her a picture of the days before his death. That New York vacation could be important. Maybe it was a trip for two and his travel companion killed him right before they left. For reasons yet to be unveiled. Maybe it all came back to those skeletons in his past.

Nico's eyes latched onto an email from Carlos Santino. It confirmed he could accept delivery of Tom's furniture the following week. Tom had emailed Carlos at 12:06 a.m. Thursday night. He'd signed off with *more to come*. At 12:15 a.m. he'd forwarded to Carlos another delivery notification. This time, a coffee table. There were no emails after that. Another sign that Tom had died in the early hours of Friday morning? Did this suggest Tom had been killed in his hotel room and his killer had carried his dead body into the building on Friday or Saturday? If that was the case, they must have pretended to be Tom. Because Chris Sheffield said he handed keys to Tom at nine.

But Sheffield also left the country straight after settlement.

"Singh?" Nico called. "Anything on Chris Sheffield yet?"

DC Singh shook her head. "Nada."

Nico returned to the printout. How do you go from online shopping to calling emergency services two hours later? Had Tom looked out his hotel window and seen something happening on the street below and called 911? A fight that quickly resolved, so he hung up? Possible.

On Tom's phone, Nico opened an email with confirmation of his travel details. "Huh." she said, frowning. Tom's flight to New York departed at 10:35 a.m. Friday. The timeline didn't make sense. According to Boston Works, nine a.m. was the earliest anyone could pick up their keys, otherwise there'd be legal issues. How did Tom expect to make an international flight only one and a half hours later? Was he one of those people who screeched through the terminal, pushing things to the last possible moment? More likely, he realized his mistake and got a later flight. There was no email to confirm this, but he could have done so within the airline's booking system. He didn't have the app downloaded, though. Nico set down the phone to send a quick message to DC Singh, asking her to look into this.

"Will do, boss," Singh called from her desk.

Nico eyed her computer screen. She had a new email. The fingerprint analysis of the package found in Tom's apartment had come through. As she read the report, a surge of adrenaline rocketed through her body. There were two sets of prints on that package. Prints that didn't belong to Tom. And one of them matched a set she'd taken only a week ago, lifted off an innocuous glass of water in the interview room. Things were finally clicking into place.

"Nico," Patterson said, stepping up to her desk. "Where's Jackson?"

"I think you meant to say *DS* Davis," Nico replied, her eyes narrowing.

"Right, yeah."

"What's up?"

"Nothing new. Jackson not here?"

She sighed. "I don't know where he is. Talk to me."

"We've got someone who saw something at the Aurora the weekend our vic was killed." He thumbed behind him at a woman standing next to a uniform. She wore a tiny purple skirt and a leather jacket Nico immediately coveted.

Nico followed Patterson over. The woman stopped chewing her gum to eye Nico. "You gonna drop the charge?"

Nico glanced at Patterson. He shrugged, as if he didn't mind.

"If you give me something good," Nico said.

"It's about that building... been in the papers. The Aurora."

"The newspaper?"

"What, you think I'm ignorant? I read the news every single day." She made an annoyed sound and crossed her arms.

"Sorry. Carry on. Please."

"I was near there on Friday night. Right outside."

"Friday the 5th?"

"I guess."

"What did you see?"

"I was chatting to one of you...."

"One of whom?"

"A cop. Trying to chat me up." She chuckled. "Didn't matter in the end. Anyway, I looked up and saw her."

"Her?"

"Yeah. She was climbing around the side of the building." She shook her head. "Some Instagram shit. You know, selfies in dangerous places."

A woman scaling the building. *On Friday fucking night.* A slow smile crept over Nico's face. This wasn't an Instagram challenge. No, this was a professional doing what they did best. Someone who could disappear over the side of a high-rise without so much as a backward glance.

This was Gemma Cross.

"Patterson, find a picture of Gemma Cross and get a proper ID."

Nico finally had her. Because it was Gemma's prints on that package in Tom's apartment and it had to be Gemma climbing the Aurora that Friday night.

Finally, Nico could connect Gemma to Tom.

Nico ran back to her desk and grabbed her phone and keys. She dialed Carlos Santino's number as she jogged out of the room. Straight to voicemail. "Damn it," she hissed, entering the elevator. No matter, if she couldn't tailgate her way inside, then she'd buzz apartments until someone opened the door.

When she pulled up outside the Aurora, Penny Pritchard was at the entrance. "Hey," she called out, leaping from the car and hurrying over. "I need you to let me in. Police business."

Penny looked uncertain. "Oh, um...."

"You want to be charged with obstructing justice?"

Penny's eyes widened. She ducked her chin and opened the door. Nico pushed roughly past and ran to the entrance to the stairwell. "Open it," she barked. Penny, looking pale, lurched forward and obeyed. Nico ran through and up the stairs to level four. She hurried down the corridor to Gemma's apartment, but before she could knock, the door swung open. Jared walked out backward, tucking in his shirt. As he turned, his eyes latched onto Nico, the goofy grin dropping from his face.

"Fuck," he said.

"Apparently."

40

I follow Jared into the hall, then stop. Oh. Shit. Nico is here. Outside my apartment, only a few feet away, her face turning red. Jared's expression makes a lot more sense now.

Nico's hands clench into fists as she flicks wild eyes from Jared back to me. "I thought you didn't know Tom Bollard," she growls.

"We've been through this," I huff. "Never heard of him, never met him, never spoke to him."

"You deny meeting him? Going to his apartment?"

"Sure do."

"Care to explain how your fingerprints ended up in his apartment?"

I draw back in surprise. "They did?"

"Don't play dumb with me, bitch."

"Whoa, Nico, take it easy," Jared says, lurching forward to plant himself between us.

"I've never been fingerprinted." I glare at her. "How did you get a match?"

Jared turns wide eyes to Nico. "Nico? When did you print her?"

Nico scowls.

And then I remember. I'd accepted a glass of water in the interview room. Like a rookie. Like a dumbass. Damn. I'd been totally off the police radar and now they have my prints on file. Sven had specifically warned us about this. It had literally been part of my training.

"That's illegal," I say, even though it's probably not. A sneaky but legit move.

Nico shoves Jared to the side and steps closer. "Someone saw you scaling the building that Friday night."

Oh, shit.

Nico catches my expression and smiles. "Did Tom see something he wasn't supposed to?" she continues. "Or were you hired to kill him? Is that your gig? Are you a killer for hire?"

Jared's eyes bug out. "Nico, what—"

"Get out of here, Jackson. I'll deal with you later. Fucking a suspect? You're unbelievable."

"She's not a—"

"She sure as shit is, you fucking idiot."

"Language, Nico, language," I say.

She turns violent eyes to me. A pulse of adrenaline rockets through my body.

"Nico—" Jared starts.

"You're compromised," she hisses. "Scram."

"I can't leave you alone with her." He moves in front of her again. "Not like this."

"Jared, it's fine," I say, pushing him away, my pulse thundering in my ears. I tilt my head to smile at Nico. "Won't you come inside, Detective," I say, opening the door wider.

"Gemma, no," Jared tries again. "Nico, please."

We both ignore him.

Nico strides inside, slamming the door behind her. We face each other. As she glares at me, eyes burning, I check the surrounding area for breakable things. I'm already pretty fond of my apartment and everything in it. I didn't think this invitation through, but what else is new?

She takes a step closer, her jaw working. "Let's have a chat," she says, her expression making it clear there'll be no actual talking.

I take a step back and transfer my weight to the balls of my feet, tensing my muscles to prepare for whatever's coming next. "Okay, *this* definitely isn't allowed."

"If a tree falls in the forest and no one is around...."

I straighten. "Huh?"

Nico rolls her eyes. "I won't tell if you won't."

"Are you forgetting Jared is standing right outside the door?"

At least, I hope he is.

I'm trained for this, the inevitable physical altercations, but so is Nico. And I don't have vengeance igniting my ass. She's clearly not messing around, and this is almost certainly a mistake.

So Doctor Foster, how's that intelligence theory looking now?

"If you get blood on my carpet—" I start.

Her arm swings out, a cat swiping at a slow-to-catch-on bird. I lurch to the side, a gust of air kissing my cheek. She recovers quickly and raises her hands again.

"You box, don't you?" I pant, dancing from side to side. She jabs at me again, and I duck, again. But then she charges, tackling me to the ground. Okay, that hurt.

41

My bottom lip is bleeding, my head throbs, and I have an ugly bruise on my right hip. But I'm alive and not in jail, so I'm counting this as a win.

"Keep still," Penny says as she dabs at my face.

"It hurts."

It doesn't, not really—my pain tolerance is high—but Penny is being motherly and my neglected inner child is soaking it up. Sol, once he recovered from the disruption to his little universe, had slunk out of the spare room and did his best to console me, purring loudly against my chest. But sometimes you need to talk to another human being. And when I described myself as an adrenaline junkie, that's not what I meant. Facing off with Nico was a thrill, yes, but she's not all bark and no bite. She, for sure, has teeth. When Jared finally came to his senses and burst into my apartment to literally drag us apart, I was relieved. When it comes to getting physical, I prefer my one-on-one sessions to go a different way.

"Are you going to tell me what happened?" Penny asks, sitting back to study me.

It's a good question—am I? But how can I offload on Penny when I just ratted her out as a potential suspect? Because that's why Jared had been at my apartment at all. At least, at first. I called and said I had intel. A suspect for his list. But Jared already knew about Penny's past with Tom. She confessed earlier today. In a weird twist of universe synchronicity, she'd called Jared and told him all about it less than an hour before I did the same. Which means I betrayed her for nothing. This is why Jared and I ended up in bed again. I'd felt bad and sex feels good and neither of us has much willpower. That Nico caught us is just bad luck. She's now not in any position to arrest me, though. Silver linings.

"Gemma, are you in trouble?"

Yes, Penny, I am, but I can't tell you about it.

She gestures at my bruises. "Should I call Detective Jackson?" she says, sounding almost hopeful.

"Ha!" I blurt, then start to laugh.

"What's funny?"

"Oh, Penny." I let out a sad sigh.

"Gemma." Her voice softens. "Who did this to your face?"

I raise my gaze to meet hers. "Detective Davis."

Penny's eyes turn to saucers. "A police officer? But they can't... but surely—"

"It's against the law? Sure is. Technically. It still happens, though."

Penny might have condo-life adulting sorted, but she can be naïve about other stuff.

"I kind of invited her to, though," I add.

"You did what?"

"It's a long story."

I look into her anxious face. I need her as an ally, and I want to tell her the truth. Because I'm tired of lying and I have to clear my conscience about tattling on her, at least.

"Penny, I did something stupid. I was feeling desperate and…"

"Gemma, you're scaring me."

"I know you've been lying about the murder victim. You were at high school with Tom Bollard."

The color drains from her face.

"Why did you lie?" I ask.

She sighs. "I got such a fright when I saw him in the locker. I recognized him even through the plastic. I guess I panicked." She stands and starts pacing the room, then abruptly stops. "Gemma, we dated in high school. Briefly." Her face twists. "But I honestly haven't seen him in years."

"You went to the same university."

"Different campuses. Different programs. I literally never saw him. Not a single word. And I didn't kill him, I swear. I should have admitted I knew him straight away, yes, but I thought I might be a suspect because I was the one who found him. I didn't know what to do, so I lied. And at first I tried to find out as much as I could about what happened to him, but then I got overwhelmed and decided I should stay as far away from it as possible."

I nod. Explains her attitude U-turn, at least.

"And I've come clean since then," she continues. "I've explained our history to the police, I swear."

I believe Penny didn't kill him, but being a good judge of character is not something I would put on my résumé. If I had a résumé.

"I'm sorry for lying to you," she adds, wringing her hands.

"All good, Penny. Seriously." After a pause, I add. "And the wrongful death lawsuit?"

Penny's head snaps up. Suddenly, her eyes are like ice. "How do you know about that?"

"I, uh, George mentioned it."

"*George*? What did he say?"

I stare at Penny's furrowed brow and her flinty eyes. The hard line of her mouth.

"Uh..."

"How *dare* you?" she snaps. "How dare you snoop into my life as if it was nothing. As if it was something to gossip about."

"That's not what—"

"Get out, Gemma. Now."

Her whole body is shaking. Penny is smaller than me, but she's furious. I'm not interested in another cat fight this evening. I didn't enjoy the first one much.

So I leave.

At Bar 605, I drain my first martini, then signal the bartender. Same again. I'm not cut out for a normie life. *Obviously*. No matter how hard I try, crap follows me around. And now I'm infecting other people. Is it time to give up? Sven will probably take me back. I could work off my so-called debt.

As the bartender slides over my drink, someone sidles up to my left.

"Gemma, isn't it?"

I turn to see Leighton leaning against the bar. "Someone's been in the wars." He points at my lip.

I did my best to cover it with lipstick, but I guess I'm not fooling anyone.

"Leighton, right?" I say without interest. "Where's Cassie tonight?"

He shrugs. "We're not exclusive." With a boyish smile, he hops onto the barstool next to mine. Apparently, me not telling him to fuck off straight away is an invitation. "Plus, she's not really my type," he adds.

"Oh yeah? What's your type?" I ask, already tired, because I know what his answer will be.

Leighton waves his hand in my direction and gives me a leery smile. "Raw. Sexy. A little wild."

I take another sip. I'm only tolerating this douche because I need a distraction. A hit of dopamine. I can get loaded or climb into bed or crawl across a building. Which is it going to be, Doctor Foster? You want to place a bet?

Leighton leans closer. "What do you say? Should we get out of here?"

I down the rest of my drink and grab my bag.

42

NICO

Nico pushed away the bowl with a disgusted sigh. She couldn't even enjoy noodles right now.

"No good?" the waitress asked, pausing next to the booth.

"Can I get the rest to go?" Nico said. Maybe she'd be able to stomach them later.

The waitress stayed at the edge of her table. "You okay? You look tired. And," she frowned, "your face is sore."

Nico gingerly touched the bruise on her cheekbone and sighed again. "I'm fine," she mumbled. She forced a smile. "Fine."

But she wasn't. She'd been suspended. Off the job until she could get her shit together. That awful meeting with Sarge had been twenty-four hours ago, and she hadn't seen Jared since. He'd called a couple of times and the person who'd banged on her door last night was probably him, but she'd ignored it. What could he say? How could he apologize for screwing the suspect, then ratting *her* out about the fight? Two strikes and he wouldn't get a third.

How could he have slept with her? After what Nico had shared with him. Had they lain around in bed laughing about what an idiot Nico was? Discussing the case? Or Nico's life? She let out a heavy sigh. Now that she'd blown her lid, released her rage, she felt hollow and alone. Weighted. Like someone had tied an anvil to her neck, dragging her into oblivion. But one that didn't include the mercy of sleep, apparently. Just awful, echoing wakefulness. Buzzing, relentless awareness. Tired but wired.

Feeling as if her whole body was made of lead, Nico pushed herself up and out of the booth. As she emerged onto the street, her phone vibrated in her pocket. She pulled it out and checked the display. Tatiana. She sent it to voicemail. She didn't have the strength to talk to her sister. Tati always knew when something was wrong.

Inside her apartment, Nico threw her tote onto the kitchen island and watched as it skidded across the fake-granite surface. Her *Pocket Size Puzzles* book fell out, but her bag carried on its merry way to land with a thud on the floor. Nico exhaled. "Fuck you." She hurled the words at her bag. As if it had done this on purpose.

Nico sniffed the air, frowning. What was that smell? Meaty, savory... familiar. "Dammit," she hissed, hurrying around the breakfast bar. She'd forgotten about the container of leftover noodles she'd tucked into her tote. She ripped off a wad of paper towels and kneeled on the floor to mop up the mess, then dumped the bag and container in the sink.

Nico wandered into the dark and still of her living room. Normally she liked this, a balm to the bedlam of the station and the city, but right now it felt ominous. She dropped onto the couch, letting her body meld with the furniture, willing herself to relax. But her rattling mind wouldn't release her. She stood up. She could go out. She could find a familiar face at a cop bar and nurse a drink while other people's noise filled the silence. Because sometimes existing in the proximity of someone who knew your name was enough. But what if word had already spread? And she wanted to put this mental energy to use. Sarge be damned.

Nico waited outside the station until ten p.m., then scuttled inside, head low. Nico immediately felt calmer. For once, the chaotic yet consistent hum felt good and normal. Drunken disorderlies downstairs. Uniforms gritting their teeth and pushing through the worst shift on the roster. The dedicated night owls zipping happily around, making the most of the space with fewer people getting in their way. Jared wasn't the type to hang around unnecessarily, it was obvious he had a social life. But DC Patterson was prone to lurk at any hour, so Nico worked quickly to photocopy the Bollard case file.

When she stopped by her desk for a final check, her eyes latched onto a yellow post-it note. Chiandra Chase, it read, with a Yorkville address listed underneath. The Kimberly Dallant missing person case, Nico suddenly remembered. Chiandra was Kimberly's best friend and Nico had been in the process of setting up a meeting with her when....

Nico glanced over her shoulder to check for watchful eyes, then photocopied that file as well, as minimal as it was. A long sleepless night stretched ahead of her, Nico already knew, and she'd be damned if she'd spend it tossing and turning and allowing her subconscious mind to turn her grief into a funhouse nightmare.

43

Don't worry, Doctor Foster, I didn't do it.

If you thought I was going to sabotage my new life beyond repair, you can relax. Last night I left Bar 605, went for a run, then came straight home to dive into a bottle of wine. I didn't doink that creep Leighton. Cassie is sweet and doesn't deserve someone shitting on her relationship. I mean, Leighton is obviously already doing that, but I don't need to participate.

I've messed up with Penny, though, and I'm still number one on the suspect list because of my dumb dopamine brain. Because I just *had* to climb the Aurora that first night. I explained away my fingerprints on that package for Tom, but it's not enough. And even though Nico is now off the case—worth a split lip, for sure—I'm not in the clear. Life as a normie is way more angst-ridden than I expected. And there's more interaction with police officers than when I was a criminal.

Feeling heavy and sore, I dress for yet another run. Despite how crappy I feel, I need to move and sweat. The monotonous motion is soothing. It calms me down and helps me think.

By the time I get home, I've resolved to make things right with Penny. I even bought pastries on the way home to help me beg for forgiveness.

Once showered, I get dressed, slap on a little makeup—just to be polite—and select the nicest bottle of wine in my stash to go with the eclairs. Some might argue it's too early for drinking, but I am not one of them. I suspect Penny isn't either. Either way, it's part of my peace offering.

As I descend two floors to Penny's apartment, I practice my best rueful expression. Outside her place, I knock and wait, feeling that strange tug of déjà vu. But this isn't a brain glitch; I have literally done this before. And it probably won't be the last time I show up at Penny's with an apology treat.

She opens the door, which is a good start.

"I'm sorry I dug into your past," I say to her pinched expression. She doesn't reply, but I carry on. "I had no right, but I was desperate. Detective Davis is trying to pin the murder on me."

Penny eyes me, biting her lip. She's far from convinced, but she hasn't slammed the door in my face. So what should I say next? How did Danni do this? She always knew the right angle. To make things go her way. What does Penny need to hear?

I take a breath. "We're neighbors, Penny. Unless one of us sells, we're going to be bumping into each other all the time. We could try to avoid each other, but neither of us wants that, do we? I moved in here because I didn't want to be isolated, which I've only just realized, properly. You did too, right? So why don't we talk it out and I'll promise never to go behind your back again?"

Tears spring into her eyes, and after a moment, she nods. "Okay."

She lets me inside, then puts the pastries on plates, the wine in the fridge, and makes coffee. I guess it is too early for Penny.

Once we're on the couch, she sets her shoulders and turns to face me. "I should apologize too. I overreacted, but it's still so raw."

"Raw?" I echo.

She takes a large gulping breath, then tells me her story. It's a heartbreaker.

Five years ago she'd been happily shacked up with a husband and a kid, living her best life in a beautiful ranch-style bungalow in Bayview, until disaster struck. Her six-year-old son contracted meningitis and died after an overworked and arrogant emergency room doctor sent them away, muttering about hysterical parents. They won a wrongful death suit—kept out of the media as part of the settlement—but it had destroyed their marriage and shattered Penny into a million pieces.

After they sold the house—she couldn't stand living there with the ghost of her boy—she wanted to move somewhere completely different and start fresh. She rented an apartment in a large complex and signed up as a volunteer for a meningitis awareness charity. Our building manager Carlos is also a member—he lost a niece—and it was Carlos who told her about the Aurora condos. Struggling with loneliness, Penny realized that living in a small and community-oriented building might be exactly what she needed. And so, she purchased her condo and resolved to build a new life. Just like I had.

As she finished, she brought out a framed photograph of her son, the thing she'd overreacted to that first day I'd hung out in her apartment. It had been sitting on the side table, but the moment I'd knocked on the door, she'd realized she wasn't ready to talk about him. She'd shunted it under the couch, but I, all eagle eyes and no tact, had seen it poking out.

When Penny wipes away what looks like the last of her tears and takes a shuddering breath, I lean forward and clasp her arm. "I'm so sorry, Penny."

"I'll probably never stop hurting. Not completely. I—"

Her phone rings, startling us both. She checks the display. "Oh, it's Cassie. She's confirming our pre-dinner drink later today." She makes a sheepish face. "I invited her over after you and I...."

"Had a fight?" I give her a small smile. "You were going to replace me with Cassie?"

She looks down. "No, I...."

"Why don't we all hang out?"

As soon as the words leave my mouth, I remember the Leighton situation. I have to tell Cassie. She needs to know she's dating a creep. Because chicks before dicks, right?

"You're sure?" Penny says, lifting her phone.

I nod. "Let's do it. Let's start a girl gang at the Aurora."

44

NICO

C hiandra Chase was a familiar face, Nico realized as soon as Chiandra opened her door. A model and the ambassador for an underwear brand of which Nico was a loyal customer. Their sports bras were the only ones Nico wore, and stepping into Chiandra's beautiful two-story apartment, she felt both intimidated and weirdly emotional. Probably the lack of sleep, Nico mused as she accepted a bottle of chilled water, wishing it was coffee. But Chiandra wasn't the type to fuss about in the kitchen making hot drinks for other people.

They settled in the living room, a large and minimally furnished space with a seventies style depression in the middle that immediately conjured up the idea of retro fondue parties. Nico pushed this away and focused on Chiandra, sitting across from her with her legs tucked up and waiting expectantly.

Chiandra was several years off thirty, but her face had been filled and plumped and botoxed into ageless, almost inhuman beauty. Chiandra didn't look younger than her age, just... smoother. Nico had seen this before, watching her twelve-year-old niece absorb a makeup tutorial on YouTube. Nico had wondered why her niece was taking advice from someone in her thirties until she learned the woman was only just twenty. Young girls probably couldn't see it, especially with Instagram filters clouding their judgment. To Nico, it was a strange new world. But she herself likely seemed alien to people like Chiandra.

"As you know, Kimberly Dallant is officially a missing person," Nico began. "I'm here to figure out where she might be. Can you tell me what's been going on in her life recently?"

Chiandra fixed her eyes on Nico. "Normal stuff."

"How often do you see each other?"

"A lot. Brunch, hot yoga, events. Sometimes we have shoots together. I see her at least twice a week, usually more."

"Anything unusual happen?"

She shook her head, her hair tumbling around her shoulders. There was something artificial about the movement. As if she'd practiced it before. A go-to modeling move, perhaps?

"And the last time you saw her?" Nico continued.

"Thursday night. We went out."

"The date, please?"

Chiandra eyed Nico coolly, then lifted her phone to check her calendar. Nico waited, still trying to find her sense of gravity. She felt scratchy and unsettled and discordant. As if the normal rhythm of conversation was off. Nico watched Chiandra, now scrolling. Was it this woman's expressionless face? Flawless in a photo, yes, but unnerving in person. Her forehead was like a marble counter, her eyelashes fluttering repeatedly and her lips moving only as much as needed. Like talking to a living doll. Or an AI image.

It was messing with Nico's normal process. She wasn't paying attention to all the little cues she usually gathered during routine questioning. Nico's fatigue, perhaps. Or maybe because they weren't visible on this inert landscape. Nico's mind drifted to a friend who studied behavioral analysis and lie-detection techniques. Did botoxed faces put a spanner in the works? Or did liars still exhibit the same telltale signs? Shifting eyes, overly detailed explanations, fidgeting fingers.

"Thursday April fourth," Chiandra said finally.

"And where were you and Kimberly?"

"A club called Spider. Just chilling. A normal night, but I had an early call, so I left around midnight. She stayed, there were a few familiar faces around—"

"Names?"

Chiandra shook her head. "Can't remember. Acquaintances, at best. Spider's on Instagram. You could check there."

"Right."

Scouring social media wasn't always Nico's first instinct, but it often yielded clues.

"I asked Ley already, but he hasn't heard from her either."

"Ley?"

"Her ex. They only broke up a few weeks ago."

"Can you give me his contact details?" Nico asked.

Chiandra let out a heavy sigh. "Sure." Keeping hold of her phone, she peeled herself slowly off the couch. Either exhausted or intensely bored.

As Chiandra ambled out of the room, Nico wondered why Ley's number wasn't in the iPhone she had clutched in her hand. But when Chiandra returned, she handed over a business card. "Thought this would be easier. He works a lot."

"Thanks."

Nico read the card, sucked in a breath, and looked up. "Ley is Leighton Matthews?"

Chiandra let out a hiccup of laughter. "Leighton. Makes him sound like such a nerd."

"So Leighton and Kimberly were together?"

Chiandra lifted one shoulder as she considered the question. "They dated for a while."

"Exclusive?"

"Not on Kimberly's end." Another little laugh. Nico watched, amazed. Almost no facial muscles used at all.

"Kimberly's agent lodged the missing person report, but what do you think? Are you worried or is she just away somewhere?"

Suddenly Chiandra leaned forward, the most animated Nico had seen her.

"Honestly, it's possible she went on vacay. A couple of times in the past, she got all overwhelmed or whatever and just had to leave. Normally she tells me, but one time she didn't." Her eyes shifted to the side.

"What was different about that?" Nico pressed.

"Look, she'll probably show up tomorrow and be, like, *sorry*. And then spin it so everyone thinks she's mysterious and cool."

"You're not worried about her?" Nico blurted, her voice suddenly hard.

Chiandra's eyes flickered, then narrowed. "Of course I am. Underneath. But Kimberly is strong." She lifted her chin. "She can look after herself."

What if she's living a secret life, though? Maybe she's in over her head and you're supposed to be her best friend, but you didn't notice.

Suddenly, something deep inside Nico surged up, crested, and landed. With it came a rush of exhaustion, slamming into her like a rogue wave. She leaned forward, her elbows on her knees, trying to gain control over the swirling, eddying sensation. She swallowed. What was she doing here? What was she trying to achieve? Kimberly Dallant was off in the Swiss Alps at a mountain retreat, while Nico was scrabbling in the dirt, digging her own grave.

"Ma'am, are you okay?" Chiandra said.

Nico blinked. "Not really," she said without thinking.

When Chiandra recoiled, Nico waved it off. "Kidding," she added.

But she wasn't.

45

When I return to Penny's apartment a couple of hours later—Penny had errands to run and Sol was due scratchies—Penny tells me that Cassie is on her way.

"Just a heads up," I say. "I'm going to have to tell her something, and it's kind of a bummer."

Immediately, Penny's face creases into a frown. "Why, Gemma?"

I sigh. "I don't *want* to. A couple of days ago, I saw Leighton with another woman. Maybe it wasn't a date, but last night I bumped into him at a bar and he hit on me."

"Oh." Penny's mouth turns down. "I think she really likes him. Poor Cassie."

At the sound of a timid knock, Penny jumps up and answers the door. "Cassie, come in."

"Thanks." Cassie steps inside and turns to me. At first her expression is uncertain, but then her eyes widen, almost excited. "Gemma, what happened to your face?"

"Long story."

"I love long stories," she says eagerly, studying me.

"Cassie, listen."

I've got to get this Leighton thing off my chest.

"So... Leighton—"

"Sorry, Gemma," Penny interrupts. "Can I get you a drink, Cassie?" she asks, giving me a *look*. As if I'm doing this wrong. I make a *go ahead* gesture. Penny has probably staged a boyfriend intervention before, unlike me. I'm happy for her to take the lead.

"Thanks, Penny," Cassie says. "Whatever you're drinking." She eyes the coffee cups, still on the table. The pastries are long gone.

"I was about to open the wine Gemma brought over."

I nod. You can't get into the stuff we're about to get into without proper drinks.

"Sounds great," Cassie says.

"How's it going with Leighton?" Penny asks once we're all set up. "Are you still dating?"

I eye Penny. Smart move. Suss out the situation first. They might have already broken up, for all we know.

But Cassie is smiling widely. "He is so sweet."

Sweet? And I thought *I* was a poor judge of character.

"In what way?" I ask, genuinely curious.

"Flowers. Whisking me off to spontaneous lunches. Being super interested in my life. He actually cares." She beams. "He looks like a player on the outside, but he's not."

"Yeah, but he tries," I blurt.

Cassie frowns, chewing her lip, then her expression lifts. "Oh, yes. Leighton told me."

My eyes bug. He did?

"Told you what?"

"That there'd been a misunderstanding. At the bar," Cassie continues. "He said you might have gotten the wrong idea when he came over to say hello."

Nobody misunderstood anything. Except maybe Leighton and his own appeal.

"That's what he said?"

Cassie nods. Her eyes shift to Penny, as if gauging her reaction. Penny's face is blank. Totally neutral. When Cassie turns back to me, her smile is almost patronizing. "He was really cute about it. He didn't want to get between us."

Wowser. Does Cassie really believe this or is she dancing in the land of denial because it's less painful there?

"I hope there are no hard feelings," Cassie adds anxiously. "You're not into him, are you?" She wrinkles her nose. "I get why you might be. He's so great. But I'd hate for that to cause a problem."

I take a controlled breath. "No, Cassie. I am most definitely not into him."

"Good, good."

"Something to nibble on?" Penny says brightly, disappearing into the kitchen.

Thanks for the backup, Penny. But maybe she recognizes a lost cause when she sees one.

Cassie leans closer and drops her voice. "Gemma. The other night, at dinner," she begins, seeming nervous.

Okay, we're getting into that, are we? I wait, bracing myself for another truth grenade. Think you've dealt with your trauma? *Kablam*.

"I asked what you're doing here, but I didn't mean it like you shouldn't be here. I just find you intriguing." Cassie tilts her head, her eyes examining mine. "You've inspired me to create a new character. Someone like you. Messy but likable. Who sometimes does bad things or maybe just the wrong thing. Maybe involved in some stuff she shouldn't be, but strong and smart and interesting," she finishes, smiling expectantly.

She's calling me a hot mess and borderline shady right to my face.

I mean, she's not wrong, but still.

"I'd love to get your blessing. As my official muse, I guess."

I bite my lip. "I don't know, Cassie."

She draws back. "What?"

"I mean...." I trail off, flailing my hands as I try to explain. But explain what? I'm trying to keep a low profile because I have a lot of secrets. Also, I don't want anyone digging into my psyche, thanks very much?

"It makes me uncomfortable."

"Oh." Cassie's eyes go wide. "I thought you'd be flattered."

"A little, maybe. But I'm mostly uneasy."

Cassie's mouth tightens. "Is this about Leighton?"

"No." I clench my jaw. "And there was no misunderstanding," I add under my breath.

"Pardon?" Cassie says, eyes blinking fast.

"Cassie, I know you want—"

"I can't believe you're being like this."

"Like what? Warning you that you're getting involved with a total douche? You could do so much better—"

"Just leave it," she hisses. "You don't understand what—"

"Here we go," Penny says loudly, returning with a tray of complicated-looking snacks.

Cassie stands up. "I've got a headache." She raises one hand to her head.

Unconvincing, Cassie.

"I'm going to go," she continues. "See you another time?"

She doesn't wait for a response, virtually running to the door. With a quiet click, she's gone.

"Is she okay?" Penny stares after her, frowning, then turns to me. "What did you say to her?"

"It's the Leighton thing. There's no way I misread that."

Penny grimaces. "I figured as much. You can't tell people what they're not ready to hear." She pushes over the tray of food and smiles hopefully. "But you'll stay?"

I eye the little snacks. "Sure."

And not just because of the food. Now we've cleared the air, I have something to ask her. But I'm going to ease into it this time, warm her up first. So for the next couple of hours, we drink wine and share dating disaster stories. We decide Cassie will have to learn about men like Leighton the hard way.

"Poor thing," Penny says, draining her glass. "So what now? Maybe a movie?" Her face is flushed and her eyes bright. A little tipsy and open to suggestion. Perfect. Here I go.

"Penny?" I set down my glass. "I have a proposition."

46

NICO

Parked outside the Aurora the next morning, Nico slouched low in her seat and slid on a pair of oversized sunglasses. A gift from her niece last Christmas, cheap and not remotely suited to Nico, but finally useful: large and dark enough to hide her identity, as well as the evidence of her run-in with Gemma.

Her gaze drifted to the Baymax figurine sitting on the dash, then slid away. Nico had taken the Marvel toy from Izzy's car because it reminded Nico of the two of them riding around together. If not working on a case, then just cruising and shooting the shit or grabbing food. Nico picked it up and held it in her hand, a smile playing at her mouth. But the pleasant memories quickly dissipated, leaving her only with the ache of grief. Nico shook her head, banished Izzy from her mind, and shoved the figurine into the glove compartment. She slammed it shut and returned her gaze to the entrance to the Aurora. She'd come here today with rebellion in her blood. She couldn't let this go. She wouldn't. Not when she was so close, and not when Jared ruled-by-his-dick Jackson was literally screwing with her case.

Nico picked up the copied file and thumbed through, reviewing the information. On CCTV near the hotel Tom stayed at before the Aurora, he'd been picked up only three times. Each time, alone. No warrant yet for the hotel lobby footage, but it had to be imminent. The skeleton in Tom's past remained a mystery, and, as suspected, the cameras at the Aurora had been offline until Monday. According to Boston, the mistake was human—a simple case of plugging in the wrong date. But Nico didn't buy it. So who was responsible and why?

She rubbed her eyes and returned to the file, picking up the photographs of Tom's apartment. She sucked her teeth in frustration. Something was pinging in her brain. Something she'd seen that didn't make sense. She went through them once again, stopping on the image of the red suitcase by the door. Nico found its catalog of contents and ran her finger down the list. Tom had clearly packed this bag to take on vacation. So where was the evidence he'd changed his flight to a later time?

Nico let out an annoyed sigh. They had to have missed something. But what? She inspected the photos of the lobby, the locker area, the garbage and utilities rooms, and finally the small equipment room. She stopped on a wide shot of this space, mostly taken up by two large shelving units. This time, something jumped out at her. A phone charger plugged into the socket in the far corner. Nico frowned. Why? Someone who didn't charge their phone overnight and had to plug it in wherever they went? But why down there? When Nico checked the rest of the photo, she noticed a small portable heater. The Aurora had state-of-the-art air conditioning, but maybe it wasn't installed everywhere. Because why would you need to heat (or cool) tools and bags of fertilizer?

Nico's attention was suddenly pulled to movement at the entrance to the Aurora. Marco Esposito, stepping through to the street. Nico lurched out of the car. "Marco?" she called, jogging over to meet him at the door. "Detective Davis," she added with a smile.

He tilted his head, seeming wary. "Yes, I remember."

"Carlos is late," she lied. "Would you mind letting me in?"

Marco glanced behind her as if expecting to see someone else, then nodded. "Sure." He swiped his fob and held open the door.

"One more, please?" Nico asked, pointing at the door to the lockers.

"I really have to—"

"Thanks." Nico forced her face into an even wider smile. "I appreciate it."

Face tight, Marco marched over with Nico in tow. "There." He pushed open the door, then hurried away before Nico could inconvenience him further.

But when Nico reached the door to the equipment room, she found it locked. Damn. Should she risk calling Carlos? Did he know she'd been suspended? As she retraced her steps, she noted the temperature. Not as warm as the lobby, but not cold. It was spring, but this area didn't have access to sunlight, which meant it was likely included in the air-con system. So what was the small heater for? A backup in case of a power outage? Possibly, but what could it do except heat one person?

Nico opened the door leading out to the lobby and held it ajar with her foot in case she was lucky enough to catch another resident passing through. As she waited, she let the situation roll over in her mind. If residents were supposed to access the equipment room, it would be on the same fob system. Damn, she needed Carlos. But she was already dancing on thin ice. No, she'd pass on the lead to Jackson. It didn't matter how pissed she was with him right now, clues mattered.

As Nico let the door swing shut, a beep and a swish pulled her attention to the back entrance. Tobi Hart stood just inside, eyes locked on Nico's, body frozen.

"Tobi?" Nico said, brightening. The Aurora gardener was just the person she needed. "Can you—"

Tobi slammed her hand against the door release and ran out again.

"Fuck," Nico hissed, taking chase. But Tobi was fast, and she knew the area. By the time Nico reached the garden, Tobi was gone.

Why did she run?

Nico's phone rang. DC Singh.

"Singh, what's up?" she answered, still a little out of breath.

"Do you feel like owing me a favor?"

Singh, Nico was discovering, was ambitious. Having a detective sergeant owe her a favor, even suspended, was an excellent position to be in.

"What have you got?" Nico asked.

"A notification just came in... Guess who was on an inbound flight from Mexico last night?"

Nico sucked in a breath. "Chris Sheffield?"

"You got it. You want the address?"

"You bet your ass I do. But don't—"

"Tell anyone? Of course not. And remember, you owe me now."

"Sure." Nico disconnected and hurried down the side alley that led to the front of the Aurora. By the time she'd climbed into her car, the address had come through. Only fifteen minutes away.

But when she pulled up outside Sheffield's house, Jared and DC Patterson were already there, standing at the door. Nico jumped out of the car. "Where is he? Where's Sheffield?"

"Nico, you can't—"

"Fuck you, Jackson. Tell me."

"Whoa, Davis," Patterson said, stepping forward. "You're so far outta line—"

"He's not here, Nico," Jared interrupted. "And you shouldn't be either."

"Where is he?"

Jared sighed. "He came home and left town again, straight away. The neighbor saw him. He had bags with him. I think he's on the run."

"We can trace his plate," Nico said.

"*We* can. You can't."

"Jackson," Nico began.

"What?" Suddenly, he seemed angry. "What's your plan here, huh? Keep pushing until you make this suspension permanent?" He turned to gesture at Patterson; a phone in his hand and a challenging glint in his eyes.

"Just go home, Nico." Jared's face softened. "I'll let you know what happens."

47

Penny takes in my outfit—loose jeans and a tank—and frowns. "You said we were going sleuthing."

I eye her for a moment, suppressing my smile. She showed up at my apartment this afternoon as planned, wearing all black—baseball cap included—and carrying her flashlight. Not only is our building well-lit, this isn't a covert operation. She's finally playing ball, though, so I keep quiet.

Last night, I'd landed on the way to convince Penny to get involved. I simply said I need her help. Detective Davis believes I killed Tom, so I have to figure out who actually did. I told her I'd run into Nico before, we'd had an altercation, and she was out to get me. The truth. Mostly. This, she accepted without a single question. Maybe because she's no longer hiding her own connection to Tom.

I now have a real asset on my team and I'm only just realizing how much I miss this, working in a partnership. A pulse of something raw and hot slams into my chest. Damn you, Danni. Why did you have to go? I swallow, blink a few times, then push it away.

"Are you going to change?" Penny gestures at my clothes.

"I can. If you want me to."

"Do you have anything appropriate?"

"Ha."

"What?"

"Nothing, never mind. Yes." As I open the door to let Penny inside, I glance over my shoulder to check Sol isn't strolling around the living room. He tends to hide, but Penny is the type to snoop, so I change quickly. I pull on a pair of black leggings, a black t-shirt and my converse hi-tops. I emerge and hold out my arms. "Do I pass?"

Penny nods once, eyes bright. "We should start with the scene of the crime."

"Agreed."

In the lobby, Penny swipes us through the door that leads to the lockers. "The police took away the evidence days ago," she says, now seeming uncertain. "What are we looking for, exactly?"

"Not sure," I admit. "But this is where we found Tom, so maybe there's something important here. He was obviously killed during that first weekend, sometime between Friday and Sunday morning, but when and why?"

"Apart from you, everyone came down here at some point."

"Did Tom, though?" I say. "Did you see him at all?"

"No."

"Which is kind of weird, right?" I pull a face. "He was probably in my locker the whole weekend."

Penny grimaces. "You should get it professionally cleaned. Sterilized. I can recommend someone?"

"Sure, thanks. Okay, back to the body. Let's go over what you did that day. Who you saw."

Penny's nose scrunches up as she thinks. "I came down first thing Friday to look around, then met my movers at the entrance. After they'd finished with my furniture, there were a few boxes I wanted to put directly into storage, so I had them bring them straight here. That was around midday. I was directing them where to go, so I paid little attention to anything else. But when I popped down again in the afternoon, I saw George." She taps her lips with her forefinger. "You know what? He's been weird about it. He didn't want to admit it, remember?"

"What was he doing?"

Penny shrugs. "Just looking around."

I gesture at the stark concrete space. "Just taking in this epic environment?"

I move to the utilities room and try to open the door, but it's locked. There's no key fob access pad, so it must use an actual key. Same for the equipment room. I, of course, have all the tools to get inside, but how would I explain that to Penny? And if we can't get into these, then neither can the other residents.

I carry on to the garbage room door and Penny follows. We both peer inside.

"Boring," I say, turning away.

"Hang on." Penny says, her eyes bright. "It's gone now, but it was definitely here on Friday morning."

"What's gone?"

"As soon as I got my keys, I did a tour of the entire place. I even looked in here, and there was a large black bag right there in the corner. I noticed because it looked brand new and even though it was just one of those cheap canvas ones, I wondered whether I should rescue it and give it to charity."

"You didn't?"

"I had a lot on my mind," Penny says defensively. "I planned to come back once I was settled, but forgot."

"How big?" I ask. "Big enough to hold a body?"

She nods slowly. "I think so, yes. Tom wasn't a large man."

"What time was this?"

"No later than nine-thirty on Friday morning. I thought maybe the contractors had left it but now I'm wondering.... Oh." Penny's eyes go wide. "The detectives asked me about bags. They wanted to know what kinds of bags Orson took into storage."

"Orson, huh."

"But he didn't move his things until Saturday, and I definitely saw it on Friday."

"What about George?" I say.

"That wasn't first thing in the morning."

"But he could have come in before you, then later removed it. Or changed the hiding spot or... I don't know. You said you saw him looking around."

"You think George is capable of...?"

We both fall silent.

"Oh." I snap my fingers as a memory pops into my brain, "I heard George and Marco having a fight the night of the rooftop drinks. They were talking about blame and someone said *not my fault.*"

"What wasn't?"

"That's when Marco stormed off."

"Let's go talk to George," Penny says, her eyes flashing with excitement.

We take the elevator up and knock on 301. After a brief delay, George answers. With something paused on the TV, an array of snacks on the table, and Marco out, we obviously interrupted George enjoying alone time. He wasn't happy to see us even before we started hurling questions at him.

"Look, I didn't want to say anything in front of Marco, but yes, I dumped some stuff on Friday," he says grumpily. "And yes, I was hiding something."

Penny's hand flies to her mouth. George rolls his eyes. "Not the body. As if I would say that. No, just a couple of Marco's things. They're *so* ugly. One lamp and a hideous painting." He shudders. "I was going to pretend the movers lost them."

"And you used a black canvas bag to move them to the garbage room first thing?" Penny says excitedly.

"No, I put them in a normal trash bag and took it down that afternoon."

"Oh." Penny is disappointed.

"That's what your fight with Marco was about?" I ask. "I heard you two at rooftop drinks."

George shakes his head. "No, he still doesn't know I got rid of them and he'd better not find out." He waggles his finger. "Our fight was one we'd had before. About a family trip coming up. It's turning into an absolute fiasco."

"Huh," I say.

"Did you seriously suspect me?" George's voice rises. "Why would I kill that guy? I've never even heard his name before."

He has a point. People don't go around murdering other people without a reason.

"Okay, well, thanks anyway," Penny says, offering George a small smile. "Sorry to interrupt. We should organize another get-together once this murder business is resolved."

"Sure," George says unconvincingly.

In the hall, Penny and I face each other.

"We should tell Detective Jackson about the bag," Penny says, a blush of color warming her cheeks as she gets out her phone. "I'll tell him to come to my place."

Penny goes pink every time she mentions Jared. She definitely has a crush, but how deep does it go?

"Penny." I push away her phone. "This is kind of awkward, but," I take a breath, "are you into Jared? I mean, Detective Jackson? Because you should know that we, uh, hooked up."

Her eyes pop open. "Oh my goodness, Gemma, is that allowed?"

"It was before the investigation started." I grimace. "Sort of. But no. It's not. At least, not for him."

"Wow."

I wait, but she says nothing else.

"Are you...?" I trail off. She frowns, waiting. "Penny, I don't want him to get between us."

Penny laughs. "Thank you for thinking of me, but I'd never go for someone like him. He's too...." She waves her hand and makes a funny face.

"Yeah, he is."

"But nice to look at." She winks.

"He sure is," I agree, my shoulders dropping as the truth bomb is safely detonated. I'm getting good at this.

Jared doesn't pick up, so Penny leaves a message and disconnects.

"Oh." Penny frowns at her phone.

"What's up?"

"Cassie has posted something." Her eyes meet mine. "It sounds weird."

48

Nico eyed Jared through the peephole. "Why would I talk to you? You ratted me out. Got me suspended."

He frowned. "You think *I* told Sarge about your bust-up with Gemma?"

"You really expect me to believe—"

"It was Carlos."

Nico rested her forehead against the door and sighed. Good thing she hadn't called Carlos from the Aurora earlier today. It might have been the final nail.

"Penny told him everything. That you threatened her outside the building. That you forced your way inside. He looked at the security footage and saw you with a ripped shirt and actual blood on your sleeve. He complained directly to Sarge. I guess he isn't a fan of yours."

"Could this be a new angle on the case?" Nico said through the door. "Maybe Carlos doesn't want me snooping around? Or someone higher up?"

"Or maybe you were way over the line," Jared said, quietly, but still audibly. "We both were."

She clenched her jaw.

"Please, Nico. We need to get past this."

With a heavy sigh, Nico straightened and flipped the latch. She stared blankly at Jared for a few seconds, then returned to the couch. "There's beer in the fridge," she called over her shoulder. "I'm having one."

With the hiss of a bottle cap being released, Jared took a seat next to her. He held his beer out toward hers as if to say *cheers*. When Nico didn't move, he clinked the bottle against hers.

"That bruise has come up nicely." He nodded at her cheekbone.

"What do you want, Jackson?"

"Listen. I shouldn't have slept with you know who, but I can't change that. And more importantly, I get that it felt like a betrayal, but it wasn't. Honestly. It had nothing to do with you."

"Thanks."

"You know what I mean."

Nico continued to stare straight ahead, her beer resting on her leg, dampening the denim of her jeans.

"If it helps, our first hook-up was before I was assigned to the case. But I take full responsibility for the other times."

"How many?" Nico asked, her voice hard.

"Three, or maybe four, depending on what you count—"

Nico held up her hand to stop him.

"I shouldn't have kept sleeping with her. The investigation is open, and she is a part of it." He let out a low chuckle. "I guess willpower isn't my strong suit."

"No shit." Nico took a sip of beer. "So why didn't you tell Sarge about my fight with Gemma? Carlos beat you to the punch?"

"Pun intended?" Jared said, waggling his eyebrows.

Nico rolled her eyes.

"I'm not a hypocrite," he said. "We've both been messing with a suspect in a case." He leaned forward to rest his forearms on his thighs. "But, Nico, you've got to let the Gemma thing go."

"Do I?" she snarled, unable to control the sudden rage in her throat. "What about the fingerprints?"

"The ones on the package that Gemma picked up and left near the mailboxes? The one Carlos confirmed he took up to Tom's apartment because Tom was away? Carlos's prints were on it too, remember?"

"And the witness who saw her scaling the building?"

"They couldn't make a firm ID."

Nico turned to him. "What? Why not?"

Jared shrugged. "The woman fits Gemma's general description, but when Patterson showed the witness a photo, she said she couldn't see her face."

Nico took an angry pull of beer. "How much clearer do you need this to be spelled out for you?"

"Even if she was, uh, climbing the building that night, it doesn't mean she killed Tom Bollard."

"Your gigantic hard-on for her doesn't make her innocent."

A smile played on his lips. "It's not *that* big."

Nico threw her eyes toward the ceiling and leaned back.

After a moment, Jared continued. "Nico, you've got to ask yourself what this is really about. Tom Bollard, or...."

They both let the question drift away.

"And maybe she *was* there that night at the Barrington's apartment. But maybe she wasn't, Nico. She has an alibi. There isn't any evidence of her being there, except for—"

"Me." Nico sat up. "*Me*. I saw her."

"You've been through a lot. Seeing her on her own balcony could have triggered something and your brain created a false memory. Either way, it doesn't relate to this case. You're letting it cloud your judgment."

"She still could be—"

"We've got a new lead."

"We do?"

"We found another link between Tom and Romanov."

Nico sucked in a breath. "Don't leave me hanging."

"Tom was indebted to Romanov."

Nico nodded eagerly. "How?"

"Nine years ago, Tom got screwed over at work. Set up to be the fall guy, maybe. He lost his job and their savings, *and* he put their house on the line. He was already drinking too much, and he wanted the debt off his shoulders, so he tried gambling. I don't know whether the debt came from Romanov directly, or if Tom got a loan from him to pay someone else off, but you know the timeline. His life turned to shit."

"Tom owed money to Romanov?"

"Maybe not just money. Romanov had something on Tom, I think. Whatever it was, Tom owed him. And I think Romanov used him for financial dealings. The kind of transactions you only want someone who you've got dirt on to know about."

"Alice Thornston did say Tom was a financial whizz," Nico said. "How'd you get all this?"

"Mike from organized crime."

"He came through, huh?"

"And Patterson. He's been around the block a few times."

"Patterson's an asshole."

"Maybe, but he's got useful contacts."

Nico let the comment slide away. In the distance, the wail of a siren pierced the room. Her gut clenched, as if a reminder. She was supposed to be out there, doing her job, instead of stuck here. Trapped in the sin bin.

"Did Romanov have something to do with Tom getting kicked out of his old apartment?" she asked.

"Let's just say finding a connection between that building owner and Romanov isn't difficult. It's looking like Romanov engineered Tom's move into the Aurora. Because while Tom owned that condo on paper, the money for the deposit appeared in his bank account overnight."

"Shit," Nico breathed. "Romanov paid for it?"

"We might never prove it, but I think so. You know what Mike from org crime told me? One of Romanov's inner circle, a finance guy, died at the end of last year."

Nico sat back, nodding slowly. "Suddenly Romanov has an opening in his team. And who better than someone he has the dirt on. He wanted Tom there. Entangled. Ensnared."

Jared nodded. "Tom was right about never getting away." His phone buzzed. He checked the display, then sucked in a breath.

"Something good?" Nico asked.

"We've got a lead on Chris Sheffield."

49

Outside Cassie's door, Penny clutches at my arm, eyes wide. She might be mostly sensible, but she has a dramatic side, for sure.

"You want me to knock?" I say.

"Yes."

"Is this a good idea? Cassie basically told me to back off the other day."

"I know, but she didn't reply to my message, and—"

"Penny, you sent those less than half an hour ago. This is the opposite of backing off."

"But I'm worried. Her post sounded... depressed."

I study her face. Is Penny overreacting or reacting the right amount? I'm not great at this stuff, and I suspect Penny has good instincts.

"Maybe she confronted Leighton, and he broke up with her?" Penny says.

"And since this was her first attempt at dating...." I make a face. "Should we have brought ice cream?"

Penny lifts her chin. "We're here now. Let's just see what's what."

"Okay."

She gestures at the door again.

"Me?"

She nods.

"Fine." I lean forward and knock.

When Cassie answers, she seems flustered. "Oh, hey."

"Hi, Cassie," Penny says brightly. "Is now a good time for a visit?"

Cassie glances behind her, then turns back with a goofy smile. I know that look. *Just Got Laid.* On tiptoes, I look over her shoulder. Sure enough, Leighton is inside, looking like a cat that got the cream. Or is it a canary? Whatever. Leighton is smug and douchey. He raises his eyes to mine and smiles.

"Are you feeling okay?" Penny asks.

"I'm honestly fine. Better than fine," Cassie says, quietly but earnestly, eyes bright.

I guess she and Leighton figured out the sex thing.

"Your Facebook post sounded..." Penny trails off, searching Cassie's face.

"Facebook?" She frowns.

Suddenly, the door swings wider. "Hello, girls." Leighton grins. "What are you whispering about out here?"

"Girls? Do we look like eleven-year-olds?" I huff.

Leighton chuckles. "Come in," he says, as if this is his apartment. He tilts his head at me. "Glad we can get past our misunderstanding, Gemma."

I scowl. I understood him perfectly.

"How's your novel coming along, Cassie?" Penny says conversationally as we follow Leighton and Cassie inside. "You've been working to a deadline, right?"

"Nearly finished." She blinks and clears her throat. "And I've already started plotting out a new one. It's not the steampunk series." She shifts her eyes away from mine. "It's going to be a standalone mystery thriller with a bit of a romantic storyline."

Leighton sighs. "We talked about this, babe. You want to keep it tight. Sure, pop in some sex, but keep your readers entertained with action. Don't lose them with any boring lovey-dovey stuff. It's what readers want."

"How would you know?" I say.

"Recent research shows—" Cassie begins.

"Trust me, babe."

"You're mansplaining the publishing industry to a successful author?" Penny's voice rises to a squeak.

Leighton makes an irritated sound. "Mansplaining? Hardly." He forces a laugh. "It's fine, it's fine. Relax. Hey, let's not ruin a good time. Let's change the subject," he says smoothly. "What's the word on the dead guy?" he adds. Cassie looks horrified. "Sorry, babe," he pecks her cheek, "was that too blunt?" He laughs. "I tell it like it is, you know that."

"Actually, Gemma and I are looking into who killed him." Penny lifts her chin. "We even found a clue."

Leighton gives us an indulgent smile. "Had a few glasses of wine and decided to snoop around the building, did we?"

Penny and I exchange a look. That's exactly right, but Leighton doesn't need to know.

"What kind of clue?" He waggles his eyebrows and smiles again.

God, this guy is such a dick.

"I saw a bag in the garbage room," Penny says, "and it could be important."

Leighton smirks. "Why?"

"It was there on Friday morning."

"Someone threw away a black bag on moving day? That means nothing." Leighton spreads his hands.

"We didn't say it was a big clue," I say grumpily.

"Yeah, well," Leighton waves his hand dismissively. "You probably should leave it to the police to catch the guy." He leans forward. "Or girl. Equality, right, ladies?"

I want to slap him. Hard. But he's the type to call the police. Which won't go well for me.

"Hey, did you go to the doctor, babe?" Leighton says abruptly, turning to Cassie.

Her eyes go wide. She glances from me to Penny, seeming embarrassed.

"Everything okay?" Penny asks.

Cassie raises one hand to her temple. "A few memory issues, that's all. It's just stress."

"What do you mean?" Penny asks, leaning closer.

"She keeps forgetting where she's put her keys, and having conversations with people. I'm a little worried, to be honest." Leighton says, sounding concerned. Or at least, pretending to.

Cassie gives him a wobbly smile.

"And that message from your publisher?" he continues. "The one you can't remember getting."

Cassie bites her lip and frowns. "I, uh. Yeah. Um, I don't know." Her face creases.

"Reminding her of what she's forgetting maybe isn't helpful," Penny says.

"Yes, it is. She needs to be aware of the situation. If something is wrong with her brain, then—"

"With my brain?" Cassie says.

Leighton gives Cassie a squeeze. "I'll look after you, don't worry. Whatever happens. Even if the old noggin fails you." He knocks the side of her head. Cassie tilts away.

"Hey, that's—" I begin.

"Stay out of it," Leighton says. His voice suddenly loud. Harsh. "Don't you two have anything else to do?"

I blow out an irritated sigh. "Cassie. This guy? Really?"

"Gemma." She glances at Leighton. "That's not very nice."

"I agree," I say. "Whatever. This has been super fun, but I'm out of here."

Penny follows me to the door. "Call me," she says to Cassie, who just blinks in response.

Out in the hall, Penny turns to me. "He's awful."

"Total asshole," I reply, my brain spinning and whirring. All that stuff about Cassie's memory is bugging me. Cassie is naïve and inexperienced in some ways, but she isn't scattered or dozy. And I don't like how involved Leighton is in her memory issues.

"Penny, have you heard the term gaslighting?"

She nods, her eyes going wide. "For sure."

"I heard this story a few months ago about a husband gaslighting his wife until she had a nervous breakdown and he got her committed and then took their property and money and ran off with someone else." I think for a moment. "Maybe it was a movie?"

"Gemma?" Penny says, dropping her voice. "I think Cassie is worth a lot of money. Like, *a lot.*"

50

I say goodnight to Penny and return to my apartment. We'll get together tomorrow to solve the Cassie problem. Whether Leighton is merely a controlling douche or he's angling for her money, we're getting her away from him.

I'm looking forward to a hot shower and quality chill time with Sol, but as soon as I let myself inside, I know that won't happen. My first clue? The smell of sandalwood. One infuriating detail about Sven is that he wears the absolute best-smelling cologne. Because yes, Sven Karlsson is in my apartment. Again.

"You've got to be kidding me." I sigh. "How do you keep getting in?"

"Don't pout, Gemma, you're too old. It doesn't suit you."

"You can hardly talk. You're at least ten years past poutable age."

He scowls. Sven's rapidly disappearing youth is maybe the only thing that gets under his skin.

"What are you doing here?" I ask. It's bad enough that he's invading my space, but this time he has Sol perched unhappily on his lap. Sol raises his large green eyes to me and lets out a mournful yowl.

"Yeah, I'm not happy about it either, Sol. What are you doing here, Sven?" I repeat.

"Come now, what way is that to greet your old friend?"

"Friends don't blackmail friends, Sven."

"Blackmail is such an ugly term."

"But appropriate. What do you want?" I step farther inside, flicking my eyes from Sol to Sven. "My time isn't up yet."

"I'm not happy with your progress."

"How would you know?"

"The company you keep.... I can't tell whether it's brilliant or idiotic. But either way, I've decided you need more motivation. A push in the right direction. Or, as they say, more skin in the game." He pats Sol roughly on the head. Sol squirms, gives him a disgusted look, then meows again at me.

I freeze. "No."

"Yes." He smiles. "But the good news is I don't care whether I get the diamonds or the money. So I'll give you more time. Two days. But that's all." He stands up. Sol meows and I lurch forward, but Sven holds him tightly to his body.

"Give him to me," I growl.

"Not until you—"

"I don't have the fucking diamonds, Sven."

"The money then."

"I... I.... How much are they even worth?"

"The diamonds alone are two million."

"Right, like I have that lying around."

"No?"

I fold my arms across my chest.

"I have expenses, Gemma." He tilts his head. "I'm not walking away from this empty-handed."

"Of course not. Why would you take responsibility for the shitstorm of a job *you set up*," I spit.

"I've always liked you. Had a soft spot even, and I know you've lost Danni. So I'm prepared to go easy. To make you a deal."

Despite my history with Sven telling me I should know better, I feel a surge of hope.

"I'll settle for my cut. One million, and we'll call it even," he says.

I grit my teeth, shaking my head. "Asshole."

Sven narrows his eyes. "Watch it, young lady. You're not too old for a spanking."

"Ugh."

He stands, tucking Sol under one arm like a football.

I reach out. "Please."

As he saunters past me, Sol lets out a final howl.

"Sven! Please. Give him back." A sick swirling gathers momentum in my stomach. I would tackle Sven, except he's always carrying. Always. And I can't risk Sol getting hurt.

"You know what I want," he says, his eyes bright.

And with that, he's gone.

I stand motionless near the door, trying to calm my racing heart, trying to ignore the pounding in my ears. I double over, my hands on my knees, desperate to catch my breath.

51

NICO

Nico placed her coffee on the dash and rubbed her gritty eyes. Had she slept at all last night? And when would Jackson call with an update on Sheffield? She checked her phone. Nothing. She scrolled to DC Singh.

"What is it, Davis?" Singh answered, her voice wary. "I can't help. You know I can't."

Nico sighed. Someone had warned her off, obviously. Or maybe Singh knew when to cut her losses. "Has Jackson been at the station today?"

"Haven't seen him."

"Heard anything about Sheffield?"

"I'd love to help, Nico, but—"

Nico hissed her displeasure and disconnected. Damn.

A rap on the window startled her. When she turned, Jared was eyeing her through the glass, a wry expression on his face.

"Jesus. Don't creep up like that."

"You should be more aware of your surroundings, Nico. Especially when you're not supposed to be anywhere near the Aurora." He nodded at the building.

"I'm halfway down the street. I'm barely even on Cannon."

"Right." Jared made a face. "You look like crap."

"Thanks," Nico said dryly.

Jared strolled around the car and climbed into the passenger side.

"How'd you find me?" Nico asked.

Jared spread his hands and smiled. "I'm a detective."

"What's the word on Sheffield?"

"He used his credit card in a restaurant in Hamilton."

"What's he doing in Hamilton? If he's on the run, why stop there?"

"It's his hometown. Maybe he's hiding out? Maybe it's a ruse? Local cops checked the parents' house, but nothing. I'm headed there next to sniff around myself. It's only an hour away." Jared gestured through the window at the building beyond. "But right now I'm here to talk to Leighton Matthews."

Nico sat up. "You're working the Dallant case."

Jared eyed her. "I'm not the only one, apparently. When I interviewed Chiandra, she asked me if the other detective was okay?" He cocked an eyebrow. "Are you? Okay?"

Nico shrugged. "I'll be fine."

"Nico, I—"

"Leave it, okay? It's not your problem."

He sighed. "But it kind of is."

Nico looked away, but she could feel the weight of his eyes on her face.

"What's your take?" Jared said into the silence.

"On Chiandra?" Nico asked. "Hard to read." She turned to him. "What about you?"

"She doesn't seem concerned about Kimberly, but it might just be that they're not that close. I mean, on paper they're best friends. They spend a lot of time together, but maybe they're more like work colleagues." He gave her a smile that Nico couldn't interpret. She ignored it and gestured at the entrance to Tiles & Textures.

"Are you going in?"

Jared opened the door, swinging gracefully out of the car. After a moment, he leaned down. "What are you waiting for?"

Nico lifted her eyebrows in surprise. "You're not worried about Sarge?"

"Sarge who?"

Nico yanked the keys from the ignition and scrambled out.

Leighton Matthews met them just inside the door, almost as if he'd been waiting.

"Detectives," he said with a wide smile.

"You remember us," Jared said, holding out his hand for Leighton to shake. Nico stood back, letting Jared take the lead.

"Of course." Leighton leaned forward. "A murder investigation right across the road. How could I forget?" The smile dropped off his face. "But you're here about Kim, right?"

"How did you know?" Nico asked, unable to help herself.

"Chiandra called."

"We have a few questions," Jared said.

Leighton glanced around his display room. On one side, a couple were looking at samples. On the other, a man on his phone stood near the door.

"Ben?" Leighton turned to direct his voice to the back. "Can you cover the floor for ten minutes?"

"Sure."

Nico and Jared followed Leighton up one flight of stairs to an apartment-slash-office.

"This fully functional?" Nico asked.

"Does the apartment function?" Leighton said with a smirk.

"Does the toilet flush? Does the stove work? Is there a bed?" Nico said, a warning in her tone.

"Yeah. I stay here sometimes if I have to work late or have an early delivery."

"Where's your actual house?" Nico asked.

"Richmond Hill."

"Tell us about your relationship with Kimberly," Jared said.

"We stopped seeing each other a few weeks ago."

"Let me guess, she wanted to settle down, but you weren't ready?" Jared said with a light but leery chuckle that made Nico's stomach roil. As if they might start talking about Kimberly's body or her prowess in bed. But this was an act, Nico now knew. Jared was building rapport with Leighton, which meant dropping to his level.

"Nah, she wasn't interested in getting serious. Kim was too much of a party girl for me." Leighton gave them a rueful smile as if to say *you live and learn*. Nico took in his too-tight, ripped designer jeans and his form-fitting white t-shirt. Leighton looked exactly like a guy who pursued 'party girls'.

"We broke up, and I moved on. I hoped she had too, but this kind of disappearing act, it's classic Kim."

"When did you break up, exactly?"

"We had *the talk,*" he air quoted this, "on a Tuesday night about three weeks back   ."

"Tuesday the second of April?" Nico asked.

"Sounds about right."

"And when was the last time you spoke to her or saw her?" Jared asked.

"That same Tuesday night."

"Nothing since then?"

Leighton shook his head.

"You don't seem worried about her disappearance," Nico said.

Leighton's jaw tightened. "Like I said, she's taken off before."

"For two weeks?"

"Maybe not. But who knows what she gets up to with her shady friends."

"Shady?" Jared raised an eyebrow.

"I don't have names, but at clubs she's always able to get stuff, you know? Her and Chiandra. And they're friendly with guys that people tell me are *connected*." He lifted his hands. "It was too much for me. I'm just a normal guy. A business owner."

"Was Kimberly hanging with those people that Thursday night?"

Leighton shrugged. "You'd have to talk to the people Kim was partying with. Trace her phone."

"Her phone is off. Last tagged at a club called Spider at about one a.m."

"Sounds like you should visit Spider and talk to the staff," Leighton said, as if this might not have occurred to them.

Nico narrowed her eyes. "We're talking to you. Where were you?"

"Probably at home, asleep." Leighton turned and walked into the office. He leaned over to open an appointment book on the desk and flipped back a few pages. "Yeah, I was. I got an early night because I had a car picking me up first thing for a golf weekend with the guys. Trust me, you don't want to start those already tired or hungover."

"What time Friday morning?" Nico said.

"Six a.m."

"Can anyone corroborate that?"

"Sure. My assistant booked the trip; she has the details. I was with four guys the whole time."

"We're going to need those names," Nico said.

"Don't hassle them, okay? They're clients. Big ones."

"We'll hassle them as much as we need to," Nico said.

Leighton eyed her, his jaw working, then pulled out his phone. He wrote four names and numbers and handed it pointedly to Jared. "I need to get back downstairs. I have orders to oversee."

"We'll release you when we're good and ready," Nico said.

He raised cold eyes to her. "What are you even doing here, *Detective* Davis? Aren't you suspended?"

Nico stepped toward him, fists balled. "How the fuck do you know?"

Jared's hand was on her arm. Gentle but firm. "Easy," he whispered.

Leighton smiled. "I have my sources."

Nico swallowed, her jaw working. She couldn't let this sleazeball get the better of her.

Jared turned his back to Leighton. "Nico?" He waited until she made eye contact. "I got this. I'll finish up and catch you up in the car."

"Fine," she hissed.

Nico walked the length of Cannon Street before letting herself inside the car, breathing easier. For a couple of minutes, she did nothing except stare into space until her phone beeped. A message from Jared.

Run a search on Kimberly and Romanov.

52

Penny is outside my door. Again.

"Gemma?" she calls.

I can't deal with this right now. Sven has Sol. My insides won't stop curling and clenching at the thought of him shivering with fright. Like the night I rescued him.

"Gemma?" Penny knocks louder.

I yank open the door. "What?" I bark.

She draws her head back, eyeing me with alarm. "What's wrong?"

"Sol is gone," I blurt.

Penny frowns. "Sol? Who is Sol?"

I sigh. "Sol is my cat. Mr. Solomon. He has gray fur and green eyes and an entitled attitude. He's the best thing in the world."

Penny's eyes go wide. "Oh."

"We're not allowed pets, I know."

"You're not expressly prohibited, but you are supposed to get approval first. I'm sure the condo board, once it's properly set up, would approve a cat."

My lip wobbles. "Yeah?"

"Of course."

"They won't take Sol away from me?"

"Didn't you just say he's already gone?"

I swallow. How do I explain about Sven?

"My, uh, ex took him back."

"Can he do that?"

"Apparently."

"Gemma, I'm sorry, I really am, and I promise to help you with Sol, but Cassie's situation could be urgent."

"And Sol's isn't?"

"If I can help you do something right now, I will. Just say the word."

Penny waits, her eyes boring into mine. Finally, I shake my head and sigh, rubbing my temples. "I'm not sure how I'm handling that yet," I admit. "Why is the Cassie thing suddenly urgent?"

"She was supposed to do a radio interview this morning. I tuned in to listen, but it was canceled."

"She said she hated doing interviews. Maybe she couldn't face it."

"But why this one? Cassie doesn't strike me as someone who'd cancel out of the blue. And radio must be way easier than a live TV show." Penny fixes her wide eyes on me. "I looked up her agent. We should call and ask."

"Won't she tell us to mind our own business?"

"It's worth a shot."

"I assume you've knocked on Cassie's door and called her, right?"

"Of course."

"And you're the one who'll make the actual call?"

"I just need someone with me."

"Okay, let's do it." I wave at Penny's phone, clutched in her hand.

She nods and lifts it to her ear. "Yes, uh, Liz Roundtree, please. What? Um.... Regarding Cassandra Pike. Okay, thanks." Penny holds the phone away from her face. "I think she's getting her," she says excitedly. "I wasn't sure if I should ask for her pen name or not, but knowing her.... What? Oh, yes," she speaks into her phone. "Penny Pritchard. No, I don't know where she is. That's why I'm calling you." She casts stricken eyes at me. "Uh-huh. Will do. Thank you." She disconnects. "Cassie texted to say she couldn't make the radio interview and Liz hasn't been able to get in touch with her either." Penny clutches at my arm. "Gemma, I'm really worried."

A tuneful melody sounds from Penny's phone. "Rats. I have to pick up a check for the charity and deliver it to the hospital."

"Now? Can't they send it by courier?"

"We give our donors the VIP treatment. Without the personal touch, they won't keep contributing."

"Can't you do it another time?"

"They were so hard to get hold of." Penny makes a face. "I was going to find Cassie's mother's contact details and try her. Maybe you could do that while I'm out?"

There it is, that pixie Penny persuasion.

"Fine."

It will distract me until I figure out what to do about Sol. And Sven.

"Excellent. I'll be back as soon as I can. Keep me posted."

Once she's gone, I take my phone and laptop over to the couch. An image of Sol jumping up to the armrest to join me surfing the net pops into my head. I push it away, ignoring the tightness in my chest. We'll get Cassie sorted, and then we'll focus on Sol. Everything will work out.

Where can I find Cassie's mother's name and phone number? Maybe she's listed. It might be as simple as checking the online directory. Turns out, it is. There are a few Pikes, but only one Pike, C., in East York, where Cassie used to live. Hey, maybe I'm good at this.

I order a rideshare, throw on a clean shirt, and grab my bag. When I get downstairs, my car is two minutes away. I'm about to walk through and wait on the street when I see Tobi just inside the main doors. She's wearing non-gardening clothes—loose jeans and a white tank—and has her hands and face pressed up against the glass of the door like a kid, staring outside.

"Tobi?" I say. "Everything okay?"

She whirls around. "Wow, you're great at sneaking up on people."

"I should be a cat burglar, right?" I grin.

What is wrong with me?

I stand next to her and look out the window. Cannon Street seems quiet. "Waiting for a delivery?" I ask.

She turns to me, eyes clouded with worry. "No, uh, I.... Hey, have you heard anything about the murder investigation? That guy, Tom."

"Have I ever," I say before I can stop myself.

She cocks one eyebrow, clearly interested.

"Long story." I wave it off. "All I know is they're still investigating," I finish. Partly true.

Her eyes linger on my face, seeming to want more, but my phone buzzes. "That's my car," I say.

Tobi presses the door release and holds it open for me, but doesn't follow me outside.

"I'm going east. Can I drop you anywhere?" I ask, gesturing at the waiting Prius.

"No, I'm staying here for a bit. See you soon, maybe."

"Sure."

I climb into the car, disappointed. Why does it feel as if I might not see her again?

53

NICO

Leighton had suggested that Kimberly frequented under-world-funded clubs, and this neighborhood was close to Romanov's turf. They already had Romanov's connection to Tom. If they could link him to the missing Kimberly Dallant, it might complete a triangle that solved two cases.

Nico searched and scrolled and clicked, feverishly reading any article that looked vaguely relevant. Finally, on Instagram, she found a photo of Romanov and Kimberly together. Some club opening downtown. A group shot. She sent this to Jared and continued scrolling, finding a couple more at other events. She nodded to herself. A missing model was definitely in Romanov's wheelhouse. But how did it all fit together?

She tapped her pen against her lip, thinking, then scrolled to DC Singh.

"Davis, I—" Singh answered.

"This isn't me calling. It's DS Jackson."

A pause.

"What?"

"He wants you to look for a concrete association between Kimberly Dallant and Alex Romanov."

Silence.

"Singh, this might break two cases. You want to be part of that or not?"

"I'm sending the information to Jackson direct, okay?"

"Fine."

As Nico disconnected, Jared emerged from Tiles & Textures.

"Leighton give you anything on Romanov?" Nico asked him as he leaned down to her window.

Jared shook his head. "How about you? Find anything?"

"Check your phone. Kimberly and Romanov have attended a few of the same events. I've asked Singh to keep looking."

"I have to follow up on Sheffield, but meet you back at your place in a few hours?" Jared said.

"Sure."

Jared turned to leave, but Nico called him back. "Hey. Thanks for... you know."

He gave her a crooked smile and a salute, then jogged back to his car. Nico stared after him, a fist gripping her chest, heat stinging her eyes. Then, just as suddenly, she felt numb. Deflated. She blew out a breath and shook her head. This goddam emotional rollercoaster.

As she started the ignition, she saw a taxi pull up outside the Aurora. Nico watched Marco Esposito emerge, laden with bags, then awkwardly swipe himself inside the building. A taxi, Nico mused as the car drove away. Kind of old-school. But then Marco is in his fifties. Maybe he doesn't use rideshares.

Something in her brain shifted. Held up its hand, asking for attention. A puzzle piece still looking for its place. How had Tom gotten to the Aurora? Had someone helped Tom move? Did he have a car ferreted away somewhere? Had he hailed a taxi the old-fashioned way and used cash? Because Nico couldn't remember seeing anything to indicate how he'd actually moved his belongings.

She grabbed her phone and dialed. DC Singh picked up immediately.

"Davis, it's been like two minutes."

"This is something else."

"Neat."

Nico smiled at Singh's dry retort.

"Listen, I'm going to be reinstated any moment, and we both know it. Once I'm back, I can ignore you like the others do, or keep sending stuff your way. Singh, I can get you on track to becoming a detective sergeant in Homicide. You want that, right? I can tell you do. You'd be good at it."

"Yeah?"

Nico could hear the eagerness in the young DC's voice. "First, nothing new on CCTV, right? None of the other cameras picked up Tom in the days leading up to his death?"

"No."

"Have you got access to Tom's phone?"

"Right now, no."

"Can you get it?"

"Davis, I—"

"All you have to do is open his email spam folder and tell me if there are any recent rideshare receipts in there. Or if you can, check his bank statement."

The line was silent.

"Singh?"

"I'll call you back."

Nico disconnected and started the car.

Tom. Romanov. Kimberly.

Something never going away.

Maybe it went back farther than they thought. Was the destruction of Tom's marriage directly related to his death? Nico had to find out.

As she turned into Alice Thornston's street, she checked the time. Nearly five o'clock, which meant school was out. But Alice and the kids could be at activities. Nico caught herself. She shouldn't assume Alice was doing all the childcare. Likely, though, since Alice didn't have a job. Nico pulled up outside the house, her gaze landing on the empty driveway. Nico could wait. She pushed her seat back as far as it would go, then pulled the illicit case file copy onto her lap. Where on Tom's timeline was the crucial incident? The thing that would never go away? That maybe led to his death. She found a blank piece of paper and started mapping out what she knew of his jobs, his gambling problems, his DUIs and his divorce.

She tapped her pen against the name of the company Tom had worked for before Five Star Finance. It was familiar. She grabbed her phone and typed it into a search engine and a few minutes later, had her answer. The firm had gone bust a few years back after a money laundering scheme was uncovered. In the week after Izzy's death, Nico had become obsessed with Romanov and his dealings. A blurry episode of investigative mania, trying to distract herself from the pain of reality by working nonstop for five days until she'd literally collapsed and given into grief. But in that brief period she'd dug up some good stuff, ultimately handing it over to organized crime, and one of the nuggets had been Romanov's peripheral involvement in this company. The reason the name had pinged in her brain. This could be something. As Nico added it to the timeline, Alice's car swung past her into the driveway.

As Nico stuffed the file into her tote and swung open her door, two children tumbled out of the SUV.

"Go straight inside and wash your hands," Alice called as they disappeared through the open garage door.

"Alice?" Nico said, meeting her at the trunk of the car.

Alice turned, startled. "Oh. Yes. Detective Davis." She tilted her head. "Have you found...?"

"No, I have a few more questions."

She frowned. "But Tom and I barely spoke in recent years."

"It's about when you were still married."

She gave Nico a tired smile. "Give me a hand with the groceries and I'll answer your questions."

"Deal," Nico said, taking a bag from her. "Do you know Kimberly Dallant?"

Alice's mouth twisted. "The name is familiar."

"She's a model."

"Right. I've probably seen her in a magazine?"

Or heard about her disappearance, Nico thought to herself.

Inside, as Alice made coffee and put away groceries, a children's TV show blaring from another room in the house, Nico sat on the couch with Tom's timeline. She cast her eyes around the room, noting the orderly photo albums on the shelf and the chronological photos in frames on the wall. Nico's gut was telling her Alice would be an excellent source of information about Tom in those years before they divorced. Alice didn't know what went wrong for Tom, but maybe a few extra details could help Nico put it together.

Nico's phone buzzed. "Singh?" she answered. "What have you got? Something concrete between Kimberly and Romanov?"

"No, but there were rideshare receipts in Tom's spam folder. Three in the two days before his death."

Bingo. Nico smiled. "Send them through."

"Romanov?" Alice said, suddenly in front of Nico, a coffee in her hand and a funny expression on her face.

Nico went still. "You know that name, don't you?"

Alice nodded.

54

Outside a mid-sized bungalow on a suburban street, I knock. A tired-looking middle-aged woman wearing an apron answers.

"Yes?" She has either flour or icing sugar on her cheek and if vibes were printed t-shirts, hers would say *OVER IT*. And this can't be Cassie's mother. They don't look remotely related.

"Hi. I'm looking for...." I stop. I can't say *Cassie's mom*. I'm not twelve and here asking if my friend can hang out after school. "Mrs. Pike."

"You are?" she says, clearly surprised.

I frown. "Does she not live here?"

"No, she does, it's just... she doesn't get many visitors."

She opens the door to let me inside. It's a basic-looking house, but it has expensive and kind of ugly furnishings. Nothing like Cassie's apartment style.

The weary lady leads me into a living room, then continues through a swinging door into the kitchen.

"Yes?"

I turn to see a woman reclining on a huge sectional sofa in front of a TV so large it's almost a home movie theater. Flickering on mute is a shopping network. "Mrs. Pike?" I ask. She nods. "Sorry to bother you, ma'am," I begin. Not my favorite word, but if there ever was a ma'am, she's it.

Given what Cassie said about having to care for her, I expected an invalid. But Mrs. Pike looks healthy. Robust, even. Her brown hair is fluffy around a soft-looking face. Her skin looks as if it never sees the sun and benefits from repeated applications of expensive moisturizing cream. But maybe her disability isn't visible to the naked eye.

"Yes?" she says, sounding annoyed.

"I'm a friend of Cassie's. She's not here, is she?"

"A friend?" She frowns.

"Yes." I frown too.

Mrs. Pike makes a tsking noise. "*No*, she's not *here*," she says, as if it's an idiotic question and I should know better. "She moved out."

"I know, but I can't get hold of her."

"You couldn't have called me to ask this?"

"I tried." Once. "No one answered."

"Francesca?" she screeches toward the kitchen. We both eye the swinging door. It stays motionless, but a loud silence somehow pushes through. The kind of quiet that means the person heard, but they're hoping there's no follow through.

"Now that I'm here," I say quickly, because I don't want to stress out poor Francesca further. "Have you talked to Cassie today? I'm worried."

"Worried?"

I want to ask Mrs. Pike whether it's really necessary to repeat every single question, but, like a hero, I don't.

"Cassie didn't turn up to an appointment. I thought maybe she came to see you."

"It's her fault for leaving me."

"What's her fault?"

She sniffs and lifts her chin. "Whatever's happened to her."

Geez. And I thought *my* parents sucked.

"So you don't know where she is," I confirm. "Or where she might be?"

Mrs. Pike shakes her head and pointedly picks up the television remote. A second later, the TV is blaring.

"Well, thanks Mrs. Pike," I say, moving toward the door. "You've been super unhelpful. I can totally see why Cassie moved out. Byeee."

55

NICO

Nico opened the door to Jared, pulse already quickening. "You said you have something?"

"Yeah." He studied her face. "You too?"

Nico rolled her eyes. "As much as you're a pain in the ass, Jackson, I can't deny you're good at reading people."

He grinned. "It's a gift. So what is it?"

"I know what Romanov had on Tom. At least, I've worked up a theory."

Jared let out a whistle. "Maybe we all should be suspended from time to time."

Nico gave him a wry smile. "After Tom lost his job, he hit the bottle and the casino. That's how he first got tangled up with Romanov. Gambling debts. A few months after that, Tom got a sales job that involved traveling around the province to sell and implement 'financial solutions'."

"Sales? I thought he was an accountant."

Nico shrugged. "Whatever got him fired probably ruined his reputation. During that time, he traveled a lot and Alice, his ex-wife, kept track. For tax reasons but also for herself. Ease of mind."

"She kept a log?"

"She's an organized woman. Got files on their entire life together. Alice had heard of Romanov, by the way. Tom once mumbled his name after returning from a trip. He'd been in bad shape, coming off a bender. She saw Romanov's name on a couple of inbound calls in the following days, but Tom wouldn't talk. But those details helped with my timeline. I got a window."

"A window? For what?"

"For when Romanov properly got his hooks into Tom. Tom's skeleton. His ghost. The thing *never going away*. I cross-referenced his travel dates and locations against missing persons and unsolved homicides. I figured whatever Romanov had on Tom, it had to be bad. Dead body, bad."

"And you found something?" Jared whistled. "Holy shit, woman."

Nico shrugged. "It's not definitive, but I think Tom could have been responsible for an unsolved car accident eight years ago. A missing person. A twenty-two-year-old college student's car was found smashed up on the side of the road, but she was nowhere. Since she'd recently had a fight with her boyfriend and drove away angry, investigators figured she caused the crash then disappeared."

"One of those convenient runaway explanations that makes no actual sense."

"Exactly."

"You think Tom was driving drunk and caused the accident?" Jared asked.

Nico nodded. "Maybe, yeah. Drunk or high or too tired to drive. Who knows. Either way, I think he called Romanov to help him out. Like I said, it's not concrete, but it tracks."

"In terms of lifelong debts, that'll do it," Jared agreed. "But how did it lead to his death?"

"That is still to be determined. But I got another piece of intel. Tom had rideshare receipts in his spam folder. Get this. He got picked up from the hotel at one a.m., Thursday night. Or, I guess, Friday morning."

"He left the hotel in the middle of the night?"

"Guess where he went?"

Jared waited, eyes expectant.

"Drop off was Cannon Street, but—"

"The Aurora. Why?"

"Related to Romanov, maybe," Nico said. "The start of events that led to his death. Something to do with the Aurora camera system being off?"

"According to Sheffield, that was an accident."

Nico's eyes went wide. "You got to him?"

"He was in Hamilton for a funeral. That's why he came back from vacation early. Said he had no clue anything had gone wrong at the Aurora."

"You believe him?"

Jared took a moment. "Honestly, I'm not sure."

"But he cooperated?" Nico asked, raising her eyebrows.

"He admitted to entering the wrong date into the security system at the Aurora, but said it was a mistake."

"What a surprise," Nico said dryly.

"Could Sheffield be working for Romanov?"

"I wondered too," Nico said. "But I found no connection to Romanov outside the Aurora. And if Romanov was responsible for the disabled cameras, why go to all the trouble of getting Tom set up at the Aurora just to kill him straight away?"

"Something could have gone wrong between them."

Nico sighed. "Romanov as the connecting factor makes sense in a lot of ways, but in one major way it doesn't. Romanov isn't dumb. He wouldn't have dumped Tom's body at the Aurora, a building in which he owns two condos. Why put yourself in the line of fire unnecessarily? I don't see it."

"Maybe he's just that arrogant?"

"Maybe," Nico said, her voice low.

"Okay, let's park that for a moment, because my news is that Penny Pritchard saw a large black canvas bag in the garbage room at around nine-thirty Friday morning."

Nico let out an annoyed gust of air. "I specifically asked about the bag. I even showed her a photo."

"Yeah, she apologized for that. She forgot. All she could think about was her own connection to Tom."

Nico narrowed her eyes. "Do we believe her?"

"My gut says yes."

"Okay, so the large black bag was in the garbage room as early as nine-thirty Friday. Trace found Tom's hair in it, which means it could either be Tom's bag or the way he was transported to the locker."

"Or both."

"Right. Or both." Nico thought for a moment. "Sheffield was on site at nine. He could have given Tom his keys and taken him up to his apartment and killed him, then used his bag to dump the body."

"Pretty risky, with people like Penny Pritchard roaming around."

"True. But still possible. And we still don't know if anyone helped Tom move. Maybe he brought his killer into the building with him."

"I asked Sheffield if anyone was with Tom that morning when he picked up his keys, and he said he didn't think so, but it was hard to be sure. A lot going on." Jared held up a flash drive and lifted his eyebrows. "But this might tell us."

Nico grabbed it from him. "The hotel lobby footage?"

"The one and only. Where's your laptop?"

Nico pointed to her desk in the corner. Jared brought it over and they huddled together on Nico's sofa; two pairs of eyes fixed on the screen.

"Start it Wednesday morning. Maybe we see Tom with a familiar face in the days leading up. Or someone with him Thursday night," Nico said.

They both leaned closer to watch as people scuttled back and forth through the lobby. Tom appeared once on Wednesday afternoon, alone.

"He had a rideshare receipt for a trip to his doctor on Wednesday. Lines up," Nico said, eyeing the time stamp. "Keep it running."

On Thursday, early afternoon, Tom strode across the lobby to the exit, then returned at seven. Alone. At a little before midnight, he emerged from the elevator bay, still solo.

"There," Nico said. "Here we go."

They watched Tom amble through the lobby to take a seat at the hotel bar. A moment later, the bartender brought him a bottle of soda water and a glass. For about ten minutes, he sat there alone, doing something on his phone.

"He's buying a bed and a coffee table," Nico said.

"How could you know that?"

"His emails. He sent the delivery information to Carlos at around this time."

On screen, another figure appeared, walking into the bar and taking a seat next to Tom.

When the man turned, Jared sucked in a breath. "Chris Sheffield. That fucker lied to me."

The bartender poured Chris red wine. He raised it and clinked his glass against Tom's, something of a toast.

"They seem pretty chummy, don't they?" Jared said.

"Look." Nico pointed at the screen as Chris slid a small bag over to Tom.

The picture was black and white and grainy, but two sets of keys and fobs were visible through the clear plastic bag.

Chris shook Tom's hand, then strolled out of the hotel. Tom left too, but reappeared half an hour later, wheeling a trolley. On it were two large black canvas bags, a medium-sized red suitcase, a smallish cardboard box and two larger ones clearly containing the TV and the TV stand they'd found in his apartment. They watched him drop his key card into the drop box and then wheel his belongings outside.

"Now we know why he went to the Aurora. He got his keys early," Nico said, turning to Jared. "He fully intended to make that Friday morning flight, but his killer got to him first."

56

NICO

Nico paced her living room, reeling off the facts. "Tom met Sheffield at midnight and got his keys. He checked out at around one a.m. and transported his belongings to his new apartment. He always intended to make that flight. He thought he'd be out of there by dawn. We know he made it to the Aurora because the stuff he walked out of the hotel with is in his apartment. And we know he called 911 at two-thirty, but we don't know why."

"Maybe Sheffield followed him because he knew the cameras were off and it was the best time to make his move. They struggled and fought. Chris killed him, then fed us that bullshit story about giving his keys to Tom at nine to expand the list of suspects." Jared pulled out his phone. "I'll get Patterson to pick him up. He needs to explain himself."

"He sure does."

As Jared made the call, Nico went over to her desk and picked up her copy of the case file. Jared, seeing the illicit photocopies, shook his head and smiled. "You're a nightmare."

"I'm dedicated."

She opened the file and pulled out the images of Tom's apartment. "He'd already packed for his vacation, so he left the red suitcase near the door, ready to go. He unpacked his clothes and a few other belongings, but having lived in a furnished apartment, he didn't have much and needed to buy more." Nico held up a photograph and pointed at the measuring tape visible near the window. "Maybe Tom was taking measurements when Sheffield knocked on the door."

"Why would you drop a measuring tape to open the door?" Jared asked.

Nico frowned. "Yeah. Why not walk over with it in your hand?"

"Chris had keys, so maybe he didn't knock. He walked in and Tom realized what was about to go down. He tried to call 911 from where he stood, but Chris ran over and stopped him and the rest is history."

"It fits," Nico said, nodding slowly.

Was that it? Had they cracked the case? But why? Why did Chris want Tom dead?

Jared's phone buzzed. "Jackson," he answered. After a moment, he flicked wide eyes to Nico.

Her gut clenched in anticipation. "What is it?" she hissed.

"Thanks for the heads up." Jared disconnected and let out a low whistle.

"What is it?" she repeated.

"They found Kimberly Dallant's body. Downtown. In the water."

Nico held his gaze. "Something tells me that's not all."

"Nope, it sure isn't."

57

Penny will be caught up at the hospital for another hour. What happened to this being urgent, Pen? Whatever, I guess it's not so long. I type a quick reply to say I had no luck with Mrs. Pike, then jog downstairs to knock on Cassie's door again. Nothing. Utter silence. She could be out doing something totally normal, but I'm getting a bad feeling. My eyes drop to the lock. "I know you," I whisper. I reach out my hand, then snatch it back and hurry away.

In my apartment, I pace my living room, adrenaline rattling around my body. Do you know what this is, Doctor Foster? Because I do. I remember this one. Your words landed at the time and it stuck with me. When we get all panty and angsty like this, it's not because we don't know what to do. It's because we've already decided what we're doing, but are struggling to come to terms with it.

Which means this adrenaline isn't anxiety. It's excitement. Because this feels like my old life. Inside, the old Gemma is warming up. Stretching her muscles and sharpening her focus. But the old Gemma never had this niggle. The old

Gemma was just doing a job for someone else and didn't have this pulsing, picking, tapping at her brain. Is it doubt or something else? Either way, I need to dislodge it first. I can't work with this skittering energy. You can have all the skills and safety equipment in the world, but if your mind isn't in the game, you will make a mistake.

I finish another circuit, then stop. This section of carpet has gotten a lot of action recently—maybe I should get a rug so it doesn't get worn out? I shake my head and keep pacing. I glance at the armchair. If Sol was here, he'd be giving me a look. Like, *chill girl, is this necessary*? My stomach clenches. I'm coming for you, Sol. As soon as I can.

I resume pacing, then stop and start jogging on the spot. My mind won't stop spinning and whirring. I need to jostle this thing out. Should I go for a proper run? Kill time until Penny returns? Yeah, maybe. In my bedroom I pull out leggings and a sport tank. Would you look at that? I chose the slate-gray set that matches the exterior of the Aurora. My eyes jump to my silver suitcase. After a microsecond of indecision, I pull it down. I set it on the floor, then lurch upright and step back. Am I really considering breaking into my neighbor's home just because she hasn't replied to my messages? Wow. It sounds hysterical. Cassie could simply be in a sex haze. A tangle of hormones. I've been in enough to know how distracting they are. If the sex is good enough, you don't care about missing appointments or checking messages.

Maybe she and Leighton went away to focus on their life between the sheets. Did they say as much yesterday? I try to recall the conversation. Did I zone out while Cassie told us about a trip to a lake house? Some country cottage? I was too focused on Leighton's stupid smirk to remember. I frown, my gaze resting on the suitcase in front of me. We *were* talking about bags at one point, though. Did Cassie say she had to get hers from storage? No. It was about our amateur sleuthing and how Penny saw the bag in the garbage room. And Leighton and Cassie can't have told us they're going away because Penny wouldn't forget a detail like that and she's the one who started this freak out. Penny never spaces out, I'm pretty sure.

Wait.

Something is now rapping on my brain. Hard. That thing, *the* thing. The piece that doesn't fit.

Oh shit.

58

NICO

"What else?" Nico said. "Dammit, Jackson. They pulled Kimberly out of the water, and...?"

He held up his phone. A low resolution photo, clearly taken by a phone at a crime scene, showed a large black bag.

"Kimberly's body was in this."

Nico's eyes went wide. "Another black bag?"

Jared nodded. "Kimberly was last seen alive late Thursday night. Or, you might say, the early hours of Friday morning."

Nico swallowed. "And so was Tom."

After a moment, Jared lifted his phone.

"Who are you calling?"

He held up one finger. "Hi, Jennifer? It's Detective Jackson again. Do you have a second? Sure."

He turned to Nico. Muzak drifted from his cell. "Waiting for Leighton's assistant," he explained. "A virtual one. She organizes all his appointments. Remember the golf trip he mentioned?" Nico nodded. "I called, and it checked out, but.... Yes?" Jared returned his attention to the call. "You said you organized a car to pick up Leighton Matthews on the morning of Friday the 5th, but can you tell me where from? Sure, text me the booking confirmation. Thanks."

When his phone beeped a second later, he made a satisfied noise in the back of his throat, then showed Nico. "The car picked up Leighton from Cannon Street. Remember, he said he stayed at work when he had morning deliveries."

"Tom was at the Aurora in the early hours of Friday," Nico said, "and we now know Leighton was right across the road at six a.m. that same morning. Likely overnight."

"You know what my last girlfriend did when she got drunk a couple of weeks after we broke up?" Jared said.

Nico eyed him, waiting for him to finish.

"She showed up at my house."

"Why?"

He frowned. "What do you mean, why?"

"Did she want to get back together?"

Jared's eyes flickered. "No, that's not what she wanted." He eyed Nico, then nodded, as if he now understood something. "Anyway," he continued easily, "we broke up because we didn't fit into each other's lives and, honestly, we didn't like each other very much. But there was no problem with the sex. You have a few drinks, your inhibitions disappear and then... the body wants what it wants. I'd say the heart, but it has nothing to do with love."

"No?"

"The message that it's over doesn't always get from your head to your dick."

Nico nodded, the pieces finally slotting into place. "A couple of nights after Leighton and Kimberly broke up, she got nostalgic. She wanted to see him."

"And maybe she knew Leighton was at Cannon Street," Jared added.

"And now she's dead," Nico finished.

"Tom Bollard, who was right across the road from Leighton on the same night, is dead too," Jared said.

Nico pointed to her laptop, paused on an image of Tom wheeling his belongings out of the lobby. She held up two photographs of the interior of Tom's apartment at the Aurora. "You wanna play spot the difference?"

Jared's eyes moved from the screen to the photos. "Two large black bags."

59

I stand on the roof of the Aurora; the wind buffeting my hair as I check the street below for eyes. A stray smoker, someone waiting for a ride or returning home. Any sort of audience. The darkening sky is clear and I'm at peace, in control. First my left foot, then my right. I edge my way down the side of the building on route to break into my neighbor's apartment.

Are you asking why, Doctor Foster? Or do you no longer bother with that question? Maybe the reason is obvious. You were always good with details.

I'm out here because of Leighton's comment. When we were talking about the clue we'd found being a bag in the garbage room, he said *yeah, but black bags are common*. Sure, they are. But how did he know the bag Penny saw was black? Yes, this could be me leaping to conclusions. Maybe Leighton made a totally normal assumption and wasn't outing himself as Tom's killer, but I don't think so.

I have no clue why, but that doesn't matter. Because if I'm right, Cassie is in real danger. And yes, I could use a certain skill set to get into Cassie's apartment and check she's okay. Because yes, I've already picked the lock on my own door. When Sven appeared the second time, I tested how easy it was to break in. Spoiler: I'm adding a deadbolt.

But if Leighton is in there with Cassie, he'll be on high alert. Because between Penny and me, we've knocked on her door at least three times today. And picking your way into a room when someone is waiting for you, possibly with a weapon, is dumb. I might be foolish sometimes, but I am not stupid. Right, Doctor Foster?

As I edge closer to her apartment, my heart flutters and jumps and I smile. Being out here feels so good. Especially since it's not for illegal reasons. Well, this is still illegal, but rescuing your neighbor from a possibly murderous creep definitely cancels out any legal issues.

Balancing with one hand against the exterior wall of the building, I reach into the snug pocket in the front of my spandex top and pull out my phone. I try Jared again, but like my last call, he doesn't pick up.

"Now is not the time to ghost me, Jared," I hiss at my phone. Scowling, I type out a text—*Cassie 202 in danger. Tom killer. Get here now*—and send it to both Penny and Jared.

I press my nose up to the glass, but the curtains are drawn. Wait, there's a gap on the other side. I take a slow breath and inch my way along the ledge until I can peek through. On the coffee table is a bottle of water, a vial of pills, and a laptop. Oh, and there's Cassie. Lying on the couch, partially hidden by the armrest. My heart thuds. Is her neck at a weird angle? The angle you'd be at if you're dead? Oh god, am I too late? I try the window but it's locked. Lucky for Cassie, this poses zero problems for me. I pull out the basic lock-picking kit I have in the tool belt strapped to my waist. A moment later, I slide open the window a few inches, quiet as a mouse. I wait, listening, then open it wider and ease myself into the room. I look around warily, keeping low. The apartment is silent. Where's Leighton? Have I got this wrong? Am I about to wake Cassie up from an epic nap?

I move closer to the couch, bracing myself for what state I might find Cassie in. When I can finally see her face, terrified eyes blink up at me. My shoulders drop with relief. She's scared, but alive. Masking tape covers her mouth and her hands are tied behind her back. This obviously isn't the best night of her life, but I can't see blood and she's conscious.

"Are you okay?" I whisper.

Cassie casts frantic eyes to the right. I reach one hand forward to remove the tape, but she shakes her head quickly, flicking her eyes again. Making them wider.

I glance in that direction, then back at her.

"Is he here?"

She nods.

"Does he have a weapon?"

The toilet flushes.

I freeze. How much time do I have? Is Leighton a hand washer? I look around the space. Cassie hasn't gone nuts over-furnishing. The screen partition isn't opaque, and if I try to hide behind the curtain, I'll look like a kid playing hide-and-seek with a noticeable bulge and my feet peeking out the bottom. I have to go back through the window. I climb out but leave it open a crack. Hopefully, he won't notice.

A moment later, Leighton appears. He strolls over to Cassie and leans down to kiss her forehead, almost tenderly. "Don't pretend, babe," Leighton says, fixing his eyes on Cassie, almost as if waiting for her to reply, despite the tape. "You know about Kim, don't you?"

Kim? Who the hell is Kim?

"You're the type to stalk guys on social media, aren't you? Find out everything you can, right? I can tell."

Leighton takes a few steps toward the apartment door, then turns. "And those nosy bitches know I was here, so I'll have to make sure people think you're still alive for a few days until I have an alibi. Should be easy enough to arrange." He picks up the laptop from the coffee table and sits next to Cassie. "Scooch over, babe, you're hogging the couch," he says, laughing.

Okay, so Leighton's a psychopath.

"How about an email to your agent to say you're going away for a few days to get those final edits done. This last push has been giving you trouble, hasn't it, babe. Hmm, who else should I email? Gosh, you don't have many friends, do you?" He makes a fake sad face. "We'll have to tell Penny and Gemma, though. Obviously. A post on Facebook, I think. Okay, here's Penny. Look, she's already messaged to ask how you are. It's perfect. Okay. Sorry I ignored your calls, Penny," Leighton says as he types. "I'm totally fine, just going out of town to focus on writing. There." He smiles and pats Cassie's head. "Now, just a couple more emails and an automatic out of office should do it." He gets busy typing.

The little shit. Leighton *has* been messing with Cassie. He got into her computer and is likely responsible for those messages Cassie can't remember. Penny and I were right about the gaslighting, just not the reason.

"Done." Leighton closes the laptop and sets it on the table. He pulls something from his pocket and makes a weird motion with his hands. Oh crap, he's putting on gloves. He turns to Cassie, his eyes becoming glazed. Shit, it's going down. My chest suddenly tight, my pulse throbbing in my ears, I grab the handle. As he leans forward, I slide it open and leap into the room.

"Stop."

Leighton's head snaps up, his eyes comically wide. "What the fuck?" He jumps up, eyes blazing. "What the actual fuck," he repeats.

"You're done, Leighton. It's over. Get away from her."

Bang.

Someone at the door.

"Police!"

The door bursts open with a crack and Jared storms in. Leighton lurches to the right.

"Don't move," Jared barks. "You're under arrest, Leighton."

Jared whirls him around in one smooth motion and cuffs his hands behind his back, then with one firm hand on his shoulder, marches him toward the door. When he turns back to give me a wink, my panties actually catch fire. But I can't enjoy the moment because just then I realize something else. *Someone* else.

Nico is here, too.

Her eyes lock on me, her whole body still, then the moment passes. Nico hurries over to Cassie, helps her to a seated position and peels off the tape. "Are you okay?"

Cassie blinks and rubs her cheeks, red from the tape, then her wrists. "I guess." Her voice is shaky.

"Not physically harmed?" Nico says, uncharacteristically gentle.

Cassie shakes her head. "Stiff and sore from being tied up, is all."

"Feeling well enough to come to the station?" Nico continues, still ignoring me. "To give a statement?"

"Um...." Cassie turns frightened eyes to me.

"If you want a support person," Nico says, her voice suddenly hard, "I suggest asking someone else."

"I can go," someone says from the doorway.

Penny. *Finally*. The Penster is here. I'm weirdly relieved to see her. As if a grownup has finally arrived. And I guess Cassie feels the same because she runs over to Penny and then Penny is hugging her and Cassie's shoulders are shaking.

Nico lets Penny comfort Cassie for a moment, her eyes on them but all her attention on me, then says, "Take her downstairs. There's a unit waiting."

Penny nods, calm and certain, as if she's done this her whole life, then ushers Cassie out into the hall.

Only Nico and I remain. Tension hangs in the air. Heavy and full of promise. But not in a good way.

"What a shock. Gemma Cross, once again at the scene of a crime."

"Not my crime." I sigh. "I saved Cassie, Nico."

"That's Detective Sergeant Davis to you," she barks.

"I helped my neighbor out of a possibly lethal situation, and I figured out who killed Tom Bollard. It was Leighton," I add.

Nico rolls her eyes. "No shit. Why do you think we're here?"

Her gaze lowers, taking in my spandex, my climbing gloves and shoes, and best of all, my little tool belt full of all the handy essentials you need to be a burglar. A knowing smile creeps across her face and fuck. I might as well have worn a t-shirt saying *I'm a cat burglar, ask me how.*

"So?" I say when it seems as if she's not going to speak.

"So," she echoes.

"Now what?"

"This reminds me of something," Nico says, tapping her chin, hamming it up. "I've got a weird sense of déjà vu, don't you?"

I stop myself from asking if she's a poet but doesn't know it and shrug.

"Goddamn it," she suddenly growls. "Just admit it. Just say it to give me peace of mind."

"Why would I be interested in your peace of mind?"

She lifts her chin. "I might drop it. Stop pursuing you."

In that moment, all my adrenaline—and with it, my brava-do—deserts me in a whoosh. I sit down on the closest chair and sigh. "I didn't kill the Barringtons. I swear."

"There was someone else there that night," she says. "Now that I know the third set of DNA found at the scene isn't yours, I can be sure. It was her blood. A lot of it."

Tears spring up. I blink them back and swallow.

"Dannielle Falducci, right?" Nico continues.

"Shut up," I hiss.

"Took me a while to find her in the system, but I did." She gives me a small smile. "And now I know what your game is," she gestures at my outfit, "I know what to look for."

"Why? I've—" I swallow. "I've retired. I've given it up. Can't you? Can't you let it go?"

Nico's head jerks back as if I'd slapped her. "Let it go?" she spits out. "Did you watch your best friend take her last breath, helpless? Unable to do anything at all?" She's shaking, color flooding her cheeks. "How dare you," she growls. "That night, I lost my partner—"

"We both did," I cry, unable to help myself. "I didn't see it happen, but you saw the blood. We both lost someone that night, Nico."

She stares at me for what feels like an eternity, her eyes burning, the muscles in her jaw working. She opens her mouth, then closes it.

And then she's gone.

60

NICO

The Pig & Parrot was busy, standing room only, but Jared had nabbed a booth. As Nico started toward him, her phone rang. Her sister. Nico held up her index finger to tell Jared she needed a minute. He made a drinking gesture, eyebrows raised, and she nodded, then walked over to a quieter corner to answer.

"Hey."

"Finally," Tatiana said.

"Yeah, I—"

"Are you okay? I know something happened. You had a meeting with the top brass, right?"

Nico let out a noisy breath. "How did you…."

But she could guess. Tati was her emergency contact and if Sarge hadn't made the call himself, Jill would have been happy to. But instead of feeling annoyed, letting irritation blister into anger, Nico smiled. These people getting all up in her business, they weren't intruding on her life. They were looking out for her. Because they cared. And really, her meeting with Sarge had gone well, despite an extension of her suspension. That confrontation with Gemma had released something. It had been an acknowledgement, maybe even just to herself. She still had to deal with the grief—properly—but at least she'd now opened the gate to allow it to happen.

And it felt good.

"Things are okay," she said into the phone. "I'm taking leave. I need to work through some stuff."

"In therapy, right?" Tati said. "Not at some ridiculous fight club or something?"

Nico smiled and glanced over at Jared, now talking to a waitress. "Yes, in therapy. I'm going to be okay, Tati. You don't need to worry."

Her sister made a small sound.

"Tati?"

"I'm here." Her sister cleared her throat. "You're coming to dinner this Sunday, okay? I won't take no for an answer."

"Yes. I... I'm looking forward to it."

Nico could almost hear Tati smile through the phone.

"Talk later, okay?"

Nico disconnected but remained where she was, riding the surge of emotion filling her eyes and her heart, then crossed the room to join Jared.

"Hey." She slid into the booth. "So? How did everything play out with Leighton?"

For a moment, Jared was still.

"Jackson?" A pulse of worry pinged in her stomach. "Please tell me...."

A slow smile crept over his face. "We got him."

"Yeah?" Nico smiled back.

"But he's trying to plead self-defense."

Nico lifted her eyebrows. "He killed Kimberly Dallant and Tom Bollard and tied up Cassandra Pike in *self-defense*?"

"I think he'll end up talking. Cutting a plea deal. When I told him we had CCTV footage of Kimberly in a taxi going to Cannon Street that night, as well as Leighton himself driving his car to the waterfront a few hours later, right where analysts think her body was put in the water, he gave it up. He has admitted nothing about Tom, but with Kimberly, he almost immediately started the, *it wasn't my fault*, song. Claims her death was a sex accident."

"You were right about Kimberly visiting for a final roll in the hay, huh?"

"Sure was. Kimberly took a cab from Spider bar to Tiles and Textures where Leighton was spending the night before his early golf trip. They had sex, and things either went wrong during or after. Leighton is trying to say that the rough sex was consensual."

Nico made a face. "Tom Bollard's death can't be played that way."

"Sure can't."

"But Leighton has said nothing at all about Tom?"

"No. We can tie him to Kimberly, but with Tom all we have is his presence across the road."

"I've been thinking about that," Nico said. "How it went down. The measuring tape by the window. Tom's phone abandoned next to it."

"So how did it go down, Detective Davis?" Jared asked.

"Tom's apartment was opposite Leighton's. Remember how his window looked directly into the second floor of Tiles?"

"Yeah. Thanks." Jared said to the waitress, setting down their drinks.

"So that night, he's standing near the window, measuring the space, figuring out whether the lounge set he's eyeing up is going to fit, when he sees Leighton and Kimberly. Maybe he watches Kimberly pull up in a cab? Maybe he only notices when they get to it in the window? Either way, when he realizes what Leighton is doing, he grabs his phone to call 911. The call cut off, not sure why, but at some point, he went outside and left his phone behind. Because Leighton didn't have a key fob for the Aurora." Nico met Jared's eyes. "Perhaps Tom's phone died, or maybe he panicked. Either way, I think Tom ran out because he thought he could stop Leighton. He thought he could save the girl," Nico finished quietly.

"Trying to make up for that mistake eight years ago?" Jared said. "That's why he ran into the street instead of finding his charger or following through with the 911 call?"

"Maybe. We'll never know for sure."

For a moment, they were quiet.

"So Leighton realizes he's got a witness and races down-stairs," Nico continued eventually. "Outside the Aurora, Leighton overpowers Tom. He has five inches and twenty pounds on the guy. He knocks him out and uses his key fob to get him back inside the building."

"And Leighton knew which apartment was Tom's because all the keys had the numbers stickered on when they first handed them out," Jared said.

"Plus Tom's light was the only one on," Nico added, "it would have been easy to figure it out."

"He takes him upstairs, probably planning to leave the body up there," Jared picks up the thread. "But then, what, he sees two generic bags and figures two bodies, two bags?"

"Tom's apartment is directly across the road, so Leighton probably worried that it would be obvious to us that Tom had seen something. That's how liars think," Nico said. "I read a psych article on it. They assume other people are doing or thinking the bad shit they're doing and thinking."

"Right. Like when cheaters accuse their partners of cheating."

"So he uses one bag to get rid of Kimberly," Nico continues. "And takes Tom downstairs in the other. Leighton had been watching contractors coming and going for months. He probably figured a body in the common area, with a long list of people who had access, would muddy the waters."

"And then Friday morning he goes off on his golf trip like nothing happened."

"And Cassandra Pike?" Nico asked. "How did she get caught up in everything?"

"According to the forensic psychologist, Leighton started dating her so he could stay close to the investigation. This, apparently, is common for Leighton's type of narcissism. He'd begun messing with Cassandra just for the hell of it until he became worried she knew he'd killed Kimberly. Based on nothing, it seems, Cassandra had no clue. The psych consult believed Leighton had developed this internal narrative to give himself a reason to kill her. He could try the self-defense approach all he wanted, she said, but in her professional opinion, he was gaining a real taste for killing. The idea of getting away with it was what got his juices flowing."

"Shit." Nico let out a breath. "Well, I'm glad we stopped him at two."

"Cheers to that," Jared agreed. They clinked glasses and again fell silent.

"Anyone mention me?" Nico asked after a moment.

He met her eyes. "No."

That night, Jared had convinced her to go home instead of to the station with everyone else. It had been the right call.

"And Gemma?" Nico asked, her stomach tight. "Any theories on why he put Tom's body in Gemma's locker?" Nico asked, trying to keep her voice casual.

Jared eyed her, his gaze heavy. "I'm pretty sure it was just a random choice."

"What about the rest?"

"The rest?" he echoed.

"Has she been left out of the report?"

"I told Cassandra she'd be doing Gemma a favor if she didn't use her name, and she didn't. Leighton was too wrapped up in himself to think about who was or wasn't there, I guess."

"Are you covering your ass or Gemma's?" Nico asked, narrowing her eyes.

"Maybe I'm covering yours." Jared's eyes challenged her, but then he dropped them and fiddled with his bottle of beer. "Nico, I—"

"You know what? Forget it. I don't even care anymore."

Was this true? Maybe. Either way, she didn't want to think about Gemma right now.

"There's only one piece of the puzzle still missing," Nico said. They now had their killer, but she liked to have all questions answered by the end of the case.

"Yeah?"

"What was up with Tobi Hart? Why did she run from me?"

"I got DC Singh to talk to her."

"Smart move. And?"

"She'd been sleeping in the equipment room for a couple of weeks before the murder."

"That explains the phone charger and the heater," Nico said, nodding. "Heating system wouldn't have been turned on, at least, not fully. In March it would have been cold in there. Did she say why?"

"Girlfriend troubles. Needed space." Jared made a face, as if to say he could relate.

Nico frowned. "She was there the night Tom died? No wonder she didn't want to talk to us."

"Didn't hear a thing, apparently. She woke up Friday morning, no clue about the body, and put in a normal day of work. Saturday afternoon, she went on an overnight camping trip. Came back on Sunday to find police all over the place." Jared took a sip of beer. "What did Sarge say to you?"

"You know, his normal wise words. Needing time to heal." She shrugged. "I am, by the way. Taking leave."

"Sounds like a good idea."

"What about you?" Nico asked.

"Meeting with him tomorrow. Not sure what he knows."

"Depends on how much Patterson knows, right?" Nico said. "But he wouldn't rat *you* out."

"Maybe I'll tell Sarge everything, anyway."

"You don't deserve—"

"I deserve what I get, Nico. I went against his orders and brought you in at the end, but I don't regret it. You're my partner."

Nico swallowed and looked down, suddenly emotional. "I don't know about that anymore," she said quietly.

"Maybe not officially," Jared nodded, "but like I said, no regrets."

After a moment, Nico said, "Sarge is decent. He'll do what's right." She turned to stare out the window, and Jared took another sip of beer.

"Sheffield has been lawyered up by Boston Works, by the way," he said.

"Interesting. Because of the security camera thing, right?"

"And because he gave Tom early access to the building. It was supposed to be a simple favor. They knew each other from years ago. Played squash together. But my guess is nothing will come of it."

"And I'm still not sure Romanov just happened to buy an apartment in a building that suddenly has a dysfunctional security system," Nico said.

Jared tilted his head. "Sarge is hardly going to go looking for crimes that might not even have been committed."

"I guess not."

"This break, it'll do you good. Probably the last thing you want to hear, but—"

"No, I know. I need it," she said in a small voice. "But whatever happens next, we got him. Leighton Matthews can't hurt anyone else. And that's something."

"That is something."

They fell silent. Nico finished her beer, took a slow breath, then dragged her tote onto her lap. She rummaged around, then pulled out her chopsticks and set them on the table.

"Am I supposed to know what this means?" he said, eyeing them. "Wait." He grinned. "I get it. You want to get noodles." He nodded. "I could definitely eat."

Nico smiled. "I know just the place."

61

So, Doctor Foster, it turns out karma is real. How else can you explain this? Brain chemicals and neuroscience won't cut it this time. We're going to have to fall back on something a little woo-woo. Because yes, I took the Barrington diamonds, but now I've had to give them back. (Sort of.) The universe balanced things out.

Look, they were spilled in a trail of glittery breadcrumbs to the balcony. I had to make a split-second decision and I'm a thief. Or at least, I was at the time. It's literally what I was trained, and hired, to do. I scooped up those fallen diamonds (and Sol) and I got out of there. Once I got myself together and realized Sven had abandoned me, I offloaded them to a fence who wasn't beholden to Sven. I used half of the money to buy this apartment and put the rest in my bank account. I now realize that was a dumb move because it's the same account Sven helped me set up. Maybe that's how he knew. Or maybe he put two and two together and got me. I don't know what happened to the rest of the jewelry or to Danni. I probably never will.

So yes, I stole those diamonds, but Sven stole them right back. Or close enough. Because I transferred the money, as demanded, and I now have Sol back. My million-dollar cat. Totally worth it. And yes, I've installed the deadbolt. And a doorbell camera. I won't have Sven strolling in whenever he wants. So I gained a home and a new life, but I lost my best friend and I'm officially broke. I have a mortgage-free condo, but no delicious nest egg to support my indulgent lifestyle. So there you go. Karma.

Sol pads through the living room, throws me an *I'm still pissed* expression, and carries on into the kitchen. He plants his bottom and looks at me expectantly. "Yeah, yeah." I follow him in and spoon out an extra helping of the chicken livers I guilt-purchased from the butchers yesterday. He meows once, then tucks in. Is Sol milking this for all it's worth? Sure is. I don't blame him; I'd be doing the same.

I pick up my notebook. The upshot is I now need an actual job. Not a pretend one to cover up my past, but one that will mean I can buy food for Sol and me. And pay my bills. Because there will be bills, right? Yesterday, I found a letter in my mailbox which I suspect is my first. It was kind of thrilling to see my name printed next to my address, though, so I'll hold onto that feeling for a few more days before finding out what it contains.

Sure, I could sell this apartment and buy a cheaper one to live off the difference for a while. But who wants that hassle? And yes, the people in this building might have something to do with it. George and I are still finding our vibe, but we'll get there. Cassie has already said she wants more Girl Gang hangouts. And that she'll definitely listen to me about the next guy. Which means I have to stick around and guide her through the terrible world of dating. Her first boyfriend turned out to be a murderer. If I don't help Cassie, she'll get eaten alive. And not in a good way.

I haven't heard a peep from the police department. Pretty pleased about that. At first I was surprised. When I thought on it some more, I realized Nico wasn't supposed to be there. And Jared had also crossed a line. A couple of them. Multiple times. Both detectives have something to gain from keeping me out of it. Another win for me. But I might never see Jared again, which is kind of a bummer. See? Balance.

In my notebook, I flick past my amateur investigation notes and write a new heading. *Job*. I stare at the blank page. Nope. Too big to deal with now. I'm feeling restless. I stroll into the bathroom and take an Everything shower because who knows where this evening might go. I choose an outfit designed for movement—stretch jeans, a crop tank and my hi-tops. I pull my hair into a sleek topknot, pair a dusting of mascara with a bold red lip, then head out.

I find myself at the club Danni and I used to go to after we'd finished a job, when residual adrenaline still buzzed around needing release. Usually, I'd find someone on the dancefloor to take home. Tonight, I now realize, isn't about that. It's about liberating the knowledge I got the other day from Nico. A final confirmation. One I was hoping would never come.

That I'll never see Danni again.

The beat pulses in my chest, throbs through my body. I become one with the music and lose myself to the moment and I feel good, so so good, until suddenly I'm wrecked. Grief pushing at my eyes and weighing down my limbs. All at once, I'm desperate to be at home and cuddled up with Sol.

So I leave.

When I let myself inside, Sol is chilling on the new couch—it arrived this morning and we're both in love. He blinks and gives me one sleepy meow. "Hey, bud," I say, fresh tears welling up.

Just as I go to join him, there's a knock at the door. It's only ten, but this is late for unexpected visitors. Then again, Penny seems to live by her own visitation rules.

I check the peephole. Nope, not Penny. With an involuntary flutter in my stomach (and lower), I open the door. Leaning with one arm raised and propped against the doorjamb, exposing lean abs above the waist of his jeans, is Detective Jared Jackson.

"Hey," he says.

"How did you get in here?"

"Police business," he says with a lazy smile.

"Liar," I say, but I'm smiling too.

He raises both hands. "Truth. I had released evidence to return. I dropped it off and was about to drive away when you pulled up in the cab. It would have been rude not to say hello."

I tilt my head. "Hello."

He shifts position and lifts his chin. "You enjoyed watching me arrest Leighton the other day, didn't you, Ms. Cross?"

Heat floods my cheeks, and then everywhere else.

"Ms. Cross?" I arch one eyebrow.

"Uh-huh." He grins.

"You can't call me that without dealing with the conse-
quences, Detective."

"That's the point." He leans closer. "Aren't you going to
invite me in?"

I almost say yes. Of course I do. But when my mouth opens,
a *no* comes out.

"No?" he echoes.

No. Because I need tonight on my own. Or at least, just me
and Sol. Hey, maybe I'm finally learning how to control my
dopamine brain.

"Honestly? I'm exhausted."

He makes a sad face, then straightens and cocks one eyebrow. "But another time?"

"Another time."

As I close the door, I smile.

Are you proud of me, Doctor Foster? I hope so. Because I
care what you think. Honestly. I always have, I just didn't realize it back then. So much of what you said still rattles around
my head. Part of me must have been paying attention.

Remember those wide-legged pantsuits you used to wear?
One in every color, it seemed like. I used to mock them re-
lentlessly in my head, but I fully get the appeal now. I wouldn't
mind a couple of those snappy suits for whatever is coming
next. And those glasses. Those huge, round, seventies-style
tortoiseshell spectacles. I want a pair of them too, I've decided. Look, I don't know what my point is, except to say, again,
that you were right. About a lot of things. Which brings me to
your final nugget of wisdom.

*Find what you're good at to be happy. Find your people to feel
like you belong.*

People and purpose. I heard you. And I did that once, criminal world or not. I can do it again.

So, thank you, Doctor Foster.

62

Saturday, a little after four, I take a shower and throw on a summery maxi dress. I give in to Sol's demands for a pre-dinner snack—I'll be having one and I'm no hypocrite—then head up to the rooftop. It won't be dark for hours yet, but the fairy lights look pretty and feel festive. The air is warm and there's a lightness to the atmosphere. Or maybe that's just me.

Penny, Cassie, George, Marco and even Orson sit around the two tables in the middle. I join them, plunking down my new ice bucket with a bottle of prosecco and six plastic flutes.

"I thought we could celebrate." I pour everyone glasses, then raise mine in a toast. "Here's to Tom Bollard, poor guy," I say.

"And to fresh starts," Penny adds, meeting my eye.

"And chicks before dicks," Cassie says with a mischievous grin.

I lift my glass. "Here, here."

"Hey," George says snippily.

"Not you," I retort. "You're not the dicks we're talking about and you know it."

He nudges me, a small smile on his face, and a sudden pulse of emotion surges up, hot and fast. I take a gulp; the bubbles tickling my nose, trying to hold it together. It's been a crazy month, but things are actually looking pretty good now.

"So, what's our first project?" Marco says.

"Project?" I say.

"For the Aurora crew."

"The what?" Orson says.

"Is that the name?" George asks, wrinkling his nose.

"We can workshop it," Penny says brightly.

"What about *squad*?" Cassie offers.

"I like squad," I say, leaning back in my chair.

"Oh, look who made it," Penny says. I follow her gaze to the rooftop door where Tobi Hart stands. A crop top and short shorts, a sixer of beer, and a packet of chips.

I smile.

Dear Reader

I hope you enjoyed reading *Gemma and the Ace Detective* as much as I loved writing it. (And rewriting it.) If so, please leave a review at the online bookstore and/or Goodreads, BookBub etc. Getting reviews is especially hard for indie authors so I really appreciate it! If you'd like to reach out email: margotdrewdelaney@gmail.com or follow me on Goodreads, BookBub, Pinterest, Bluesky, or YouTube.

If you want more of Detective Nico Davis, check out ***Wild Sweet Perfect Dead***: psychological suspense meets police procedural in this college thriller and murder mystery.
If you want another light-hearted mystery, try the FREE novella ***Killer Focus***. Three lakefront cottages, two deadly secrets, and one grad student who can't mind her own business.

Acknowledgements

A huge thank you to my readers and reviewers, Jane, Lisa, Cynthia and Barbara.